A Dead Polar Bear

on a Sledge

Alison Lane

Broad Oak Books Ltd

A Dead Polar Bear on a Sledge

A Dead Polar Bear on a Sledge

Published by Broad Oak Books Ltd

Cover Art Copyright © 2020 Sam Jarman

Be kind, for everyone you meet is fighting a hard battle.
Attributed to Plato

There is no debt greater than that which is owed to those who hold your hand as you go under, and don't let go until you are safely on dry land again.

Thanks are not enough, but this book is for you.

AJL 2020

A Dead Polar Bear on a Sledge

About the author

I have been writing all my life for fun and the love of it, but a few years ago I started writing and didn't stop until I finished a novel six weeks later - this was 'A Dead Polar Bear on a Sledge', a funny and sweet story of Jen, a women in her late thirties stuck 'in a village by mistake' trying to cope with infidelity, loneliness and finding love in all the wrong places. My second book, 'Cover Version', is a fun and light-hearted contemporary romance and a bit more of a wish-fulfillment. I recently started a third novel, again in the contemporary romance genre.

I also blog non-fictional and (hopefully) humorous observations on modern life, at www.inavillage.co.uk - my first published book, 'In a Village By Mistake', is a short collection of those writings. I began by thinking I would write something serious, but it always comes out with a lot of jokes. A bit like my own life - nothing apart from love and laughter really counts after all. I have to fit my writing around work, children, family life and volunteering in the community - but I think you always find time for what you love. And I love telling these stories, and letting these (flawed, funny, annoying, human) characters live and breathe for a few hundred pages. It's a hard thing to let your creations live out in the world, but it's exciting too. I hope you have as much fun reading as I did writing them.

For more information on my books and to join my email list, please visit my website:
https://www.alisonlane.co.uk/contact
https://www.amazon.co.uk/Alison-Lane/e/B08JKYHSFT

Follow me on Facebook and Instagram
https://www.facebook.com/alisonlaneauthor
https://www.instagram.com/alisonlaneauthor/

Thanks and acknowledgments

Writing is easy, the American sportswriter Red Smith famously said. You just sit down at the typewriter, open up a vein and bleed it out, drop by drop. Apologies to those who were abandoned and ignored during the (literally and metaphorically) draining process of writing and editing of this book - in particular, Rebecca and Annabel (remember, neglect is character-building) and most of all the ever-supportive Andy Lane, who is about as far from being Chris as it is possible to be.

The wonderful artwork for this book was designed by the talented Sam Jarman (www.instagram.com/s.jarman_illustration/). It was incredibly moving to see the places I had only imagined come to life, and in particular to see Jen dragging her poor broken heart around the village of my imagination. You captured it all so perfectly, and I am truly sorry for giving you such an appallingly graphic simile to work with. I really hadn't thought it through.

This book took a very short time to write but a very long time to wrangle out of my laptop and to send out into the world. My heartfelt thanks go to those wonderful people who encouraged me along the way. I am blessed with amazingly supportive family and friends and I am hugely grateful for all your suggestions and comments and sarcasm. Especially the sarcasm. My grateful thanks must go to Angela Spence for her continued faith in this book and its characters and their story. I couldn't and wouldn't have got this far without you. It's indisputably your fault. I can never thank you enough.

This book is a work of fiction and all of the characters and events are from the febrile place that is my imagination. Any resemblance to any persons living or dead, or any events that you might vaguely remember, is purely coincidental.

Like many writers, I imagine, I have become ridiculously protective of these characters and nervous about letting them out and about on their own. Take care of them, won't you?

AJL December 2020

CHAPTER ONE

PROLOGUE

THE FOREST

A nap. It tells you everything about how low I've sunk, that these days I often have a little nap after lunch. Like a toddler, or an old lady. I'm so exhausted from the effort of dragging my broken heart around all day, like a dead polar bear on a sledge, that I have to lie down and close my eyes, just for a while. Shut them tight against the glare of reality. In the haze of the blind-drawn afternoon, I slip into a half-dream.

I am standing in a forest, the kind of forest I have never been in, not in real life. The sun slants through the tree-trunks, slicing me through with blades of heat and light. I can feel the cool of grass-blades between my toes, and beneath that the solid warmth of the earth. For just a minute, the briefest of moments, I feel a sort of queasy peace, a vertical hold.

And then, I catch a glimpse of you, through the trunk-louvre, through the giddy patchwork of leaves. Just at the very periphery of my vision, moving fast and now stopping, stopping to watch me. The flash of your eyes, startling me in the darkling shade, brighter than the flashes of sunlight. And now and then the glint of sunlight on your skin, on the raven-wing of your hair. Like a hunter, I catch the scent of you on the breeze, sharp and citrus, above the earthy warmth. Like the prey, I feel my blood pounding in my ears, my breath ragged and torn from my lungs, and the timpani-beating of my heart, my aching, broken heart.

I am woken by the horror-movie screeching of the School-Run Alarm.

THE SCHOOL-RUN

At some point, without me noticing, 'school-run' became an adjective, and a frequently used one in my life too. As in:

1. The School-Run Alarm: 2.45 (no repeat, no snooze) leaving just enough time for
2. The School-Run Makeover: splash of cold water on face, toilet-paper sweep of splurged mascara, quick spray of deodorant, followed by dumping of tracksuit bottoms in favour of
3. The School-Run Dress: you know, the kind of dress you just throw on over your bikini when it's time to dash to pick up your gorgeous children at the end of a long afternoon lolling about in your garden. Or, in my case, to throw over the manky vest that I've been sleeping in for most of the afternoon. Actually I quite like my School-Run Dress. It makes me feel like I am stepping into costume, ready to play (though, granted, not very convincingly) the role of
4. The School-Run Mother. The slightly late School-Run Mother, not quite school-running but certainly school-jogging fairly briskly, wishing she were still in bed.

THE PLAYGROUND

Time was when I liked going to school. I liked the classrooms; I liked the library. And the music room, the labs, the computer room (singular in those days) and the art room and the kiln. Oh yes, the kiln, I loved the kiln. The changing rooms? Well, perhaps not so much and I was certainly never keen on the playground. I made a good school girl: keen, hard-working, competent. Really very good at sums, even hard ones.

Well school isn't what it used to be. The classroom door is closed to me, except for those awkward parents' evenings, legs splayed on undersized chairs and me writing random stuff in a notebook. (Why? Who do I think I'm kidding? Do I really think that the teacher is impressed, picturing me filing these notes away in the file marked 'Academic Progress'? She already knows that most weeks I can barely remember to sign the homework diary.)

Now all I get is the playground, twice a day, five days a week. I am a permanent new girl: pointless, gauche, self-conscious and not quite sure what to do with my hands. Trying not to make eye contact with anyone but the other misfits. I often wish Carrie were here, but she's got her impeccably behaved and boatered children, Rupert and Jocelyn, at St Matilda's, the prep school, where they keep them busy until 5pm. No Ruth either, because she has a proper job healing the sick and sends her Mum to collect her twin girls. It's just me and Mel, mostly.

So the playground was always a stressful place, but these days it has some pretty devastating associations. For it was here that I received the rather upsetting news that I had accidentally married a faithless twat.

CHAPTER TWO

JULY

NOT MUCH LIKE GRANGE HILL

So this is how I found out that my marriage was over.

I am in the playground, avoiding eye contact by keeping my gaze resolutely on the middle distance. I stand close to Mel, admiring her new dress, a delightful cheesecloth and macramé number. We start a bit of vague, aimless chit-chat to fill that yawning gap between 2.58pm and the appearance of the children at the classroom door. Behind us, toddlers screech their noisy impatience; undisturbed, a baby naps serenely in its pushchair, chubby legs sticking out from under the navy sunshade like the Wicked Witch of the East. I can feel my phone buzzing in my pocket, but it's too late, too close to pick-up time, to answer it.

But today my avoidance tactics aren't enough. For here is Imogen, PTA Clipboard Woman, and she's got me spotted. All the sliding eye-non-contact in the world won't dissuade her.

Hold on, though, something's not quite right. Normally women like Imogen approach me with only two possible facial expressions: Rota-Firm (usually involving the Clipboard) or Oh-I'm-Sure-You-Haven't-Forgotten (translation: I am bloody sure you *have* forgotten you flaky waste of space excuse for a mother, and I'm completely delighted about it). But there's something different playing around Imogen's Touche-Eclatted eyes. Something like... sympathy? God help me, pity?

'Jenny! Darling! How are *you?*'

Fake-concerned tilt of the head. Syrupy tone. Oh God, it's bad. I feel my phone buzzing again in my back pocket. I can't think what to do. Think Jen, think. The children? Something wrong with the children? No, that makes no sense. Why would Imogen be telling me? The PTA mafia aren't in charge of passing on news of dead or injured children. Not yet, anyway.

'We were so sorry to hear, *awful* news, I mean it must have been a terrible shock for you.'

Imogen gives me her best am-dram approximation of friendly concern. I feel the bile rise in my throat. We? Who's we? The PTA? The entire village? Is this *awful* news posted on the bloody church noticeboard?

I feel giddy and breathless, a heady cocktail of fear and anger making my head spin. My phone stops buzzing, for just a brief pause, then starts again.

My throat feels dry and cracked, but I manage to say, 'Thanks. I appreciate it. Look, sorry, I just need to take this phone call...'

I fish out the phone and hold it between us, a half-apologetic barrier. Imogen doesn't even bother to hide her disappointment that I have denied her this moment of high melodrama. I turn to Mel, but I see my confusion and concern mirrored in her face.

'Mel, can you get the kids, I just need to ...' The phone is buzzing again, a ticking bomb, a vibrating grenade in my palm.

Behind the bike-sheds the air is cooler, damper. I wonder if children still snog and smoke behind the bike-sheds? Not in Lower Worthington of course, but maybe in The Town. Christ I'm really stalling now, letting the precious seconds tick and stretch. Gingerly, I turn the phone, read my future written in my palm.

Chris mobile 7 missed calls

Behind the bike-sheds. A refuge from the world, but if this were the film of my life, the strings would be screeching, and an extreme close-up would pick out my dilated pupils, and the beads of sweat on my upper lip.

The grenade starts vibrating again. If I don't answer it, I won't have to know. I won't have to start to deal with it, whatever it is. I won't have to be the mother, the adult, the grown-up. I can just be a child again, hiding from the future, living in the moment. But even as I think this, I can feel the last precious moments of fragile-normality, of the-time-before, dribbling away, like the last remnants of water from a turned-off garden hose.

I press the screen and put the phone to my ear.

'Jen? Jen, are you there? I.... I've been trying to ring you.'

I am trying to identify the emotions in my husband's familiar voice – pain? guilt? panic? – when I see Mel coming towards me, her features crumpled with horror and her mouth pressed tight.

And to my husband of eleven years, my darling, the love of my life, the father of my children, the man I trust completely, the man I promised to love for ever, I say, 'I don't want to hear it. Not from you.'

And I hang up.

PARTY FUN

With immaculate timing, my husband's infidelity becomes common knowledge precisely three days before our daughter's fifth birthday. Don't worry though, because Chris doesn't blame himself for this unfortunate juxtaposition. He is a victim of circumstance, it turns out.

'It's not like I planned for this to come out now, you know.'

We are sitting on the patio, drinking tea and attempting to

have some sort of sensible conversation about what to do. It's the day after Revelation Day and two days before the Bloody Party.

'Don't keep calling it the Bloody Party. It's Rosie's day and that's really unpleasant.'

'Oh fuck off Chris.'

I really should try to stop saying that, or at least limit myself to some sort of daily quota. Because that's pretty much all I can manage at the moment and even in my highly emotional state I can see that it isn't the basis for productive dialogue. To a random passer-by, or maybe a drone with a camera covering above us, we would probably look like a normal couple, having a normal chat. Well, unless they could hear. Or lip-read. It all looks very civilised; I'm feeling murderous.

But I got most of my screaming out of the way yesterday. By the time Chris finally skulked home, I had heard the story from a few different sources, but the details were consistent.

My husband, kind, reliable Chris, a dull and boring something-in-IT type, has been knocking off Romily from the Big House. Romily! From the Big House! It's almost hilariously unbelievable, right up until the point that it's true. They'd met on some parish council business and he had helped her with her laptop when it crashed just before Christmas (Christmas! Seven months!) then there had been some cosy pub chats and things had progressed from there. And although there had been some talk in the village (none of it ever reaching me of course), they had kept it all pretty discreet until Romily had lost her phone down the side of the bed and her husband Edwin had heard it buzzing. And thence discovered some damning evidence in the form of, it was rumoured, sexting. This had rather affected the balance of Edwin's mind, and he had sought out Romily in the lunchtime crowd at the Red Lion. A showdown ensued. Two hours later, the news was all over the village, before reaching me via the unspeakable Imogen.

Now a number of questions arise from this story, not all of which, at the point we are having our 'Bloody Party' chat, have been thoroughly explored; some of which never will be I suspect, on the grounds of taste:

1. When the heck has Chris had time to conduct an affair, when he's always too bloody busy to come to sports' day, have lunch with my mother or help choose a new washing machine?

2. Did Chris join the parish council just to see if he could get a bit on the side, nice and close to hand?

3. Has Romily never heard of password protection? Amateurs like Romily should not be allowed to start adulterous affairs without some sort of basic lessons in covering your tracks. Infidelity 101. Loser.

4. Did he ever screw her in the Big House? Did they do it in the pool, in the tennis court, in the herb garden, under the shade of that rather impressive wisteria avenue? Is he, in other words, the lover to her Lady Chatterley? (I am finding this aspect inappropriately hysterical. Hysteria is my back-stop position right now.)

5. Sexting? *Really*??

But right now I am not asking any of these questions. My throat is hoarse from yesterday's circular but cathartic yelling. I have no real energy for any more confrontation tonight. Although I can't quite resist one more nasty dig.

'So, when were you planning for this to come out? Was there a schedule? I mean how early are we for this revelation?'

Chris has spent the night with his mother (and not with Romily, but I can't quite read the significance of this just yet); my mother-in-law's delight at this turn of events must only be exceeded by her joy at the prospect of having Romily as a new daughter-in-law. Quite an upgrade.

'I don't think I can bear to have you at this party.'

Chris sighs, and looks like he might cry again. Oh Jesus.

I say, 'Oh come on, really? You think I am being unreasonable?'

My voice is rising to a tone and volume that I need to try to control. Michael is playing on the X-Box and Rosie is watching CBeebies in the kitchen; I hope that both are turned up loud enough to drown me out.

'It's just ... well she's only five once. It seems so hard to miss it.'

Calm, Jen, calm.

'Well perhaps you could come in the morning and see her open her presents.'

A cracking compromise. How mature and reasonable of me. Chris just holds his head in his hands, his fingers tight against his scalp. My eye is drawn to the contrast of white knuckle and dark, thick hair. Despite myself, despite my hot anger (or maybe because of it) I feel the stirrings of lust, straining and inappropriate. And then, the sickening backlash of pain. This handsome man, the object of my desire and the source of so much pleasure for most of my adult life, is no longer mine. He has rejected me, betrayed me, lied to me, dumped me, ditched me, left me for another. For ROMILY from the BIG HOUSE.

His voice, his beloved voice, is broken with emotion and self-pity, 'It's just so, well, so sudden, so quick. I just can't get used to it.'

For the first time, I could hit him. I have never hit anyone in my life, but right now, if only I knew how, I would very much like to smack my fist against his stupid, reckless, ridiculous flesh and hear him cry out with pain.

'Chris, you utter utter *twat*.'

'Sssshhhhh, the children will hear for God's sake.'

The children, now he thinks of the children. I have to go inside, sit on the sofa hugging Rosie onto my lap and watch some mindless cartoons for a while. Otherwise I might smash his perfect, boyish face against the glass patio table, and we'd never clear up the mess before the Bloody Party.

ON YOUR OWN DOORSTEP

Back when I was Jennifer Dottridge of 3R, my tutor Mrs Addison wrote in her end-of-year report that I was 'relentlessly cheerful.' Well on the surface, to the casual reader, that might seem like a compliment. If you're 13 and, let's say for the sake of argument, a pretty perky sort of person. It was only years later that it occurred to me that what Mrs Addison was saying here was: 'Jennifer is incredibly annoying.' And, I think it's fair to say, she may be speaking for a fair proportion of my acquaintance.

Time has passed, but nothing has changed, not really. My cheerfulness is still pretty relentless, and still, I guess, incredibly annoying. Not much more than 24 hours after I crouched, sobbing, in the rough grass behind the bike sheds while Mel told me the Awful News about my faithless twat of a husband, here's poor Mel again, having to hear all about the Silver Lining to this situation.

I say, 'You know, Mel, I don't normally let people in. I like to think I can cope with everything, by myself. Well maybe this will make me grow up a bit, start accepting that I can't do everything by myself.'

Dear kind Mel, total saint that she is, squints a little but refrains from laughing out loud at this total bullshit. Instead she smiles, and nods.

'Darling you are terrifically strong. Really amazing. We all love you, you know.'

Poor Mel, she's got nothing for me, really. Because my bullshit is true, to an extent. I don't let people in and frankly Mel doesn't really want to be let in. She likes it much better when I am cheery and chatty and normal. This role reversal is disconcerting for her. She leans forward and strokes my arm.

'Ghastly for you, just ghastly.'

Carrie arrives with three cups of tea. Carrie has made a lot of cups of tea over the last twenty-four hours and will surely make many more over the coming weeks and months. In fact, I may suggest she goes out and invests in an urn.

'Right so here's what I've done today.'

Briskly practical, Carrie is the kind of woman who should really be fighting wars, or at least protecting the Home Front. Running the pre-school, and the fete, and the church flower rota, well it keeps her busy enough but the world of warfare is the poorer for her absence.

She goes on, 'You know Ruby Becker?'

Do I? Do I know Ruby Becker? Christ, I can't think. I shouldn't have had that glass of wine when Chris left, but I can't face bedtime without it.

'Ruby, Ruby Becker?' Impatient now, even a little irritable. 'Lives by the church? Well anyway'- giving up on my neighbourly ignorance - 'she's got her nephew staying with her, some sort of Victorian name like Jethro or something. He's had some sort of trauma, haven't found out the deets yet but anyway he wants to be a teacher and he's been fab with the kids at Sunday School and he does the Scouts or Cubs or whatever and anyway he's coming to help.'

I say, 'Christ Almighty Carrie, you are making no sense at all. What are you saying?'

Carrie sighs deeply. Exasperation is like sweet balm from her: it shows she cares.

'Ruby's nephew, Jethro. He's a lovely young man and he's coming to help, at the party. I thought he could be a good babysitter for you, now you don't have a man about the place.'

Ouch. No I don't have a man about the place but why would I want a spotty, awkward teenager? I don't know much about teenagers but I definitely don't want one in the house. I don't have the room. And anyway teenagers make me nervous. Too late now, though. Carrie's asked him and Carrie's requests in the village have a power that is nothing short of a Papal decree.

LESS GRUFF, AND SOFTER

So Jethro comes, an hour before the party starts, except he isn't called Jethro at all. His name is Edgar, well 'Ed, if you don't mind'; his response to my questioningly-raised eyebrow is to say, 'My mother is a Brontë fan.'

'Edgar Linton? You're named after Edgar Linton? He's a great character.'

'Oh yes, he's amazing. Always going pale and trembling. And married to a woman madly in love with someone else. That's pretty much every man's dream.'

'Well, he's very... amiable.'

'True, true, I mean who wants to be passionate and heroic when you can be *amiable*?'

'It could have been worse I suppose,' I say.

'Yes. My brother is called Heathcliff. He's blonde, skinny and five-two. He runs a surf-school. He calls himself Becker. It was either that or hang a few dogs, just to get in character. Oh and I have a sister.'

A beat. I fill it. 'Cathy?'

'Villette,' he deadpans.

Although this isn't all that funny, it makes me laugh out loud, for the first time since The Bike Shed. It's just so delightful to talk to someone about books (even in this slightly elliptical way) and even more wonderful to talk about, well, something else. Even for a short time, I'm not the abandoned wife. If Ed knows my terrible sad story, he's hiding it well.

He is also, rather wonderfully, helping me with the preparations. Without asking, he is observing what needs to be done and doing it. We are setting the table, in a pretty companionable way for two people who met ten minutes previously.

Ed says, 'Do you have some games or something planned? Or would you just like me to improvise something?' I try not to look too panicked - I have, of course, planned absolutely nothing - and then the door flings open and Rosie bounces in.

'It's my birthday!'

Ed says, 'Yes I heard that. Happy birthday. Are you having a good day?'

'What's your name? I don't remember inviting you.'

My daughter is terrifically shy. It's a terrible curse. We are thinking of getting her some professional help to deal with it.

Ed laughs, 'Actually your Mum invited me. I have some good ideas for games. Would you like to hear them?'

'My Daddy isn't coming. Do you want to see my new swingball?'

And the two of them go into the garden, continuing their extremely random conversation over a very violent game of swingball. I wonder for a moment if I should warn Ed about my daughter's wild competitiveness, but the boy seems pretty much able to take care of himself.

Thank God for Carrie and her powerful decrees, because the presence of Ed makes the party not only bearable but, unbelievably, actually quite enjoyable. I sit around the patio table chatting with Carrie and Mel and Ruth while twelve squeaking five-year-old girls play dressing up, musical bumps and some sort of complicated dancing competition. At any one time, he appears to have at least two pink princesses holding his hands, but miraculously he is still able to bring us all a cup of tea about half-way through and beat the birthday girl at swingball, again. (No concessions for her age; I like that.) He even encourages the picnic tea onto the lawn; by the time I have handed out the party bags, he is already shaking out the picnic blanket and folding it neatly.

I am enjoying myself so much, in fact, that I almost forget the prickly issue of payment; I haven't even asked Carrie what she has offered.

'Come and have a glass of wine with us!' Jesus, is the boy even old enough?

'Thanks but I think I will get off. I am pretty knackered to be honest.' I am frantically windmilling to Carrie, to find out how much to pay him. He is sliding towards the door and Carrie, true to form, is completely ignoring me and chatting to Mel about the price of biscuits or some such. I follow Ed into the hall where his exit is stalled by a flying tackle from Rosie.

'I like you! Will you come again?'

Well said, Rosie. Oh to be five years old, and able to speak the truth without fear. He laughs, to his credit, in a surprisingly unscared way. He is probably used to having girls grabbing his legs. It's quite possibly a daily occurrence.

'Rosie, let go, let go darling. God, thank you, really I can't thank you enough. Can I bring the money round later? I am sorry I haven't sorted anything out. Really, you were great. I am so grateful.'

'Don't worry Mrs Grey. I loved it, really. Mrs Stanford said you might need a babysitter? Well maybe you could think of me if you do? I need to earn something, you know, to pay my way.'

'Yes, yes of course. Well thank you again.'

Awkwardly, I hold out my hand to shake his, like some retired Army Captain or something. God, he's going to think I'm mental. But he shakes it, and smiles. 'Goodbye, Mrs Grey. It was lovely to meet you. And you Rosie.' Rosie is gazing up at him, with a look of nothing short of worship.

'Kiss! Kiss!' And he reaches down and kisses the top of her head, then says, 'Goodbye, birthday girl.'

And then he's gone, leaving us both feeling a little dazed and sorry.

PLAYING THE WRONGED WOMAN

You would think that all those novels I had read about the dumped woman, the wronged first wife, would help to give me a clue about how to behave appropriately. But no. As usual, Jen is scrabbling around for her motivation. I am no more dignified, no more serious and certainly no more sympathetic a character than my usual flippant self.

'Jennifer finds it hard to take anything seriously,' said my geography teacher Mrs Winter on that 3R end of year report. Well, she should know. I mean, if you can't take geography seriously, then there's no hope is there? If I can't rearrange my features into a semblance of dignity while learning about oxbow lakes, well, being ditched for someone thinner, richer and prettier, that's hardly likely to stop the endless glib remarks. If anything it's only likely to raise the hysteria stakes.

(She's not younger, though, Romily - well done Chris for avoiding that particular cliché. Marries a woman four years his senior; dumps her for one a good clear decade older. Nice work. Interesting quirk of character there, Chris. Can't quite put my finger on what it says about you Chris, but it'll come to me, I'm sure.)

Part of the problem is, I haven't been dumped since I was 14 and I find myself falling into Jackie clichés. Listening to my gloomiest records, eating nothing but cherries all day, buying a new outfit from Top Shop - I wonder if any of these would make me feel better? Perhaps I should write to the Just Seventeen problem page about it all:

HELP! My fella has run off with another girl! I feel really down about it. I keep thinking it's something I did wrong. Maybe it was my habit of spitting on my mascara? Or maybe I should have got rid of my Five Star tapes? How can I win him back?
Love
Jenny.

Dear Jenny,
It's always horrible when a relationship ends, but the sooner you start to get over him the better. Trying to win him back is just a way of prolonging the pain – and it won't work. Move on, and start looking for someone who wants you and likes you enough not to treat you this way. Keep yourself busy with friends and hobbies, and you will be amazed how quickly this fella will seem like history.

That's all well and good when you're 14 and all you have to bind you together are some borrowed (now scratched) Oasis CDs and a half-eaten stick of rock from that bus-trip to the seaside last summer. When you see your husband's eyes mocking you from those artfully-lit, stomach-churningly-tasteful, happy-bloody-family photo-on-canvas monstrosities on the dining room wall, it's a bit harder to put the bastard out of your mind.

It's even harder when the bastard won't actually leave.

IF YOU WANT TO LEAVE ME, WHY ARE YOU STILL BLOODY HERE?

Separation is not quite what I thought it would be. I mean, for a start, I anticipated an element of actual living apart, maybe even a bit more room in the bed. Well, no joy there. The trouble is, you see, it's all very complicated. Apparently. I mean he misses the children (bites lip) and Romily (Romily! rolls eyes) is looking for somewhere for them to move together but she's so bloody busy with the business and blah blah blah. For a couple of seconds after this particular excruciating conversation I sense he's contemplating asking me if I would help with the house search. Gosh wouldn't that be terrifically civilised and grown up and twenty first century? The schools break up soon so I will have some time on my hands. Well, I might actually agree, if only he had the balls to ask me. If it meant I could have him out of the way so I could start to get used to being alone, then I think I could stomach it. I wouldn't mind telling people either; it would show me in a marvellously mature light.

And I am being very mature about it, apparently. Everyone is terrifically proud of me and all that. I am not really sure that I have a choice about this. What else could I do? Turn up bleary-eyed for school pick up? Swap the School-Run Dress for rent garments and mantle? Chuck paint at Romily's house? Except of course it isn't just Romily's house, it's Romily and Edwin's house, and I guess Edwin's day wouldn't exactly be brightened if I started lobbing Dulux at his property. Seems a bit mean-spirited really. I mean my husband already nicked his wife, and while I don't blame myself for that (well, not all the time) I can't imagine Edwin's mood would be improved by having to deal with me getting hysterical.

Except I'm not. Hysterical that is. I am just extremely bloody miserable. And surely even the playground Mums can tell that? Surely they aren't fooled by my 'brave smile'? Surely they don't think I'm drifting around serenely and coping wonderfully well? Playing the tragic heroine brings a number of expectations with it, and one of them is a pretty much constant requirement to lie, blatantly, through your teeth about how you are.

'Yes, I'm doing fine. Thank you, you're very kind, but no I don't need anything. Gosh yes, very amicable. Well we've been friends for a long time and that's not about to change any time soon. You know, for the children.'

Sometimes, just occasionally, I imagine what it would be like to tell the truth.

'Christ, no I'm terrible. I can't sleep at all at night, then can barely stay awake in the day. Do I need anything? Is there anything you can do? What I could really do with is someone to look after my children because I can't, I really can't. I am irritable and snappy with them. Especially with Rosie, she looks so much like Chris that sometimes I can't stand to look at her. And Michael, he's so gloomy already I just can't bear to think what this is going to do to him.

'Oh and the other thing I need is a gun, quite a big one because I want to kill them, my husband and his rich, sophisticated and beautiful lover, not injure them or anything but actual, certain, immediate death. I don't want them to suffer. I just want them gone. So I don't have to face being civil to them for the rest of my life. But my consolation is at least she's too bloody old to have a baby, so I don't have to deal with that.

'And although I love my children, so very much, there are times when I wish I didn't have them because I am desperate, longing to run away, somewhere far far away from all this appalling pain and mess and misery where I could start again and not have to be strong and loving and bloody relentlessly cheerful. And I would never have to see him again because he's no friend of mine and never will be again, because friendship can't ever include causing another human being quite this much horrible pain.'

CHAPTER THREE

AUGUST

I MUST STOP FUCKING SWEARING SO FUCKING MUCH

It's Polly on the phone. I lie on my bed to talk to her, supervising the children through two closed doors and down thirteen stairs. It's for the best though; Polly is a shocking swearer and I can't risk mirroring her language. The last thing I need right now is for the children to start effing and blinding in front of ROMILY (eye roll).

'For fuck's sake Jen, it's so fucking obvious.'

As well as Olympic-standard swearing, Polly specialises in straight-talking. For a woman who has never, to my knowledge, maintained a relationship for longer than that tricky six-week anniversary, she has a lot of good relationship advice to hand out. Presumably because she's not using any of it herself.

'You need to get back to fucking work.'

I lie back onto the bean-bag pillow, a remnant of the days when I used to prop myself on it to feed my wriggly babies. It still smells vaguely of sour milk. It's curiously comforting, a faint whiff of a time when all I had to worry about was chafed nipples.

I say, 'It really isn't that simple.'

I suddenly feel very very tired.

Polly says, 'I could get you some work, I could find something for you tomorrow.'

'I have been looking, honestly. I had a look on-line today. They all want someone digitally savvy.'

'Well you can get digitally savvy. You are online all the bastard time.'

I snort, 'Hanging out with the internet sprites on KeyboardMums. Oh yeah hold on, I'll just update my cv.'

'Look, I'm not saying go back into fucking publishing. It wasn't a proper fucking job anyway. But there's all sorts of crap you could do. What about sales, or marketing or some of that soft bollocks?'

I say, sarcastically, 'Or maybe I could retrain as a lawyer?' Polly laughs so loud and so long that even I am gratified, although she isn't the hardest audience to please. Polly likes to play the hard-nosed barrister type, and I thought she would find that idea amusing, but even I could not have hoped for quite this level of amusement.

'Yeah, yeah, good one. No, they don't let squirrels practise law, Mare.'

Oh yes, Polly also does nicknames. Mare, as in Old Grey Mare, and short for Nightmare too I guess; sometimes Squirrel as in Grey Squirrel short for Half-Squirrel, as in the jumpy woodland creature that, given my clumsy awkwardness in the human world, she maintains, must be part of my genetic heritage.

'Anyway it isn't the skills, it's the hours and the energy and the childcare and I just can't be arsed, frankly.'

'Jesus, sorry to break this to you, Mare, but you have to be arsed. You can't be wifey-wifey any more. You have to be hard-bitch divorcee. Hard-bitch divorcee has to worky-worky.'

I know this is true, but God where to start? I mean, the very idea of sorting out the childcare is just too much for my addled brain to deal with. And how would I even begin to afford it?

'Well actually there is something I have been thinking

about. I am going to try writing again, send a few articles to some old contacts. I have a few things that might sell. And,' I hesitate, because I haven't yet said this one out loud, 'I thought about teaching.'

'Oh fucking hell. Of course you have. Well I guess they let squirrels teach. Are you going to do that thing when you stand on tables and shout poetry?'

Now I'm laughing too because, yes, Polly knows me well and, yes, I may have searched for The Dead Poets' Society on Netflix a few nights ago.

'Not children, though. Children scare me, even my own. Especially my own. Adults I thought. Maybe.'

'Good idea. Go and do some evening class shit, then you won't be earning too much while the divorce comes through. Then you can go to Squirrel School next year, learn how to be a proper squirrel teacher. Sorted. Well that was easy. Right, see you next Saturday. I'll message you when I leave.'

And then she's gone, off to her urban life of cocktails and handbags and boring cokeheads and I am left lying on the bed, phone resting on my chest, wishing I really were a bloody squirrel.

6 REASONS WHY IT WOULD BE GOOD TO BE A SQUIRREL

1. They always look very perky and cheerful and they are quite smart I think, but they are probably unbothered by the great questions concerning the meaning of life.

2. They have lush tails.

3. Although they are basically vermin, they have a pretty good press. Children think they're cute but crucially no-one keeps them as a pet. They are more or less autonomous.

4. They can move super-fast.

5. Squirrels never have to make small talk in the playground or go to terrible dinner parties.

6. A squirrel would never, never have to be polite to the

sexy sophisticated weasel-woman who stole her squirrel-husband when meeting her unexpectedly at some horrific car crash of a village event.

LIKE AMBRIDGE ON ACID

I am in my bedroom, choosing clothes.

I hope you aren't expecting any detailed descriptions of clothes though, because I'm not very good at that sort of thing. I can't do the deets, as Carrie would say. I just don't have the vocabulary for a start; I get all confused about the difference between teal and electric blue, not to mention all that beige/ecru/stone stuff. All those years when functional teenage girls were in Top Shop getting their apprenticeship in Clothes, I was in the library, reading about life rather than living it. So my skills are pretty deficient. I can get dressed, sure. I can even go shopping – although I like to do it in second gear, just slowing down long enough to grab the clothes from the rack, but never actually stopping until I reach the cash tills. The arrival of clothes in supermarkets has been a great help too. It saves me having to go into clothes shops, which makes me nervous. I like to buy a skirt between the cereals and the toilet rolls; it seems efficient, and energy-saving. I was also pretty safe when I was working in publishing. Suits, from Jigsaw, in black, brown and, to ring the changes, sometimes in grey. And as for on-line shopping - I am crippled with indecision just even on the first page and hampered by the lack of knowledge of any of the terms - what IS a smart dress, versus a work dress and which one of those is going to be worth paying £6.99 bloody SHIPPING for?

Today though, I could do with a bit more clothes-knowledge (or at least a few more actual clothes) because I am choosing an outfit, and I am choosing it very very carefully. Because this afternoon I will make my first public appearance in my new role as Abandoned Wife at a Village Event. And I'm struggling. I need to get the costume right, because I have a message I want to get across, loud and clear, and let's face it I don't really want to actually have to talk to anyone, if I can possibly help it. I want the entire village to be able to see from the other side of Imogen's enormous garden that I am not only coping, but I am thriving. I want to look slim, elegant and sophisticated, to the extent that all will gaze upon me and wonder, out loud if possible, what kind of man would leave such a manifestation of perfect femininity. I want to look sexy and attractive, but not in a desperately-seeking-another-man way; the married women will be nervous enough in my presence already, without any need to provoke them further. A spurned woman! Cage her! Muzzle her!

Most of all, I want to appear to even the most casual observer like a woman supremely unbothered by the fact that she has been rejected, spurned and humiliated right on her own doorstep.

No matter how long I gaze in my wardrobe, I am struggling to find just the right combination of clothes to meet these disparate needs. Bugger, I should have gone shopping, although that might have made me even more desperate. Under normal circumstances I would choose something black, combined with black shoes, black accessories and - currently, coincidentally - a black mood and a black heart. But this is a summer barbecue party to celebrate the opening of the new Village Hall, and black won't really cut it. Anyway the symbolism of black isn't quite what I want to communicate either. I could do without the Black Widowhood. Chris isn't actually dead. Unfortunately.

Eventually I choose a jersey print dress with a grey and green florally-geometric pattern, to the knee, with some green sparkly flip-flops. I am pretty happy with the overall effect - just the funky side of Boden - and I consider, just for a moment, adding a hat. Then I remember at the last minute that I look ridiculous in hats and decide against it.

Although my current sticky situation has exacerbated my struggle to find the right outfit, it is a recurring problem. I never know what to wear; that's because I don't really know what role I am playing in this village. I never intended to be living in a village, and everyone around me must realise that. I exude an air of constant shifty discomfort. I never know what to say, or do, and I definitely never know what to wear.

I grew up in the faceless suburbs; I spent my early adulthood in the comforting anonymity of the city. Chris persuaded me to buy this very reasonably priced property in commuter country when I was travelling to London every day, and very handy it was too. Then one day I woke up, pregnant and living in The Archers. Chris loves it; of course he does. Why wouldn't he? He just drifts in and out, dropping by in between long trips to exotic places to fix their computers, or whatever it is he does there. (And, latterly, he has played the protagonist in a marvellous juicy adulterous sub-plot. This one will run and run.) Me, I was supposed to be living in Notting Hill or, at a push, This Life; instead here I am, lost and awkward, clutching my drink on the Dralon sofa, trying to remember who invited me to Abigail's Party.

Rosie has spent about as long as me choosing her outfit, and looks twice as funky in denim shorts and a pink floral top; even choosing her swimsuit took about twenty minutes. (There will be swimming at this party; Imogen, naturally, has a heated pool.) Michael is every inch the proto-emo-boy in head-to-toe black, accessorised with a mildly grumpy expression. He has a swimming kit jammed under his arm though; he is not so disaffected that he won't be taking advantage of the full facilities.

We can hear the buzz of noise from Imogen's house even as we close our front door. I am not much looking forward to the afternoon, but I'm glad we're invited, otherwise it would have been pretty tough to have to sit and listen to them all having fun three streets away.

I try not to feel intimidated by the palatial nature of Imogen's house; that's another thing about living in this village: everyone we know lives in a house considerably bigger and more expensive than ours. We live in the slums of Lower Worthington. Which is strange, because actually Chris and I had a pretty good income between us when we bought it. Chris has a well-paid job, really, so how come everyone else is richer than us? I am not really all that bothered about this - although Chris has been known to be a little resentful, darkly muttering about 'family money' - but it is curious nonetheless.

One reason it bothers me less than it might is that living in a relatively modest house is a pretty good way of annoying my mother. She would have adored it if I'd ended up in this kind of massive house, with endless bedrooms and reception rooms and a terrace and pool and tennis courts. She paid thousands of pounds and made many sacrifices in order to send me to the kind of smart private school that was intended to prepare me for marrying the right kind of man to bag such a prize. That plan didn't really work out, but her logic was sound. Many of my school contemporaries – pretty, blonde, shiny-faced girls with Alice bands called things like Anna and Camilla and Lucy – are living exactly the kind of life Mum had mapped out for me. The fact that I haven't joined their Joules-clad ranks is a great source of disappointment for her, and a perennial subject for complaint.

But although annoying my mother is always a plus point, that still isn't the main reason why I don't envy Imogen and her sisters-in-the-Aga-hood. Even walking around this kind of property makes me feel weary. Imagine the pressure of having to actually live in a house like this? The thought is exhausting. The housework. The maintenance. The gardening. Even if you were rich enough to afford Help for these tasks, you would still have to manage the Help, a job that I am ill-suited for, in every way. Nor would I be able to keep this place tidy, any more than I can keep my own house tidy. I am not stupid enough to think that my mess would be nicely spread out over the greater square-footage. That's not how it works. My mess would spawn, grow, multiply.

And the pressure of a music room, well, I might have to start to learn an actual musical instrument. (Again.) What possible use could I have for a tennis court? The swimming pool, well that's a nice idea in theory but in practice - I understand - a pool brings with it many pool-duties and pool-products: filters, chemicals, draining. Much better to go and use someone else's pool and then come home again, leaving them to worry about leaves in the drains and fishing out the drowned shrews.

Basically, the bigger the house, the longer the to-do list. I can't imagine anything worse.

Of course for Imogen, this is all perfectly marvellous, darling. When I was in my twenties I am ashamed to say that I used to be terrifically sneery about those Annas and Camillas and Lucys, the ones who got into the school spirit and really wanted to be corporate wives and trophy mothers. Nice enough girls; my brother Charlie went through a whole lacrosse team of them. Not very sisterly of me to be so sneery, I grant you, and - it won't have escaped your attention - I have now joined the ranks of the stay-at-home-mum. Except I don't have nearly as much to do as they have; my to-do list is much shorter, and I neglect the housework to loll about with a book as often as I can. Realistically, I have plenty of time to go to work. I am not even a corporate wife; the nearest I get to entertaining is having Ruth, Carrie and Mel round for a takeaway every few weeks. If I were organising events like this - the thank-you barbecue for the Village Hall Committee - well, then maybe I could justify my stay-at-home status. I do have my own modest portfolio of volunteer work and good causes, granted, but compared to these village chatelaines with their lovely houses, servants and extensive social calendar to manage, I am just a lazy cow.

We are in the centre of the action now, and I can't help but be impressed at this feat of organisation. It's like being in a Boden photo-shoot. (They would have to photo-shop Michael out altogether, and maybe make Rosie and me a bit fuzzy, but still.) Some children are splashing in the turquoise pool; others are shrieking with joy and excitement on the bouncy castle. The barbecue is smoking invitingly. There is a huge stripy marquee, in case the weather isn't kind; of course, the weather *is* kind - why wouldn't it be? A jazz band is playing under a sprawling oak tree, and small groups of beautifully dressed people sit around sparkling white tables, drinking from tall glasses of Pimms. And in the centre of it all, on the terrace, a podium ready for the speeches and presentations, decorated with a banner reading "THANK YOU VILLAGE HALL COMMITTEE!" This particular sight gives me a moment of lurching dread; for I am a member of this committee and I am not much looking forward to being THANKED!

Looking at all this organization and all this *stuff*, I start to calculate how much this has cost. How much for this party? How much for the caterers, the bar? The bouncy castle? How much, come to that, for the pool, for the summer-house, for the plants in this garden, the resurfacing of the tennis courts? If these people have all this money sloshing about, I think, why didn't they just club together a few grand each and pay for the new bloody Village Hall? Honestly, they wouldn't miss a couple of thousand. And it would save us all from the endless expense and time and energy of it all - the form-filling, the sponsored bounces, the nearly-new sales, the cake stalls.

I know this is all totally unreasonable. It's their money. They can do what they like with it. But it's an anarchic idea. It could be the end of the virtuous circle - good causes, committees, fund-raising. Village life would lose its core, its essential purpose, and this would lead to its inevitable collapse. We would all have to pack up and go and live in the city.

I secretly smile to myself at this thought.

I spot Carrie and Mel at a table and we join them. The children race around excitedly for a while. Carrie has chosen an excellent position, with a good vantage point for the whole party. I am glad to be sitting down, but rather wish I'd brought a book, to shield myself in case of unwanted approaches. Come on Jen, try to relax. This party is for you, partly; try to enjoy it.

I catch sight of Ed, on the other side of the lawn, with Ruby Becker. He is hard to miss, actually. He is wearing an extremely loud shirt, similar to the one he wore to Rosie's party, in blue and orange check, with jeans shorts and orange flip flops. He sees me looking at him – I look away, but it's too late. He is coming over. I suddenly feel a little flustered.

'Hello Mrs Grey. Mrs Stanford, Mrs Jackson.' Christ Almighty, good roll call; the boy certainly pays attention. 'Are Rosie and Michael here?'

'Hi Ed. Yes they're here somewhere. Do you want to sit down, shall I get you a drink?'

'Thanks but I was wondering if they wanted to go and have a swim? If they have their swim-things?'

'God, that would be lovely. Would you mind?'

'No, I was going to go in myself. Shall I go and find them?'

Carrie interrupts, 'You can take my children too, if you can find them. Rupert and Joss. I think they're on the bouncy castle.'

'Sure. Of course. What about your children, Mrs Jackson?'

'Thanks, that's kind but they're already in the pool I think, with Bob.'

'Are you OK to look after them? I mean, are you qualified?' Carrie quizzes him, intently. God, sorry Ed.

He responds, politely, 'Well I'm a very strong swimmer. And I've done some lifesaving things at school.' He smiles, reassuringly.

'OK, that's alright then,' says Carrie, ungraciously. I thank him profusely, trying to make up for her rudeness. He brings us fresh glasses of Pimms and even liberates some bowls of crisps for us, before scooping up the children. I watch his garish departing back for a moment, before turning to ask

Carrie to repeat her question.

'Sorry, I wasn't concentrating. What did you just say?'

Carrie sighs, 'I was asking about Chris. Have you heard from him?'

'Oh bloody Chris. Yes, he's in....' I search for the name of the place. 'Milan? Madrid? Somewhere beginning with M. Minerva? No hold on. I don't think Minerva is really a place. Anyway, he's due back on Tuesday and then, God help us, we're on this canal boat trip next week.'

Mel turns to me in horror, 'No! Don't tell me you are going through with it!'

'Well I don't really have much choice, do I? What else can I do?'

Mel and Carrie contemplate this question for a moment.

'Well I guess you could go on your own, just you and the children,' suggests Carrie.

'Yes. I suppose so but, have you ever been on a canal holiday?' They shake their heads. 'Me neither, and I think there's a reason for that. I honestly don't relish the idea of steering a boat by myself. It's just not the kind of thing that I am likely to be good at, or even competent at to be honest. And also, how will I manage it? I mean, looking after two children when I am steering at the same time. Going through locks? God can you imagine me trying to negotiate locks. Tying up the boat? And every time I leave the boat, I'll have to take the kids with me. I just can't see how it would work, logistically. I would just be miserable.'

I stir my glass with the swizzle stick, violently slooshing around the chopped up fruit and mint.

'I never wanted to go on a bloody canal boat in the first place. I wanted to go in a cottage like a normal family. Having to steer something is not my idea of a holiday.'

Mel says, with uncharacteristic vehemence, 'I know you didn't. You said so, many times. So why did he insist? Why would a man in the middle of an affair arrange a canal boat holiday?'

'Exactly! That's what I said to him. It doesn't make any logical sense.'

Carrie says, 'Because he didn't expect to get caught.'

We all muse upon the ultimately-duplicitous nature of man for a moment, in companionable, seething silence.

Then I say, 'I guess when you are in the middle of something like that, you need to just carry on pretending everything's normal. So risks don't occur to you, because you're not thinking straight.'

'Don't defend him Jen!' Mel is shocked.

'No, I'm not defending him. I'm just saying, I can imagine how it happened. When he was with me and the children, I suppose he just had to put Romily out of his mind. To forget about her. And when he was with her, he would have to forget about us. That's the only way you could do it, I guess. And so when he was booking the holiday on a tiny boat with his wife, he wasn't thinking - what if she finds out about my affair? Because he had put his affair completely from his mind when he was with me.'

'I can't believe you're being so reasonable about it.'

'Oh don't worry,' I laugh. 'I didn't take this reasonable tone with him. I was screaming and shouting and throwing stuff.'

Then, seeing Mel's reaction. I say, 'Not really Mel, don't look so appalled. But I am just trying to make sense of it, to get my head around it. It helps to try and see it from his point of view.'

Carrie is incredulous, 'Does it? God I don't think I would find that helpful at all.'

Mel shakes her head in agreement, 'No, me neither. I don't think I could under any circumstances spend a week on a boat with my husband if he was with someone else. Sorry Jen but I think you're a saint. I would just cancel the holiday, if I couldn't go by myself.'

Carrie adds, 'Yeah, I think that's what I would do too.'

'Really?' I am surprised. I haven't really considered this as an option. 'The children are looking forward to it, and anyway it's next week: we wouldn't get our money back. Does the cancellation policy cover unexpected infidelity? I haven't checked.' I laugh, just a little bitterly.

'Well if money is lost, then let Romily pay it,' says Mel, surprisingly nastily.

'No, the kids want to go. And they want to see their Dad. I'll just have to manage, somehow.'

'Will you have to share, you know, sleeping accommodation?' Carrie tries to phrase this question delicately.

'Yes,' I grimace. 'We will have to share a bed.' Collective sharp intake of breath. 'Bloody hell,' says Mel. 'That's tough.'

'So what are your plans for the summer?' I need a change of subject. We chat about holidays, get out our diaries, make plans for sleepovers, trips out. We negotiate when we will look after each other's children, to give the others a break. I think about telling them about my plans for evening classes, but I want to mull it over a bit longer before I talk to them about it.

The party is in full flow by the time Ed returns with the children, dressed and dry with their wet swim-things wrapped neatly in towels.

'Can we go on the bouncy castle now?' says Michael.

'Wouldn't you like to sit down and have a rest first?' This suggestion is treated with the contemptuous silence it deserves.

'I can sit and watch them if you want to go and have a swim too.' Ed's face is flushed from the swim, and his hair is slicked back and damp. With his fringe out of his eyes, I notice how thick his eyelashes are, so dense at the roots that it almost looks like he has eyeliner on. He sees me looking at him, and turns to me, holds my look until I have to look away. 'Most of the children have got out now, it's mainly adults.'

Mel and Carrie are keen; I am less so. I don't have my swimsuit with me; it's not beyond the bounds of possibility that I could go home and get it, but I am reluctant. My careful selection of clothes will all be for nothing if I have to strip off and get in the pool. I am mentally - and indeed physically - unprepared for that kind of exposure. It may well be that the whole village won't be judging my stubbly legs, but it's not a risk I am prepared to take.

'Oh come on Jen, it will be fun!' Once Carrie has an idea in her head, though, it's hard to shift it.

'Yes come on, it won't take a minute to pop home!' adds Mel. Oh great, pincer movement.

'No really, I'm quite happy here.'

Carrie again, 'But it's so hot! A dip will be lovely and refreshing.' Like a terrier with a rabbit. Drop it Carrie, drop it!

'Actually, I was hoping I could have chance to talk to you, Mrs Grey. I wanted to ask you about my text choices for next year. Would you mind?' says Ed.

We all look at him, with varying degrees of surprise and relief.

'Sure, that would be fine. What did you want to ask?' I turn to him.

'I have to choose two texts to compare, for my English Literature coursework. And one text for critical analysis, feminist probably. Or Marxist, maybe. I'm not sure, but I have a few ideas. Do you mind?'

'God, do I mind talking about books? No, I really don't.' The others have gathered up their swimming bags and are far enough away to be out of earshot. 'Thank you, that was... timely.'

'I really did want to talk to you about this, but that seemed a good time to bring it up.' We laugh. 'Your friends can be very ... forceful.'

'Yes. That's one word for it.'

We talk for a while about the poetry that he has been reading, and I make some suggestions for other things he might read. We agree passionately about the merits of Sylvia Plath, and disagree equally violently about Ernest Hemingway. (Overrated, say I. Apparently I only think this because I am a woman and therefore cannot properly appreciate the 'muscular' quality of his writing. Apparently.)

I start to tell him about my ideas for evening classes - poetry appreciation and creative writing. We chat about some possible poems for analysis, and models for the creative writing workshops. I talk to him about a few ideas I have for some magazine articles that I might try to write over the summer. He tells me about a piece he wrote for the local newspaper last year, and entertains me with stories from his school creative writing group.

All too soon, I see Imogen bearing down on us. Go away Imogen. I am actually enjoying this conversation.

Go. Away.

'Jen! You look lovely, really!'

Really? Really! No need for the note of over-emphasis there, Imogen. It makes you sound unconvincing. As if you didn't know.

'Did you see I put you down for the Couples Championship?' I feel my face prickle with horror. Surely Imogen isn't evil enough to make me remind her, here and now, that I can't take part in a Couples Championship? Because I have carelessly, negligently, lost the other half of my couple and therefore the laurels of couple-dom have been wrenched from my brow. Surely Imogen can't have forgotten that I'm the Merry Divorcee? Surely?

She carries on, 'I know tennis isn't your thing' - grimace at shared recollection of ill-fated tennis four that I was somehow persuaded to join, when I never even managed to serve - 'so I've put you down for croquet!'

She turns her clipboard around to show us. 'And you're up next! Up you come!'

Ed and I lean over to look at the sheet. There it is in black and white: Couple 6 – Edgar Becker and Jenny Grey.

No. Really? No. Surely even Imogen wouldn't be so crass, so insensitive as to pair me up with a spare child? Surely even she would realise this is the modern-day equivalent of the

Scarlet Letter – A for Abandoned Woman. It's like having to dance with your little brother at the school disco. (Which I did, for the record. Every year.)

Ed says, 'Excellent. I love croquet. Hold on, I'll just tell the kids where we are.'

I can't help but smile at his confident striding figure, and then turn my smiling face to Imogen. Laughing, I say, 'Looks like we're up for it. Will be over in a minute.'

If Imogen is disconcerted by this reaction, she has the good grace to hide it.

'Do you actually know how to play croquet?'

'Only what I've seen from Alice in Wonderland. You?'

'Yes, I'm actually quite good. In fact, don't tell anyone, but I played for my university. Little known fact, and yet another sign of my well-spent youth. Can you play pool?'

'Ha, I'm a demon at pool,' Ed says. 'Is that a good sign?'

'It's about angles and all that. And being viciously competitive.'

Ed says, 'Excellent. We are SO going to win.' I laugh at his teenage enunciation.

But he's right: we do. I explain the rules quickly to Ed. He's a swift learner. It helps that we look an unlikely pair; we lull the other couples into a false sense of security. Our combination of instinctive communication and a well-disguised but extremely fierce will to win means that we completely slaughter our first opponents, slide easily through the semi-finals and end up in the finals against Tom and Ruth. I can sense Tom getting more and more frustrated with Ruth's dithering style of play; I watch admiringly as Ed uses this against him, makes him lose his concentration and, then, we are triumphant. I practically skip back to the table with the prize: a makeshift trophy and box of Maltesers.

My mood is soon crushed, however; I had managed to put out

of my mind our real reason for being here this afternoon. There is a bustle of activity around the podium; it can't be long now until I have to go up to be THANKED! Here's Imogen again, to take us over to the scaffold.

We are shown to our chairs - yes, we are to sit in chairs facing the crowd, and these chairs have our names on them. There is a seating plan for the scaffold. Will the fun never end? It appears not. I lean over and read the name on the seat next to me: Romily Brooks. Is this really a Thanksgiving, or some sort of endurance test for my emotional resilience? A complex form of punishment for a terrible misdeed in a past life?

Of course I should have anticipated the presence of Romily. Why didn't I? Maybe I just blocked out the idea. She is on the parish council after all, and they are the ones THANKING! us. And here she is, looking willowy and sophisticated, her long glossy brown hair gleaming in the sun like an expensive racehorse. One look at her outfit - brown silk dress with white polka dots - is enough to make me feel totally outclassed, as indeed I am. Romily is Waitrose, and I will only ever be Sainsbury's. That's the brutal truth.

So I am going to have to sit next to Romily, while the entire village - more or less - gets a good close-up view of my face. Excellent. I start fantasizing about an intervention, divine or otherwise, that would mean I wouldn't have to endure this. A meteor strike, for example. A zombie attack. A rather unexpected volcanic eruption. The certain death of me, my children and the entire population of the village seems a small price to pay to avoid the next half an hour.

But it's not to be. Death must wait, and I must endure. I smile at Romily as she approaches and keep that smile firmly in place for the next thirty or so minutes. I clap politely at the opening speeches, and gaze enraptured at the extremely long slide show of photos of the process of building the new hall. I even laugh at Romily's jokes; I hope that someone, somewhere, in heaven perhaps, is taking note of these acts of extreme saintliness.

Romily thanks Mel for her beautiful mural - cue slides of the rather abstract shapes and angles of this artwork. Lots of applause, and Mel comes up to receive her gift. Next, Ruth for 'her work behind the scenes.' Now I come to think of it, I can't quite bring to mind what work Ruth did - she is surprisingly good at avoiding the actual labour and sliding in at the finishing line, arms aloft. Clapping, I smile at her in real admiration.

Carrie's 'tireless organisation' is the next item on the agenda - we all know that 'tiresome' is probably a more appropriate adjective, but yes Carrie gets things done and well deserves this applause and whatever is in her box.

And now it's my turn; my role in this was 'creativity, imagination and real expertise in wording the grant application, without which none of this would have been possible.' Well, that's nice to hear, and now I'm on my feet, shaking hands with Steve and Maggie and bloody Romily. As I turn back to the crowd I see Ed right at the front, clapping enthusiastically. He catches my eye, gives me a wicked smile and whoops very, very loudly. The incongruity of the sound of his whooping across the polite applause makes me laugh out loud; so when the camera flashes for the local paper, a second later, it captures a broad and genuine smile on my face.

I am still smiling when, some time later, we walk back to my house. He is accompanying us because, he says, 'you have too much to carry by yourself.'

'You shouldn't have done that, you know. That kind of frivolous behaviour is heavily frowned upon in this village. They will be writing your name down right now in the special book for people like you. It won't be forgotten.'

'I wanted to see if I could make you laugh. You looked like you needed a laugh. And it worked, so it was worth it.'

Evening is just starting to fall on this ravishing afternoon. I can still hear the party continuing behind us, the jazz band becoming fainter and fainter. The adults will continue for some hours yet, I guess, but I need to get Rosie to bed. The lush growth of summer makes the village paths difficult to negotiate. Every few yards we have to lift the drooping hollyhocks to get by.

I say, 'That was a surprisingly good party.'

'Did you not have high hopes?'

I say, 'Well sitting next to my husband's lover for half an hour wasn't the highlight of my week, no.'

Ed says, 'Well no-one would have guessed. I definitely wouldn't have guessed.' He hesitates. 'I don't really know why they would make you sit there.'

I laugh, 'Yes it's a good question. To see if I would cry? Ha, I showed them.'

He lifts aside some overgrown shrub branches to allow me to pass. 'No, I mean it, you were amazing.'

I let that word float around for a minute, turn it around, contemplate it.

'Thank you.' I was amazing. Ha. I know this is a kind, polite 17-year old boy but, still, that's pretty nice.

He follows me into the kitchen and puts the swimming bags and the gift box on the table. Rosie is dancing behind him.

'Eddie, come and see my bedroom!'

Ed and I both laugh. I say, 'Rosie that's a little forward.' I turn to him, 'Would you like a drink or anything?'

'No, I'm sorry but I can't stay. I promised I would go and help clear up.'

'Will you come and play tomorrow? Please?' Rosie is swinging on his hand in what looks like a very irritating manner, but if he is finding it so, he is hiding it well. I notice Michael is lurking too.

'Ed is very busy Rosie.'

Ed looks at me. 'I could take them swimming tomorrow, if you like? I mean in Aunt Ruby's pool. You wouldn't have to come, if you have something to do. Maybe you'd like some time to work on your articles, or your evening class ideas?'

Rosie is leaping around ecstatically at this idea; even Michael looks enthusiastic.

'Oh please, Mum, pleeeeeeease!'

'Go and get ready for bed, I need to talk to Ed in peace. Go!'

To Ed, I say, 'Are you sure? That would be really helpful. They would love it. You are very good with them.'

'Yes, that would be fine. OK, I'll come and get them about two, then, bring them back about 5.30?'

He is opening up the swimming bags and getting out the wet costumes. 'Is it alright if I....?' He gestures to the washing machine, and I nod, a little dumbly.

'Have you come up with any names for the groups yet?'

'No, I haven't. Have you any thoughts?'

'I'll have a think about it.'

Is it my imagination, or is the boy lingering a bit?

Hmm. Alright, be brave Jen and actually say what's on your mind. Throw it out there. Have courage. Come on.

'If you like we could talk about it tomorrow night. I mean, if you came for dinner. Tea. Supper. I could cook something to say thanks for your help. I'd like your input.'

He is fiddling around with the washing machine now, and I can't see his face. Caveat, caveat.

'If you're not busy, I mean if you don't have anything on.'

He turns round, 'Sure. That would be very nice. I'd like to help. Shall I bring a pudding? I can make a good cheesecake. My Mum showed me, it's her recipe.'

'Great, I love cheesecake.'

'It's lemon and honey.'

'That sounds lovely, yes.'

The sound of the washing machine starting up breaks the silence.

'Good, OK, well I'd better get back. Litter to pick, glasses to wash.' He smiles, 'And don't eat those Maltesers before tomorrow. They have my name on them. Well half of them.'

'Bye Ed.'

'Bye Mrs Grey.'

Ouch, must do something about that. Tomorrow, maybe.

BONNY BANKS

In the end the canal holiday isn't as bad as my imaginings. That's possibly because my imaginings are full of appalling misery and pain, but still, the reality isn't as bad, so that's something. Chris and I manage to bumble along, enjoying the scenery and putting up a front of normality that is, it would seem, fairly convincing. None of the people we meet along the canal bank is motivated to shout, 'Hold on, you're fooling no-one! You two aren't a married couple! Pull the other one.' We sit in pub gardens in what might seem like a companionable silence. We talk a great deal to, and about, the children. I read a lot. I mean, a lot.

In bed, I wear my headphones and listen to my iPod. I listen to a lot of Beethoven that week. I adopt a position in bed that minimises the chances of accidental physical contact. And the days pass, one after the other, relentlessly.

Romily has, in her efficient manner, spent our week's absence looking for a place for them to stay. Isn't she marvellous? Such a treasure. (How did she manage to get hold of a property so quickly? Money, probably. Ready cash, that always helps. Maybe she murdered the current tenants. Nothing about this woman would surprise me; she seems very used to getting her own way. I start to doubt the whole 'phone-dropped-by-the-bed' scenario, and begin to wonder if it was all a set-up, engineered to bring matters to a head.)

So the day after we get back, he is installed in a three-bedroomed love nest by the river, and I am left with a hall full of washing and two distraught children. Rosie and Michael have just spent five days enjoying their father's rare full-time attention. Now they have to get used to the idea that he will be living somewhere else and contemplate seeing him only every other weekend. That fact that this kind of sorrow and misery happens every single day, in every street in the country, doesn't make it any easier for us to bear.

It's about this time that the effort of lugging my broken heart around all day starts to really wear me down. I start to imagine that if I look over my shoulder, I can see it, huge, bulky and rotten, like a dead polar bear on a sledge.

I try not to look over my shoulder, if I can possibly help it.

CUCKOO'S NEST

'Sectioned? Ed's mother was sectioned? When?' My voice sounds ridiculously high-pitched; my hand shakes so much I have to put my cup back down on the picnic blanket, in case it spills over my lap. I am more or less a caricature of Shocked Woman.

'Yes, I know. Hideous isn't it. Apparently Ed was the only one living in the house with her and he had to call the police because she was threatening suicide. I am not sure what her diagnosis is, but she's been in and out of mental hospitals for years,' continues Carrie.

I am hoping that Ruth won't give us a quick rundown of these symptoms and offer a possible diagnosis. I love Ruth, I really do, but I could do without the doctor chat right now to be frank. I am frantically scanning my memory banks to check that I haven't said anything ridiculously crass about mental illness to Ed. Impossible to say, in fact, since ridiculously crass remarks are pretty much a staple of my normal mode of conversation.

Carrie is in full flow now. She has the 'deets', at last, and she's keen to share them. We are at the water park, and the children are all screaming with delight, running in and out of the squirting water, leaving us to have this conversation undisturbed. At least I think the children are in the water; to be honest, from here all I can see is a seething mass of bright-coloured Lycra and damp hair.

'Ruby said that the whole family is pretty traumatised.

There's an older girl too, she's gone abroad to work, in a theatre company somewhere. South Africa? And an older boy, not sure where he is.'

(Becker. Running a surf-school, I think. Unless that was a joke. It may well have been, in retrospect.)

She goes on, 'But the Dad, well he's a mess. Blames himself, as well he might.' She leans forward, conspiratorially, and whispers, 'Druggy past. Hippy types. Peace camp...' She lets these meaning-laden words hang over us for a minute, lets our thoughts run wild with imaginings of naked orgies, enormous bongs and lesbian mud wrestling.

Round here, the words peace camp are right next to Hitler, performance art and vegetarian in the Book of Evil Things. The peace camp was installed on the Downs for a few years in the 1980s and the folk memory lives on. Tales linger of corrupted local youth, rabid feminists in the supermarket with their unshaven legs and my dear, the LITTER! I am hoping we don't get to hear about the Legend of the Stolen Logs again. I am not sure I could bear it.

'And this was, when?'

'Well I think she's been bad for several years. I think Ed's seen a lot, too much for a boy his age. So I think Ed found the lower sixth was quite a struggle, and after the incident, Ruby offered to have him to stay with her this year. I don't think his Dad is in any fit state to look after him, or to look after himself. I am not sure if Dad's even working any more, and I think he's spent all the savings on trying to sort her out. Rehab. Therapy. Nothing seems to work.'

I remember Ed's words to me: 'I need to pay my way.' Jesus, poor kid.

'She's a lovely looking woman, though, his mother. Can't remember her name, something weird. Fire? Flame? Sunshine? Something like that.' I take this snippet of information with a pinch of salt; given Carrie's unreliability on the subject of names, this woman might well be called Debbie.

We all contemplate the horror and pity of this family's

situation for a moment and I can't help but feel a little guilty relief that, in fact, I only have the banality of divorce to face, the ho-hum of every-other-weekend, rather than this Gothic blood-bath. I flush at the selfishness and self-centredness of the thought.

'But he seems so....' God I really wish I hadn't started this sentence. Ruth and Carrie are looking at me expectantly, and I really have no plan for where this is going.

'Normal?' Ruth helps me out.

'Well yes I guess. He just doesn't seem traumatised or sad or hurt or anything.'

Carrie says, 'Well he's young, and bright.' (And good-looking, I think, but of course don't say.) 'I guess he has plenty to occupy him. I think he has a girlfriend.'

Ruth adds, 'Boy like that, I guess he has plenty.'

We laugh, slightly nervously. None of us have children near to sexual maturity yet, and for all of us, I am guessing, the idea of our precious offspring starting to pair up is one that is just far away enough to be amusing and not terrifying. Just about. In a couple of years' time the idea of a sexually active handsome young man in the village will no doubt be enough to have us, three mothers of daughters, barring the windows and looking out the key to the attic.

'So he's going to be here for the next year then?' I ask, as casually as I can manage.

'Well I guess so, I don't think his Mum's going to be home anytime soon. And I think he needs a little stability you know? He's going to be applying for university in the autumn I guess.'

A moment passes. We sip our tea.

'I was thinking, what would you think if I was to ask if he wanted to do some babysitting for me? Like on a regular basis? I mean I was thinking of getting some part-time work, maybe teaching some evening classes? I don't know.'

I trail off, unconvincingly, but I needn't worry: my lack of enthusiasm is lost in the tsunami of Carrie's delight. (It was, of course, partly her idea to have Ed as my babysitter, but if she remembers this she's too polite to say.) 'Darling that's a great idea! Get yourself back out there! Why not?'

She grabs me into her warm and ample chest and hugs the breath out of me. Her gesture is so genuine, so sweetly maternal even, that I feel a little emotional and have to blink away a few stray tears.

'Yes you know, nothing full on. I mean I have the copy editing and a bit of freelance stuff here and there but I might need to step things up a bit, market myself a bit more. And an adult class will be easy enough I think. Maybe, a little creative writing, or poetry appreciation or something.'

Carrie is still gushing on when she finally lets me go, about how this will be a fresh start, just the perfect thing to get my confidence back. (Er, thanks, wasn't feeling THAT unconfident but, yeah, thanks.) It's only when I lean back into my chair and pick up my mug again, that I notice Ruth eyeing me with just a note, just a hint of particular interest and, playing around her mouth, just a touch of amusement.

WORK – NOT ALL IT'S CRACKED UP TO BE

'SO, what do you DO?' What do I do? It's a good question isn't it? A perennial favourite at the dinner party. Find your pigeon hole, slot you in.

I used to quite like to say I worked in publishing. It was properly cool and glamorous. By which I mean, it sounded cool and glamorous, when in fact it was a massive amount of tedious reading and filing and sucking up to clients and sitting in immensely boring meetings.

Polly's job sounds great too: criminal barrister. Except I did a bit of court reporting when I was just out of college and let me tell you that it's very far from being glamorous either. There's an awful lot of hanging about in stinking courts, the kind of places where the furniture is bolted to the floor. There's also quite a bit of carrying massive piles of books around, and smoking. Oh, and heavy drinking. Basically, in this country they let anyone practise criminal law just as long as they can drink two bottles of claret, remain standing and still wing it successfully in the court room the next day without vomiting.

Whereas Chris's line of work, something-in-IT, sounds terrifically dull but is, in fact, just about the perfect job. He gets to sit by himself in front of his computer most of the time; everyone thinks he's terribly clever and far too important to sit in meetings. He's so dash-darn clever, his skills so precious and in demand, that he gets flown all over the world to fanny around with IT and have lovely lunches in hotels with spas and swimming pools. And, best of all, he manages to avoid lots of the hard parenting labour and yet, miraculously, has time to knock off Romily on the side. In fact, his something-in-IT skills were his killer seduction weapon. These days, 'can you come and look at my wifi connection' is the equivalent of 'do you want to come up for a coffee.' The something-in-IT boys are the Alpha males of the twenty first century: the warriors and the chieftains.

Maybe I should go back to college and see if I can be something-in-IT myself.

Since I gave up work, paid work, in the workplace with other workers, I have spent quite a bit of time, ironically enough, thinking about work. And this is what I think: it's a great big con. And we've all fallen for it. Well not all of us, clearly, but enough of us to keep capitalism going I guess. When I was working (see definition above) and long, long before, I was completely taken in by the whole work thing. How it was all terribly empowering, how we all MUST work, work, work and must earn money and buy stuff and that if we weren't working then we were a burden and time spent not working was time wasted.

And then I stopped working for anyone else. I became (although I had never heard of this acronym before, and I am not entirely convinced by it) a Working At Home Parent or WAHP. Everyone said how terribly bored I was bound to be, how I wouldn't have any adult conversation and I would be going mental within a fortnight.

That wasn't quite true. This is what I found:

1. There are adults everywhere, not just at work, and you can start conversations with people even when they aren't paid by the same employer as you. And when you don't have to talk about books or meetings or contracts or sandwiches or whatever it is you're paid to talk about, you can end up talking about all sorts of things. Flowers. Why people hate rats and love foxes. Theories of music education. The terrible price of petrol and, often, the weather. These conversations are, on average, no more or less dull than those that happen at work. They just happen in different places.

2. Loads of stuff needs doing that you don't get paid for. You'd be amazed. In the years since anyone paid me, I have, among other things, walked dogs for old ladies with bad legs, showed new mothers how to wrap their babies up nice and tight to stop them crying, Hoovered the gritty carpets of the newly bereaved, helped toddlers stick pasta onto bits of card, driven stinky old men to the hospital to get their dressings changed and, just the once, combed lice laboriously out of a very manky head of hair. I have role-played Caesarean birth with teenage mothers, made endless cups of tea, baked cakes for stalls, stood in my black suit singing funeral anthems, and played many many games of 'Pop to the Shops!' and helped put stamps into albums. Was this work? Was this more or less important than sitting in those breakfast meetings dropping Danish pastry crumbs down my Jigsaw suit and trying to concentrate on the agenda?

3. Although we place no value on all this stuff-to-be-done-and-not-paid-for, it needs doing. Capitalism has messed with our collective judgement so much that we have lost sight of that. So a child-minder is doing REAL work, but a stay-at-home-mum isn't - she's just a burden and a scrounger. (Unless, of course, you make the decision to go back to work, at which point you're the evil unfeminine bitch who isn't making the

sacrifices she should. And don't tell me that I am only talking about the women, and say what about the men? Yes, good question, what about the men? I mean, tell me about it. Really. Where are they? They're at work of course, eating sandwiches at their desk in peace and 'missing the train home' to avoid the domestic chaos waiting for them for just a little longer, and who can blame them?) What would happen if we all fell for this confidence trick and went back to paid work? Who would run the pre-schools, the drop-in centres, the mother and baby groups? If all the volunteers, the unpaid helpers and the stay at home parents in the country all went on strike for one day, then we would see that just because something isn't paid doesn't mean it has no value.

So the work I still do - the copy editing, the lifestyle articles, the odd bits of ghosting - are the smallest part of my life but I am still supposed to define myself a writer, like they are the most important thing I do rather than a rather irritating marginal item I have to squeeze in after I have done the real work of the day, the stuff that needs doing all day every day and for which no one has ever offered me a penny or a word of appreciation. Feeding your family, keeping the community together, trying to create functioning children who can manage themselves in the world - nul points. But running a class so bored middle-aged women can talk about poetry - important valuable labour.

Well I am not complaining, because soon I will have to write down my income for a divorce settlement. And I can't quite face that thought either.

ROADKILL BINGO

One thing I found really hard to get used to about living in the country is the sheer number of dead animals littering the highway. I can barely drive from my house to Ruth's without feeling that familiar bump-squish under my wheels. Rabbits I can just about cope with – their numbers are so vast, and their presence on the verges and the gardens so ubiquitous that I can reconcile myself to the idea that a few fewer might not be a bad thing; it helps, too, that no social occasion in the countryside is complete without a long rant about how rabbits are a terribly bad thing and do untold damage to crops. There's nothing like a pair of sticky-up ears and a fluffy tail to bring out the passionate orator in your average rural dinner guest.

Badgers and, especially, deer are frankly terrifying if you come face to face (bonnet to snout?) with them; early one morning I came across a stag standing in the middle of the road, proud and glistening in the pale sunlight like a scene from the lid of a shortbread tin. I have never braked so hard in my life, but the stag regarded my terrified face with cool disdain. Yeah, try running into me, he seemed to be saying. See who comes off worse.

But the kills that really make me squeal and swerve dangerously are the birds. Now the rabbit has a bad reputation for poor road sense but nothing, I tell you, nothing is as stupid at the roadside, nothing is so likely to meet an untimely end on the edge of a bumper than the pheasant. They may have been specifically bred for their kamikaze qualities; although I am not tempted by the idea of shooting for sport, I can't really imagine that these dunce-like birds offer the average sportsman or woman too much of a challenge. It is frankly more of a challenge to avoid them, in my experience.

I do my best, though; I am a pretty adept bird-swerver and at least 75% of the time I can manage to get the pigeon in my slip stream, or brake sharply enough to allow the pheasant to continue its leisurely stroll across the road. (No doubt a temporary reprieve; I imagine most of the drivers round here are not so soft-hearted or, at least, not so concerned about putting a dent in bonnet. A clapped out car is a badge of honour on these lanes.)

But this particular morning, I was not so successful. Perhaps I was distracted or maybe it was the lack of sleep, or perhaps I was just driving a touch too fast and playing the radio slightly too loud, but as I came over the crest of Worthington Hill to face the familiar tweedledum-and-tail shape of the Commonly Stupid Pheasant – well, it was too late to brake. (It's not like I can claim the bird was camouflaged. That's another thing about shooting pheasants. Surely it would be more challenging as a sport if they weren't bred so big and in such garish colours. Sparrow shooting – now that would be a sport worthy of the name.)

It was only when I got out of the car to inspect the damage that I realised that I had managed to not only clonk the pheasant into the verge but – horrible sight – I had also squashed a squirrel under my wheels too.

It's hard to distinguish the individual reasons that made up the frenzy of emotions that overtook me at this moment; like the individual drops in a waterfall, they washed over me with immense force. The sheer horror of the sight of the fluffy squirrel and its almost severed tail, the guilt at having caused not one, but two, untimely deaths in the space of a second or two, and – perhaps strongest of all – the enormous irritation at being stuck in the bloody countryside with suicidal birds and squirrels that don't realise that they should be in trees and not on roads: the combined effect of these emotions, and a range of others, less distinct, made my legs buckle. Sitting on the rough grass of the verge, listening to the ticking of my hazard lights and the far-off rush of traffic from the bypass, I wept and wept. I wept for my lost marriage, for my abandoned career, for all the pain and misery and heartbreak in the world, and because I was not, right now, sitting in Patisserie Valerie on the Marylebone High Street, where I should be.

It's only later I realised that I had missed a trick: I should have chucked it in the boot and got Carrie to pluck it. I'm willing to bet she knows how. The pheasant I mean, not the squirrel. I guess not even Carrie, game as she is for most challenges, could be persuaded to pluck a squirrel.

A TIME FOR DARING

I get Ed to help me prepare a proposal for my evening classes to take to the council offices: a PowerPoint and some handouts, sample lesson plans, the works. We spend an increasingly hysterical evening over a whole packet of French Fancies and a cafetiere of strong coffee coming up with ideas of names for these classes. We settle on "Unravelling the Silken Ties: How to Read a Poem" for the poetry appreciation class on Tuesdays and "Lasso the Muse: Writing for Pleasure and Profit" for the creative writing on Thursdays. The idea of any of the freelance writing I do being either pleasurable or profitable is entirely laughable, but this is neither here nor there. The cheesy quality of these titles seems at the time both witty and post-modern; but as I enter the earnest threshold of the municipal offices to deliver my proposal, they seem, well, just plain cheesy. Never mind, too late now.

I needn't have worried. This isn't a sales pitch after all. The woman behind the desk only wants me to sign a big pile of forms, accepting liability for this and promising to take responsibility for that. She suggests that I might want to do my own publicity as my classes are a late entry, but 'Don't worry. I think they will be popular among the book group crowd.' I am not sure whether this counts as a compliment.

I produce hundreds of posters and leaflets and distribute them everywhere I can think of, with help from Ed and the children. Ed helps me set up my own website and suggests I use it to promote my own writing and shows me ways to link into writers' networks.

Ed tells me, entirely straight-faced, that 'Aunty Ruby is thinking of coming' and then cracks up at my horrified reaction. By the end of August, though, I have 12 takers for the poetry and 17 for the creative writing, although there are 'bound to be a lot of drop-outs' says the woman at the council offices. She really is a little ray of sunshine.

CHAPTER FOUR

SEPTEMBER

SOME KIND OF PEACE OF MIND

The thing I'd forgotten about the pain of a broken heart is that it's physical. Incredibly tiring. And the healing, Christ it takes so long. And it's not linear. Sometimes I feel a bit of false progress. For hours at a time, I feel better, positive, happy even. I start to smile, sing along to the radio. I might even get a few hours, a whole night, of solid, dreamless sleep. The sick feeling will pass for long enough for me to eat a big pile of cheese on toast. I feel like I'm starting to get over it, just about on the mend, getting close to pulling myself together. And I'm wrong, because without warning, the pain is back. The queasiness in the pit of the stomach, the aching in the limbs, and the weight on the chest.

There's a reason why your teenage years are a time of heartbreak and experimentation. Because when your boyfriend chucks you, you can mope around for a bit and frankly no-one is any the poorer or wiser. You can lie weeping on the carpet like three yards of dead hedge and people will just step over you.

Trying to carry on with adult life while dragging your poor ravaged heart around like a dead polar bear on a sledge, well that's inhuman. Impossible. Remembering to buy more bloody cheese, supervising violin practice, hanging the bastard washing out – how can I be expected to care about this stuff with the poison of rotting love in my flesh, making it sting and ache and throb?

The tiny little upsets of life, the little setbacks, are so much harder to bear with this weight of misery pressing down on me. All the niggles, and the irritations: the lost car keys, the sour milk, the sibling bickering - they all scream inside my head, setting up a chain of longing. A longing for comfort and love and the confirmation that comes with it, that all this is just trivia and white noise and that life is good and the world is kind and I am loved.

But life is shit, and the world is unkind and I am no-one, and nothing and I really really don't know how much strength I have left.

BLUE BLOOD

By mid-September Ed has become a regular fixture at my kitchen table, papers and textbooks in neat piles. He has his laptop open (in fact he asked for my wifi code the second time he came here, suggesting we were now firm friends) - but he likes to write everything by hand, and often twists a ballpoint or pencil into his hair to make an impromptu manbun while he's thinking. He likes to talk about what he's working on, and I like this too. Moving schools has meant he is behind in everything and he asks me to test him and explain things to him. Luckily for me he's taking three subjects I can help with - History, French and English Lit, or 'Radio 4 A levels' as Ruth puts it. If he'd been looking for help with Physics and Maths, he'd have been right out of luck.

He's particularly behind in English Lit, which is convenient as talking about books is what I want to do all day anyway, and the feeling seems to be mutual. He's had to pick up three new texts but he's a natural literature student. I test out all my classes for Silken Ties with him and it's clear he has poetry in his soul.

'Wouldn't Ruby like to help you with your work? Might she

like that?' I ask him one day as we are arguing with some vehemence about whether Macbeth could really be seriously described as a Gothic text. Ed laughs about as loudly as I have ever heard him.

'I make her nervous with all my fancy book learning. Last week I left a pile of notes on the table and in the morning she'd used them to line the cat litter tray. No, I would prefer to study here, if that's OK.'

One Saturday afternoon in late September we are in the garden – I am attempting some pruning and Rosie is plaiting Ed's hair with ribbon while he tries to read an article about the causes of the Prussian wars. It is quite a relaxing scene - even Michael wanders outside briefly to eat an ice lolly before returning to his X Box.

Ed says, 'Ruby says you might have been to Oxford?'

'Oxford? Not usually, if I can help it. I go at Christmas for the Covered Market and sometimes for the museums. Otherwise it's always full of tourists and you can't park.'

'No, I don't mean to shop. I mean go, did you go to Oxford?'

I still have no idea what he's talking about. 'Not recently no. Do you want to go tomorrow? I can drive you if you like. It won't be too busy , the students aren't back yet.'

He says, a little flustered, 'I mean to study. For your degree?'

I stop pruning and put the secateurs down on the table, inspect my scratches.

'Dear God no, terrible place. I went to Cambridge, but that was a very long time ago. Very.'

He says, 'I was thinking I might apply. To Oxford.'

I laugh raucously, 'Dear Lord, were you? What would you go and do something like that for?'

I look at him slightly too late and realise I have said entirely the wrong thing.

'Oh OK. It was just a thought.'

I slam on the brakes, backtrack like crazy.

'Oh no, no I was just being flippant. That Oxford and Cambridge rivalry thing? The boat race? You know, I'd rather be a leper than a Tab?'

He blinks at me, still looking rather hurt and bewildered.

'Sorry Ed, sorry. I think it's a great idea. To study Lit, I guess?'

He nods, still looking rather puzzled.

'It didn't really crop up at my old school, but my new English teacher mentioned it yesterday. She seems to think it's a good idea.'

Rosie has disappeared to play on the X-Box with Michael and I am trying to recover some ground and make up for my ludicrous crassness.

'Well she would know. What's her name?'

We've moved back to the kitchen and I am presenting a range of snacks and drinks to him as a peace offering; he seems appeased.

'Mrs Awton. She says, well. She says I'm the best student she's taught in years.' He is blushing, fiddling with his Kit Kat wrapper. 'I mean, that seems quite promising doesn't it?'

I laugh, 'Yes it's a good sign. And you think you can get the grades?'

'Well I'm not entirely sure... about anything really. Mrs Awton was talking at me like I knew what everything meant and what grades I would need and I don't know anything at all. Will you help me? It's just... I don't want to get my hopes up. Will you look with me, help me understand it all? I tried yesterday but then Ruby kept asking me what I was doing and it was all ...' He throws up his hands to indicate his confusion.

So I abandon my plans for cooking dinner, order in pizza (much to Michael's delight) and we fire up the lap top and do some research. It turns out that yes, his grades are good enough. We write his personal statement, getting quite hysterical over the pretentious wording and making up fake quotes to sound more and more poncey. I create a reading list for him, packing his messenger bag with books from shelf that he simply MUST read.

We are having so much fun that we fail to notice that bedtime has come and gone and Rosie and Michael are still playing some very loud and raucous game, their shrieks becoming harder and harder to ignore. Ed and I say goodbye on the doorstep, him shifting awkwardly with his book-stuffed bag and grappling uneasily with his laptop, which no longer fits in there.

'Why don't you come next weekend when the kids are away and we can do some prep for your test.'

He laughs, 'My test!. MY test! It doesn't seem quite real.' He is suddenly serious. 'Don't mention anything to Ruby or, well to anyone really. I don't want everyone to know. I mean, it's a long shot. It's just worth a try.'

He looks so nervous he reminds me of Michael before one of his football games. 'I won't say anything, of course not. And yes, it's worth a try. You would love it there and they would be lucky to have you.'

He grins, 'Thank you, that's a kind thing to say.'

I am just about to bat this away by denying it's kindness that motivates me, when I am suddenly surprised by Ed leaning over and kissing me on the cheek.

'Goodnight, and thank you. Really.'

And he's gone and I am left rather lost for words, standing on the doorstep thinking about where his mother is right now until I can gather myself together enough to finally persuade my children that their luck has run out and bedtime has finally arrived.

ASK THE POLAR BEAR

'So what should I do, do you think? I'm sorry to ask you, but you always seem to know the right thing to do. You are always so sensible.'

Mel has been going on, and on, for what seems like many many hours about her current dilemma and I am having terrible difficulty focusing appropriately. In fact, now we have reached the climax of the story – the inevitable request for advice - I have, frankly, little to no recollection of the beginning of it. Now Mel is looking at me expectantly, and I am scrabbling around for something to reply.

Oh hold on, I have it.

'Well what does your instinct tell you?'

Good one, Jen. She'll never guess you haven't really been listening. I know, I should be ashamed of myself. Mel is a good person, a sweet kind woman who is just looking for some help and support from her closest friend. Is that too much to ask?

Well yes, it is. Far too much to ask. Doesn't she realise this? Today, it has taken everything I have just to make it through to tea-time. The dead polar bear is massively heavy and burdensome today. I was irritable at breakfast, exhausted all morning, and my nap brought no respite, only vivid and disturbing dreams. And now, I am counting the hours till the children go to bed, so that I can just lose myself for a few hours in my book, find some solace in another narrative. A narrative that makes sense, a narrative with an ending all mapped out. I need to be somewhere I don't have to think, or talk. Unfortunately, I have to do both, right now. Mel is a dear friend, but she is clueless about how close I am to the edge. My fault, probably. I should let my misery show more, perhaps; then I might get more support and understanding. But how would that work? That really would be exhausting, showing my emotion all the time. I definitely don't have the strength for that. In the end I don't really have the choice; I have to carry on as normal. Otherwise, what would happen? How would the children get to school? Food in the fridge? Clothes in the washer? I am entirely trapped by my routine and my responsibilities. Sometimes this feels comforting - at least I have a purpose - but most of the time it feels suffocatingly claustrophobic.

Mel is shaking her head. 'Oh I don't know. I don't trust my

instincts. I am useless at this stuff.'

'Mel, what are you doing? Get a plate if you want some food, sit down.'

She is standing by the hob, with a fork in her hand, picking bits of food from the saucepans. She has loaded up her fork with mashed potato and is now dipping it in the gravy before sliding it into her mouth.

'No, I don't want any food. I'm not hungry. Anyway I am on a diet. I have that wedding next week.' She starts again: potato, gravy, dip, mouth.

'Let me make you a cup of tea.' Stalling for time. 'Carrie, would you like a cup of tea?' I shout into the garden. Carrie, thankfully, comes in to say yes, and I pounce on her - my salvation! Now I won't have to admit that I haven't really been concentrating on Mel's problem, whatever the hell it is.

'Mel, tell Carrie. See what she thinks.'

Mel doesn't need to be asked twice: she's off again with her narrative. It's long and complex, involving her brother and whether she should lend him some money for another of his projects - this time, a sandwich-making franchise. Mel's brother Phil is a charming, unreliable shyster, whose one real skill is spending other people's money. That's his forte, really. Once I start concentrating, it's soon clear that what Mel wants is for us to tell her not to give him the money. We run through the pros and cons, mention all the other unsuccessful projects that he has wasted her hard-earned money on. She nods, thoughtfully and resignedly.

We all know, sitting round this table - even Carrie, who is the least perceptive person I have ever met - we all know that Mel will give Phil the money. She may, in fact, have already given it to him by now. It's just one of those repeated patterns, those recurring narrative threads, that run through all of our stories, interlinking and intertwining. The process of having this conversation, which is going nowhere and will change nothing, is far from being frustrating or anger-inducing. It's comforting. Any logical analysis would suggest it was pointless, but that certainly would miss the point. These shared stories are what binds us together. Those, and a lot of tea.

I put the kettle on again, and get a new packet of Bourbons out of the cupboard.

I AM LIVING IN A VILLAGE BY MISTAKE

As my mother always says, the only sure fire way to lose weight, apart from dysentery, is an unhappy love affair. Shallow it may be, but the reappearance of my hip-bones from the eight-year-thick layer of baby-fat is, I admit, a little cheering. And Lord knows I need something to cheer me up. I can't even remember saying yes to this Village FUNdraiser ('with the emphasis on the F.U.N.!'). Yet I seem to have spent £8 for a ticket plus babysitting for an evening that I am looking forward to about as much as the weekly horror of Michael's piano lesson.

Downstairs, I can hear Ed let himself in with a shout up the stairs, go into the living room and immediately settle down to play Top Trumps with Michael and Rosie. I am seriously considering hiring him for an hour a day for just this purpose, while I hide in the kitchen and read.

When I come downstairs, he is sprawled across the floor, a streak of colour in his checked shirt and orange shorts.

'New shirt Ed?' I raise my eyebrows.

'Yes and you look very nice too Mrs Grey. Beige goes very well with brown I always think.' He widens his eyes mock-innocently.

'I'm aiming for sofa-camouflage.'

'You will certainly merge into the background. Watch out people don't just pile their coats on you.'

'Not something that's ever likely to happen to you in that shirt. Surfer dude meets Outlander. It's a challenging look but one you are very nearly pulling off.'

For a moment I think about how much more actual F.U.N.

I would have if I ditched the FUNdraiser, let Ed put the children to bed and then sat on the sofa and engaged with him in sardonic chit-chat in front of the TV all evening. And then I allow myself to feel the force of my alienation: I have more in common with my 18-year-old babysitter than my contemporaries, my neighbours, my own kind.

I give a desultory list of instructions, although everyone in this room, even the five-year-old, knows Ed is more than capable of putting these children to bed without my intervention. Still, he's a polite boy and listens and nods in all the right places, before turning back to attempt to lose at Top Trumps before nightfall.

'See you later!' Barely a murmur. Now that Ed is sitting for us, there are no more screams of 'Don't go mummy!'

I am not sure if I like it.

ARE WE HAVING FUN YET?

The fundraiser is at Thalia's house. I have never been in there before, but I am fascinated to see inside it; it's the converted chapel and I am interested to see how the space has been used. I don't envy Imogen and Romily their enormous mansions, but I would happily swap my functional, sensible semi for this gorgeous building. I knock on the door, feeling actually quite positive about the evening.

This moment of happiness, in common with most in my current life, is pretty short-lived. Thalia's husband Robin answers the door and greets me very warmly, but I sense he is somehow uncomfortable. I wonder if this is because of my situation; not infrequently, I find people are a little awkward in my company, because they don't quite know what to say to an abandoned woman. (I understand this happens to the newly bereaved too, in which case it is completely unforgiveable behaviour.) I overcompensate for this moment of awkwardness by embracing him with excessive warmth and enthusiasm, although I don't really know him that well.

Robin is a friend of Chris's, so the other possibility is that

Robin feels guilty because he knew about the affair with Romily before it all came out. This thought occurs to me fairly often these days; I try not to dwell on it.

However, the real reason for Robin's discomfort becomes apparent when I enter into the gorgeous space of the chapel living room. I don't even have a moment to admire the beauty of the interior of this building because three things become obvious as I cross the threshold. In ascending order of awfulness:

1. everyone else is dressed extremely formally, in cocktail dresses and, saints preserve us, dinner jackets; I am wearing my stone jeans and a rather nice brown jumper;

2. on the side table I can see an array of foil-wrapped Pyrex and cling-filmed fancy bowls; everyone else has brought a dish to share for - lo - this is a bring and share. I did not know to bring, and I therefore have not brung, and I have absolutely nothing to share;

3. worst of all, the room is full, stuffed to the pew ends and stained glass windows with couples. I am the only single person in the room.

It feels like one of those scenes in a Western; the talking stops, everyone turns to look at me - the Empty Handed, Underdressed Single Woman - and the needle scratches alarmingly across the record. Thalia, a sweet kind woman, leaves whatever conversation she is involved in and strides over to where I am, rooted to the carpet in a moment of frozen horror.

She kisses me and shuffles me slightly to the side, trying to make me less conspicuous.

'Darling, I'm so sorry. I guess you didn't get my email?'

Email? Email? I feel like screeching. No I didn't bloody look at my email. Who looks at their email? I have something close to 2000 unread emails in my inbox, and most of them are just trying to sell me something. Pizza, or cheap clothes.

Or books, quite a lot of them are trying to sell me books. My email account is nothing but a source of guilt, and more work. I can't keep on top of it. It's like an extension of my car: full of crap, and getting fuller every day.

But no-one sends me anything important in an email, surely? Wrong. Oh God.

I offer to go home and get changed, and bring a dish. (But what would I bring? A half-eaten packet of salami? Six eggs? Half a loaf of sliced bread? Some mild cheddar? That's pretty much the extent of my fridge contents.) No, Thalia reassures me, it's fine. There's no need. It doesn't matter what I'm wearing anyway. (If this is true, Thalia, why the outrageous dress code in the first place? Who has a black tie bring and share? Apparently 'everyone loves to dress up' - speak for yourself.) And anyway, she says, there's plenty of food to share.

The couple thing she can't help with, so she doesn't mention. I am, effectively, the elephant in the room. The single, solitary, unmatched elephant.

Thalia, you should definitely sort out your hostess skills; this is not your finest hour. But it's interesting, actually, to be the elephant sometimes. Enlightening even. Because when no-one's looking at you, when they're all talking to each other, you get a fresh perspective. You notice, for example, how the men dominate the conversation, set the agenda. How they put down the women, in subtle ways, but effectively. How they interrupt the women, use them as the butt of their jokes, the straight man, the side-kick. Is this stuff always there? Am I imagining it, a hallucination fuelled by my bitterness, my poisoned status as wronged woman? Am I blinded, or are my eyes open to it for the first time? One thing's for certain: as a single woman in a room full of couples, I am invisible, and voiceless.

As soon as I can leave without seeming rude I make my excuses. Thalia walks me to the door. She is apologetic, 'I really am sorry about all the confusion.'

I am magnanimous. Or rather, I barely care, 'That's OK, it's no problem. Thanks for a lovely evening.'

'Listen, Jen, why don't you come round another evening, for dinner with me and Robin? It would be lovely to see you. I could cook for you. Ed Becker babysits for you doesn't he?'

Ed. Suddenly, more than anything in the world, I want to be sitting on the sofa with Ed. Where I don't feel lonely, awkward, alienated, miserable, lost. Where I can, for once in my bloody life, be myself.

'That would be lovely,' I say. Would it? Thalia is lovely, a very kind person and I'm sure Robin is too, but really? An evening with the two of them? Like Miss Bates, a lonely spinster, invited for dinner to salve their conscience. Bloody hell, I really am getting bitter. I must go home. I need for this evening to be over and I need to be home.

I say, 'Sure. I'll call you, set something up,' I lie for the third time in under a minute, and then I start to jog, then run, towards home, my sofa, and Ed.

FILM CLICHES

When I get back he is lolling on the sofa watching Love Actually. He looks comfortable and relaxed and I feel a pang of regret when he shifts to sit upright.

'Good evening?'

'Bloody terrible. Thanks for asking.'

He laughs. 'Would you like me to make you a cup of tea before I go?'

'That would be very kind. I am suddenly massively tired. It's all the smiling.'

'And all the fun, I guess.'

'Yes all the fun. That can be very exhausting.'

God this is lovely. Really lovely. Someone talking to me, someone really listening. I need to bring up Michael to be just like this, really paying attention, really tuned in. Of all the people drifting on the surface of my life, this one, just this one, seems to be actually listening. Obviously I'm paying him, so that helps. I hear him clattering in the kitchen, making me a cup of tea. It suddenly seems like the kindest thing anyone has done for me, ever. I feel a little weepy. I think I may have had too much wine.

'Mrs Grey?' Ouch. Really must sort that out.

'Yeah?'

'Biscuit?'

'Yes please. Are you having one too, or do you need to get home?'

I start to idly speculate about getting a male au pair. Possibly Polish. With dark hair and blue eyes and Slavic features. A little brooding but a marvellous cook. I am in the middle of this morally dodgy reverie when Ed returns with two cups and the biscuit barrel stuck under his arm.

'I can stay for a while. I have a free period first thing, so I don't need to be up till my driving lesson, at 9.'

'Ed, can I ask you something? Would you mind if you stopped calling me Mrs Grey? It's terrifically polite and all that but I'd rather you didn't.'

He is dipping a biscuit in his tea, sprawled again, and I feel the warm pleasure of having a relaxed male presence in the house, in the room.

'Sure. What shall I call you?' Little sideways glance. 'Auntie Jen?'

'Oh dear God.' We laugh, and my defences, my boundaries slip again. I bat him with the cushion I am hugging to my chest.

'I'll try to remember. Ma'am.'

I lean back into the sofa and we chat about the evening. I manage to make it sound more or less an amusing anecdote, and not so much of a soul-crushing experience. I am quite proud of my swift editing skills in this respect. Then we chat about the film, about even though we've both seen it so many times before, we can't help watching it if it's on. We talk about Emma Thompson's performance as the woman whose husband is having an affair (if only I could be half so convincing and touching in my role). We talk about the books we're reading, about politics, about how much he loves driving and that he's not at all nervous about the test he has booked for next week. An hour slips by.

'I should go, you're nearly asleep.'

He's right, the combined effect of the wine and the ease of his company. He takes the cups into the kitchen and I wait in the hall for the awkward money exchange, and to close the door behind him. I should go to bed but I don't, not yet; I return to the sofa and hug the cushion to myself again.

The phone buzzes.

Message Ed
Goodnight, thanks for the tea, and the chat

Right definitely don't reply. Definitely not. Go to bed, Jen, go to bed. Brush teeth, into bed, phone under the pillow. Turn off light. Stare into dark. Head spinning. Stomach churning. Phone buzzes again. I fish it out.

Message Ed
Sorry, I meant to say, thanks for the tea, and the chat Aunty Jen

He follows this message with a little winking emoji to show it's all just a jolly jape.

Oh Jesus - it's all the fault of this intimate little device, this tempting little rectangle. It's so easy to type words that you wouldn't say face to face. I think for a moment about how there's a PhD in that somewhere - the slippery intimacy of the message, the email, and the trouble it gets us into. I turn off the phone with one decisive movement and throw it over to the other side of the room, out of harm's way.

Except I don't.

A sensible woman would do that. Carrie would do that. And Ruth. Even Mel, flaky Mel would do that.

It turns out that I am not a sensible woman. I type, squinting in the dark.

Yes make sure you change my name in your contacts list... Aunty Jen. Or should that be Great Aunty Jen?

Almost immediately, the buzz back.

Oh no, that's not how you're in my contacts...
No?
No. I have you saved as Mrs Robinson...

This time, three winking emojis.

Three.

Suddenly very very sober, I turn the phone off, half-fall out of bed and run down stairs, shove it in the dresser drawer out of harm's way, next to the birthday candles and the Sellotape, make myself a large mug of camomile tea and go back to bed.

CHAPTER FIVE

OCTOBER

THE FOREST

Now, in the glade there is only silence. The birds have stopped singing. A heavy, expectant hush settles. Like me, the birds can sense danger, smell it on the breeze.

The silence flows between the patchwork of leaves, between the tree-trunks, between the blades of grass. The silence is so all-consuming, so enveloping that it even drowns out the singing of my blood, the resonant alarming boom of my pounding heart. The silence laps, unheeded, at my feet. At your feet. We don't hear it. Nor do we see the leaves, the trees, the grass. We can see only this: only each other.

Now you are close enough to see you, to look into your eyes. And to hear your words. I am finding it hard to do both of these things at once. I find it impossible to concentrate on the words when I am in your gaze. I hesitate for a moment, then make my choice.

I close my eyes. The sound of your voice, the rhythm and rhyme of your poetry soothes and excites me. Regulates my breath to a regular beat, a steady depth, to a state just beyond bliss, and just a little before sleep.

Your words fizzle and bubble in my brain, and just under my skin, opening the pores, making the hairs stand on end. They bounce into my stomach, making it twist and turn and flip, before zinging along my veins to settle inside my heart. I hold them there, turn them, cradle them. And then I lay them, with all the precious care of a mother, preserve them forever inside the very inner layers of my heart. Layers and layers of glittering perfect words.

Whatever happens, whatever you take away from me, this cannot be taken.

THERAPY, MARK I – JEN'S IDEA

'So I have an idea for a new therapy. Do you want to hear it?'

We are sitting outside, around the patio table, drinking tea. Just an ordinary Friday afternoon, but for some reason I am feeling perkier. Better. I have my bounce back.

Mel says, 'I tried CBT once, you know. I thought it was marvellous.'

I say, 'Well this is a bit like CBT Mel, only much much simpler.' They wait expectantly. Actually, I'm not just feeling better. I am feeling amazing. Better than I have for months. 'This therapy is called' - cheeky sideways look at Carrie - '"Fuck off Chris."'

'Jen!' Carrie is gratifyingly shocked. The others laugh. 'The children will hear!' Carrie is easily shocked by what she calls 'profanity'; she once saw a birthday card from Polly that included the 'C' word and I thought we might have to get out the smelling salts.

'Sorry, sorry. Alright then. Eff off Chris?'

Pursed lips, disapproving, but smiling despite herself.

'So this is how you do it. Whenever a negative thought comes into your head, for example, a thought about your faithless twat of a husband, or something tender he once said to you, you say, immediately and firmly - Eff off Chris! And this will drive out the negative thought, leaving your mind an oasis of calm.'

'Gosh that's breathtakingly simple isn't it?' Mel is amused, giggling. Even Carrie can't help but smile. 'Do you think it works for ghastly mothers-in-law?'

'I am sure it does. Give it a go!'

'OK, I will.' Pause. 'Eff off Madeleine! Gosh yes, that's super. Very effective.'

'The charm is, it's so flexible. I mean, you can think it, if in company or say, the playground. Eff off Imogen! Or you can whisper it. Under your breath, as the person walks away. Or if you are safely alone, for maximum effect, you can YELL it. EFF OFF CHRIS!'

'Eff off, Tom!' Ruth laughs, blushes. We all stare, a little shocked, and then full-on hysteria strikes. 'One prob, though Jen.' We look at Carrie, who's lost her inhibitions and is now trying to keep a straight face. 'I mean, it's a bit too simple. You need to make it a bit more complicated. So you can run weekend courses. Charge a big pile of money. Sell DVDs. Get yourself a YouTube channel. Instragram account. Celebrity Bake Off.'

'Oh yeah, you could have a retreat. "Fuck off to the FUCK OFF retreat."'

'And, for advanced cases: 'Fuck off, and go FUCK YOURSELF!'

'What are you all so amused about?' We had all been so busy wetting ourselves at my not-all-that-amusing-idea, that we haven't noticed the arrival of Chris to collect the children. His presence is not enough to stop us now, though.

Mel replies, with an utterly serious tone, 'The rise of Modernist theatre in 1930s Berlin,' and then we're off again. Chris, bemused, attempts a forced smile, and mumbles, 'I'll just get the children,' and exits, stage left, through the French doors.

For a moment, just the briefest moment, I feel a little sorry for him. But it soon passes, and then I turn to my wonderful coven, and we exchange glances, and laugh and laugh and laugh until darkness falls.

THINK OF ALL THE FUN I MISSED
One of the things I really want to say to Chris, but I'm saving

for the right moment, is this: do you think you're the only one who could have had a bit on the side? Really? When I first got married, my boss at the time, a curmudgeonly old buffer called Clive, warned me (promised me?) that the ring on third finger 'acts as something of an aphrodisiac, old girl.' I was sceptical. Surely the opposite would be true? Surely men wouldn't want the complication of an entanglement with a married woman?

Clearly, I knew nothing about men. (Do I know any more now? Unlikely. All evidence suggests the contrary.) Men - not all men, but some men - seem to like the combination of the challenge of pursuing a married woman and the minimal commitment required if the pursuit results in capture. Or maybe it's the furtive dangerous ooh-what-if-we-get-caught? business. Whatever, Clive was right. Over the eleven years of marriage I have had many (not always tempting) offers from a variety of different men. But Chris, to be honest, sometimes I was tempted. Not because I wanted to leave you but because, you know, sometimes a little attention might have been nice to relieve the boredom. It might be quite lovely, actually, to have a little passionate sex with someone new, someone who desires me. But I managed to exercise a little self-control. Well, mostly.

1. Once, at a party with Polly, I got chatted up by a gorgeous young man called Tim. Very clean cut and blond and totally into me. He spent the entire evening completely focused on me, and at the end of the evening he walked me to my cab. And gave me a hug and a kiss. And copped a little feel. I reckon I could get his number from Polly if I wanted to.
2. Michael, Polly's brother. Hard-drinking chef. Has made approximately several hundred passes of varying seriousness over the years. Would make me nice food, and then make love in chef's hat; I would only have to ask.

3. Rich, a boy I knew at school. Would have then, would do now. At the drop of a hat. (Not a chef's hat in this case. He's an engineer. But a very sexy engineer, just to clarify.)

4. Peter, ex-boyfriend of mine (do ex-boyfriends count?) who rings me every time he is in the country and tells me again how much he fancies me. An ARCHITECT this one. See, I can pull the arty ones, not just the geeks.

5. Andy, a very cute and very rich author from my publishing days, who occasionally sends me long emails (usually when he is between lovers). A standing offer, and a very tempting one actually.

6. Last week, on the bus into town, a teenaged boy referred to me as "Peng, from behind." When I got home, I googled this and found that this was a term of approbation. I appreciate I may be scraping the barrel here, but still, it all counts.

And sometimes, I think about ringing up one of these men. Although it's hard to imagine how I might open such a conversation. 'Er you made a pass at me just as I was getting into a taxi in about ten years ago. Well, a mini-cab. Yeah, well, actually, could I say yes?'

But right now the idea, the whole prospect of having a conversation with someone new, feigning interest in them, pretending that I actually care about anything, anything at all, well it's too much. Not yet.

Inevitably, of course, I find myself out on a date with a man the very next week.

NOT REALLY A GREAT NAME FOR A POET

The first four times Barry asks me out, I say no. No, no and no again. But he's a persistent bugger and the fifth time is the charm. Actually, it's not the persistence that wins me over. Nor is it the venue, or anything else to do with Barry, in fact. The fifth time of asking is just after the Mrs Robinson incident, and I am still in a state of panic. Maybe a nice normal date with a nice normal guy called Barry will be just what I need.

So I say yes. Barry looks more than a little surprised. I am not unsurprised myself.

In every way, on paper and in theory, Barry and I look like a perfectly matched couple. He is about ten years older than me (about Romily's age, as it happens). He worked in publishing for several years (like me), and gave it up to become a teacher (more or less like me). He has no children, but he does have a niece and nephew he talks about all the time. ('Lovely youngsters' he says; I later discover they're in their mid-twenties.) He is amicably divorced (as I hope I will be, if I can manage to hold it together). He is interested in books and films and politics; in fact he is active locally, and sits on the Town Council for the Green Party. He is a writer too - in his case short stories and some pretty earnest poetry - think Seamus Heaney, but without the light touch; I suspect that he would find my line in observational lifestyle articles somewhat trivial, but the remarkable similarities remain. He is also a keen cyclist (often arriving at my class with clips still in place) and enjoys long walks in the countryside, but nobody's perfect.

He is also, without a shadow of a doubt, a very nice man. Kind and gentle and interested in helping the needy and freeing the oppressed. He is the kind of man who would certainly brake for horses, even on his bike. And, most importantly, he is clearly very keen on me. He is a little too serious for flirtation, but he is certainly attentive in his earnest way. I am trying, very hard, to look forward to our evening out.

'What are you going to wear for your date?' asks Mel, a slightly mischievous look in her eye.

'Oh don't say that! I hate that word. I have never been on a date in my life.'

There is a chorus of 'Oh Jen!' and 'Don't be ridiculous'.

'I'm not being ridiculous. It's true. I have never been on a date. I'm far too old.'

Carrie asks incredulously, 'What about Chris? Did he just bop you on the head with his club and drag you back to his cave?'

I laugh, 'More or less. He was a friend of my housemate. He was in my kitchen from time to time and we chatted to each other and he watched TV with us sometimes. And then after a few weeks of that, we were at a party, got drunk and got off with each other. It's the English way.'

Ruth says, 'What a romantic story.'

'And it wasn't just Chris, that happened with my boyfriends before Chris too. You see someone in your circle of acquaintance that you like, you circle each other for a bit, snog at a party and hey presto! You're going out.'

'God wasn't life simple then?' says Mel, wistfully.

'Well those days are gone and you have a date.' Carrie laughs, evilly.

'I have no idea what to wear.' The others roll their eyes.

'Plus ça change, Jen. You never know what to wear.'

'Where is he taking you?' asks Mel.

'That's the funny thing, it turns out that I'm taking him. He emailed me earlier with his address and gave me a time to collect him. Is that weird?'

'Don't ask us, how would we know? We don't go on dates either,' laughs Ruth.

'Can I try on a few things, and you can say what you think? Please?'

So I parade around in a variety of black items of clothing and my friends demonstrate, or feign, enthusiasm. The least enthusiastic is Rosie, always very opinionated on the subject of clothes. She declares my choices 'all too boring.'

'Where are you going? Where are you taking him?' Carrie is amused by this idea.

'I've booked Retro. I thought it was an appropriate name

for a pair of Saga types like us. And it's quite buzzy, in case conversation is halting.'

Rosie is sitting on my lap, finishing my lemon drizzle cake. 'Are you going out mummy? Again?'

'What do you mean, again? Yes, I'm going out.'

'Is Ed babysitting for us?'

'No darling, Ruth is looking after you. Now shall we see if the others want any cake?' and I hustle her out of the kitchen to cover her disappointment at this news. Why isn't Ed babysitting for me? It's a good question. I couldn't bring myself to ask him; I am trying not to think too hard about why that might be.

I needn't have worried about halting conversation. Barry doesn't stop talking from the moment I pick him up in my car. (I have become increasingly irritated about this aspect; I have to clear it out and Hoover it. The whole process takes ages, and still his first comment on getting in the front seat is 'I can see you have young children!' I grit my teeth a little, but smile. Thank God he didn't see it earlier in the day, when it closely resembled a builder's skip.) I find out the reason though; Barry doesn't have a car. He likes to use his bike, or take the bus. 'The traffic is so bad these days. I don't like to add to it. And, you know, I have always been pretty serious about the environment. Member of Greenpeace since the eighties.'

Not so serious about the environment that he won't take a ride in someone else's car, though, it seems. He can reconcile himself to the horrible thud of my carbon footprint, rather than take the bus and meet me there. I suspect, from a few mildly barbed comments, he might have something to say about my four by four monstrosity - well I can't blame him for that - but I also suspect he might wait until the second date before he starts dismantling my lifestyle. I guess it might be too killing to the spirit of romance before then.

And, it appears, one woman's 'buzzy' restaurant is another man's 'too noisy to talk.' (It also turns out that the 'amicable' divorce is something of an overstatement, but this revelation comes a little later.) Barry finds Retro a little bit too modern for his tastes, and he steers me down the road towards the rather staider atmosphere (and menu) of San Carlo. Still it's pleasant to be out, and I am determined to give this my best shot.

He chooses pasta primavera ('I used to be a vegan, but I found it wasn't good for my digestion as I got older'). He recommends it to me in such an insistent fashion that I find myself ordering it, even though I really want the special - lamb shanks on bed of potato. I love lamb shanks but I feel somewhat inhibited from saying the word 'shanks' in front of Barry. It seems inappropriately specific, almost primitive, to talk about the piece of animal flesh I require in front of a vegetarian; it also has a mild sexual overtone that I would like to avoid at this stage in the evening.

I am probably being a little oversensitive about this latter aspect, because now I am out on a date with this perfectly nice man, I am finding myself almost physically repulsed by the prospect of touching him, and - worse, even - of him touching me. I am trying to concentrate on what he is saying, but vivid pictures keep floating into my mind, unbidden. As I watch him dabbing his bread into the olive oil and balsamic vinegar, I have a sudden vision of his fingers dabbing ineffectually against my breast.

I shiver a little, with involuntary horror and, also, guilt. It's far too early in the evening to be making any judgment on Barry's sexual technique. I am sure he's perfectly adequate in bed. Perfectly. I push the thoughts from my mind and try and concentrate on playing my role for the evening in a convincing manner: recently-separated woman, attractive, interesting and in no way messed up in the head.

As it turns out, my character's role is pretty straightforward: I am required to listen, politely and more or less attentively, while Barry talks. Barry likes to talk. His conversation is by no means uninteresting, but it is certainly fairly relentless. (Conversation is perhaps something of a misnomer; monologue is perhaps a more accurate description.) This is what Barry talks about (and, believe me, I am summarising):

1. The state of British politics. Now, this one is normally right up my street but Barry's narrow focus for the evening is the political scene of the late 1980s. I was there, and I remember but no matter – Barry wishes to educate me about it. In detail and at length. I try to look suitably grateful for this history lesson. I only baulk at his - rather surprising for a Green councillor perhaps - defence of Margaret Thatcher as 'a pioneer for British women in politics.' I open my mouth to start a rigorous counter-argument, but find myself overwhelmed by the potential material, and close it again.

2. Poetry. Again, pretty much my specialised subject and not a topic I thought could get boring. I thought wrong.

3. Great cycle paths of Great Britain. To Barry's credit, he starts this one with a question. 'Do you cycle, Jenny?' 'No. I don't. I never have.' Not that this answer puts him off his stride, mind you. At one point I see him put his hand in his rucksack, and I have a sudden fear that he might have a projector in there and I might be about to be treated to accompanying slide show. But, hurray, he is only getting out a tissue to blow his nose.

4. Divorce. Yes, as I say, not so amicable as all that. In fact, I would go as far as to say, a little bit testy, at least on Barry's side. The divorce petition had come as something of a surprise to Barry; I wonder, rather unkindly, whether Mrs Barry had been trying to get a word in for so long that in the end she was reduced to writing it down in desperation. Thankfully, there are no children caught in the maelstrom of this not-so-

amicable-after-all divorce - 'didn't want to increase the population, you know. I'm very serious about population size. Very serious.'

5. Women and how marvellous they are. No really, they really are marvellous. Barry is 'very serious about feminism. Always have been.' Except, you know, it's all gone a bit far now, hasn't it? I mean, it's not about equality any more. Women want special treatment AND equality. And the radical ones, well, they give the others a bad name. I find this part almost quaintly charming. Does Barry think he is being original? Does he think I have never heard this before? My arguments against this barrage of nonsense are so well-rehearsed that I have, on occasion, thought about recording them onto tape and putting them on automatic playback: 'for a defence of feminism against unpleasant, over-simplified bigotry, press 1.' But that's probably because I am one of those radical feminists, I expect.

By the time the dessert menu comes around ('I think we've had enough, don't you? Yes, just two coffees please.') I am starting to feel like we may have been caught in some sort of eddy in the space-time continuum. All sense of the normal passage of time has gone. I start to fantasise about what living with Barry would be like; terrifically relaxing, I guess. You would never have to make a decision again, or indeed express any kind of opinion or conscious thought at all.

But time passes anyway, even at this ludicrously slow pace. I am already rehearsing my excuses for not seeing him again on the drive home. (Barry's return journey topic of conversation: the laziness and selfishness of teenagers of today and how they are messing up the world we have gifted them. I smile to myself at the idea of a meeting between Barry and Ed. Now that would be worth watching.)

I pull up in front of Barry's drive, and leave the engine running.

'Thank you so much for a lovely evening.' I am smiling slightly too broadly, and my tone is over-bright, but luckily Barry is highly unlikely to notice.

'I am glad you enjoyed yourself. It's a nice restaurant isn't it?'

(Yes Barry, it is. I have been there. Many times, as it happens. Because I actually live round here, you know?)

'I did, thank you.'

'You are a lovely person, Jen, and really easy to talk to. I tried to think of subjects that you would find interesting.'

Actually that's quite touching. And thoughtful. I imagine Barry chewing the end of his biro and carefully writing down a list on a recycled pad in the hall: Possible Topics of Conversation: poems, politics, divorce, feminism. That's pretty on the button, in fact. On paper. Now I'm wavering. Maybe I should give it another go? Maybe I didn't try hard enough? Maybe just another date, to make sure?

'The thing is Jen, you know I really like you but I don't think this is going to work out. You are a lovely girl but, well, I need someone with a bit more gumption. My wife was quiet like you, and that didn't end well. But I really did have a lovely time. Well, good night, see you Tuesday.'

And with that, he's gone. I drive home in a bit of a daze, and it's only when I pull into my own drive and turn off the engine that I start to laugh.

Ruth turns off the TV as I enter the living room.

'How was it?'

'Well the good news is, I'm a lovely girl. The bad news is, I am very quiet and boring.'

'Yes,' laughs Ruth. 'That's pretty much what we say behind your back too. Thank God someone had the balls to finally tell you to your face.'

And I salvage my pride by turning the evening into the kind of amusing story that makes Ruth cry with laughter; but

I can see her thinking, thank God I don't have to put myself through this. Thank God I am married and don't have to open myself up to that kind of criticism.

Yes, Ruth, thank God. You have no idea how lucky you are, because I had no idea myself a few months ago. No idea at all.

THE F WORD

I was a feminist. I mean I AM a feminist. I went to Women's Groups, I went to Consciousness Raising, I even went to peace camp. (Don't tell Carrie. In fact, don't tell anyone. It's our secret and let's pray the police photos are never made public otherwise I may have to leave this village for good.) As a teenager I went to protests about all sorts of awful things and I sang and I chanted and I made banners with slogans. And I emerged blinking into womanhood with a strong sense of sorority, an obligation to those who had Come Before and a sturdy list of things that I thought feminists should never do, viz:

1. Take their husband's name on marriage. A badge of ownership, an outdated relic of a time when a woman was a chattel. (I wasn't quite so radical as to abandon marriage; I thought that an equal partnership, an equal sharing of child-care and domestic responsibilities was what we should strive for. Easy peasy, right? Ha.)

2. Give up work to look after children – a terrible mistake, leaving you vulnerable to exploitation and poverty. And of course, terrifically boring and not nearly so important as paid work, not to mention an awful waste of my hard-won education and a slap in the face for all the sisters who had fought and died on my behalf in previous centuries. Particularly that woman who chucked herself under the King's Horse at the Derby.

3. Have a joint bank account – economic and financial independence was the prize handed to my generation of women; to give it up for some wishy-washy notion

of 'love' would be reckless in the extreme.

4. Trust a man. They're all bastards.

Yes, well, except.

1. Well that's all well and good, but my maiden name was a bit clunky, didn't go well with my first name and no-one could ever spell it right. Whereas the clean minimalistic lines of Grey... well it was too much to resist. As a bonus prize, I also gained the same name as the actress who played Baby in Dirty Dancing. And (a new argument I picked up from KeyboardMums, this) it was only ever my Dad's name anyway, right? Right on sister.

2 It's all well and good to fight for the notion of universal childcare in principle, but then you hold your baby and the political becomes horribly, viscerally personal. To the glowing woman in her dove-grey Isabella Oliver maternity dress, Tiny Toes Nursery seemed like the perfect place for a baby to be cared for. The second time around, nine months later and with my beautiful precious Michael strapped tight in the complex weave of the Babybjorn, that cheerful line of wellies by the back door didn't seem quite so cosy; it seemed poignantly institutional. On the second tour, by the time I reached the baby room I was crying so hard that the sweet, kind manager didn't even suggest I sat down - I was making the children edgy. I was making her edgy. Or maybe they were all edgy anyway? Maybe Tiny Toes was just a plain old edgy place to be? By the time I was back in the car, my eyes were so puffy I could barely see the phone keys to dial; once Chris could work out what the hell I was saying, he told me not to worry. We could work something out, and we did. What we worked out was that I could stay at home and look after my precious baby, myself, as long as I tossed my career, my lovely job and all the

delightful things that came with it, straight onto the fire until it was burned to a pile of ash. I did it, without another moment's hesitation, without another word being spoken. Like the reckless fizzing bundle of hormones I was, it seemed the only possible sensible thing to do.

3. God I don't know; I can't even begin to justify this one. Sheer laziness? After years of balancing my accounts, well attempting to, it was a total relief to hand this over to someone else. A man, a lovely kind capable man in whom I placed my absolute trust.

4. Oh give it a rest.

CHAPTER SIX
NOVEMBER

I'LL HAVE A LOOK IN DEBRETT'S

Here's a piece of twenty first century etiquette for you - is it appropriate to send your recently separated husband a birthday card? I mean, I can't pretend I've forgotten it's his birthday; that would be ludicrous. To *not* send one would seem a little pointed - like I was sulking. And I'm not sulking. I'm not thrilled with this situation, and I am very very hurt and all that, but still, I don't begrudge him a happy birthday. I am not that petty. Even faithless twats deserve many happy returns.

Also, the etiquette of the twenty first century separation requires us to be friends, or at least maintain the outward appearance of being friends, you know, for the sake of the children. If I can manage to speak civilly to his lover, even help him pack his things to move out, then surely I can manage to buy and sign a card for his birthday.

Then why, twenty minutes after entering this shop, am I still staring at the shelves, wavering and dithering over the appropriate card to buy? I am tempted to buy one reading something like 'To my darling husband' and amend it by hand with a biro to read 'To my loathsome soon-to-be-ex-husband' but I suspect this will be less amusing in reality that in theory. Or what about a 'Thank You' card; I can personalise it with 'Thank you so much for leaving me and your children, it has been the making of us.' Or 'Sorry - sorry you're such a total arse. Hope you Get Better Soon.'

In the end I choose one to 'The Best Daddy in the World' from the children - let him feel the irony there, if he likes - and one from me with a football player on the front.

Chris hates football. I suspect even a technical geek like Chris will be able to read the symbolism of that.

ALWAYS SOMETHING THERE TO REMIND ME

The thing about getting your heart broken, getting it ripped out of your body and thrown on the floor and stamped on and kicked around for good measure, well the thing is this. It's hard to forget, and it's hard to remember.

Hard to forget because it blackens everything I do and everything I think, every minute of every day. It drains all the light from everything, so I feel like I am walking around in a permanent semi-gloom. All the little pleasures of life are watered down and twisted. Under normal circumstances I love to listen to the radio, but for the last few months, this has been hazardous. Every song has the potential to become Significant, the lyrics worming their way into my brain and making me cry, or flinch. Big chunks of my old playlists are rendered out of bounds; a yellow and black police line has been strung across, reading DO NOT CROSS – DANGER OF MAKING YOU MISERABLE.

It's not just the sad songs either. The happy ones can be even worse, because there is a risk that they will be tainted forever by association with a particular mood, or time. Songs about love can remind me of the fact that my love has been and gone, and I done got the blues. Or, worse, they can make me think of the love that Romily and Chris share. (I once nearly injured myself sprinting across the kitchen to turn off the radio when the song 'Accidentally in Love' by the Counting Crows came on. The lyrics that once seemed joyful now seem like a transparent excuse. Accident? Oh come off it. That was no accident. There is no such thing as an accident.) But worst of all, of course, are the songs that I associate with Chris, and particularly the far-off days of our early life together. It is so hard to pin down the truth when these songs send me into flashback mode; it is easy to get dragged into the idea that he was lying all along.

But then, often, it's hard to remember. As I float grimly through the days of the summer and into the autumn, I have to block off large sections of my heart and my memory, just to get through. Doors and windows are slammed down inside me, rooms are shut off in my head, until I am left, shivering but surviving, in one bare room. I try not to think about whether I will be able to open up those other rooms ever again and, if I can, what I'll find there. Will they rot away, crumble into ruin?

Yet even these radical measures don't stop the hurt. I don't talk about Chris, I don't think about Chris, I try quite hard to imagine that he doesn't really exist unless absolutely necessary. But old habits die hard, and we have a lot of shared history and language. Several times a day, a thought might pop into my head - Oh, I should save that and show Chris. Chris and I should go and see that film. What might Chris like for dinner? And I have to remind myself that Chris is gone, for good. That all the loving things he said to me, everything we shared has to somehow be divided up, separated out. How I can manage to do this without damaging everything beyond repair, I don't know. I just don't know. I just have to try and make myself forget, and hope that I can heal, and that the scars won't be too deep and tender, and that one day I will be able to shift this numb feeling in my heart.

PUT IT IN THE PANTRY WITH YOUR CUPCAKES

By November, Ed isn't just coming here to study or to babysit; we have settled into a comfortable little routine. He comes to babysit twice a week now, Tuesdays and Thursdays, while I do my classes, but he comes pretty often on a weekend too, when the children aren't with Chris to just hang out with us as a family. I pay him for the evenings but the weekends he won't take payment for, which is lucky because he's here so much it would bankrupt me. Sometimes he will pick them up from school, if I have a deadline to meet. He will take them to the park, or the library, or swimming; sometimes we go together. Sometimes I can't face it, and he takes them by himself. The amazing, the precious thing about this, is he doesn't have to ask whether I want to come or not. He picks up on my mood, and says 'Why don't you stay here?' usually followed by a little prêt-a-porter excuse, like 'I expect you have a lot of work to do' and I don't argue. I am grateful for his incredible kindness, grateful for his calm and most of all I am grateful that he never asks me how I am. Ed doesn't require me to lie, to be holding it together. He doesn't ask me to be cheerful. He doesn't ask me for anything at all.

I love the mornings we go out together, too. It is great to have another adult around, someone to talk to, someone to carry the picnic. Parenting is not the hardest job in the world, I am not claiming that. But it can be crashingly boring, incredibly repetitive and sort of draining. Having someone there, someone to push the swing for a bit, someone to hold the door when Rosie needs the toilet for the third time in an hour, someone to break up the bickering, someone to wield the baby wipes - well, it's much friendlier with two. During the week, I have Carrie and Mel and sometimes Ruth, but at the weekends they have their own family life. The weekends can be incredibly lonely. Ed slots into this role with ease; he's a natural in fact.

Just like the very first day at Rosie's party, he just sees what needs to be done and gets on with it, quietly and without fuss. This might be admiring Rosie's changes of outfit, loading the dishwasher, or advising Michael on what sort of weaponry will be most effective on the long quest to waste away his childhood fighting CGI dragons in the company of lots of Swedish teenagers called Sven. I try not to think about what Ed is getting out of this. He comes, he comes willingly and I am too low, most of the time, to be anything but selfishly, self-centredly, pathetically grateful that he is there. When he is in the house, when we are in his company, the Greys stop rubbing and scraping against each other, and start muddling along in a friendly, companionable way. He improves our mood, all of us, especially me. He doesn't bring hysterical laughter, or organise exciting activities. He just slips between us, and lets us all be as close to normal as is possible, given our far-from-normal circumstances. He is like a big squirt of WD40 into our creaking, straining family life.

One Saturday morning, when we have just returned from a rather chilly trip to the park, and I am half-heartedly tidying the kitchen, I notice he is looking out of the French windows with a decidedly purposeful air.

'Feel free to clean those windows if you like. I'll get you a cloth.'

'No, it's not that.' Uncharacteristically serious. 'It's your lawn. When was the last time you mowed it?'

'Sorry, I can hear the words, but I don't really understand what you're saying. Mow, the, lawn? Now, why would I want to do a thing like that?'

'Because... well I'm not too sure to be honest, but your neighbours must be getting annoyed. Anyway you're definitely supposed to, in the autumn.'

'I don't mow the lawn. Like I don't put air in my tyres, or go in the loft. It's just one of things I don't do. I'll get Chris to do it.'

'I'll do it, if you want.'

'Do you know how?'

'Yes of course I know how. I've done it for years. No-one in my family mows the lawn either. Well Becker might, if it was hot and there was a girl there he wanted to impress and he could do it with his shirt off. But otherwise, no, it was me.'

'You know you will really make a phenomenal husband one of these days. Either that or an excellent gay man.'

'Yes that's what my mother says.' He laughs.

I like these little glimpses of his family life. They make me feel like I am getting closer, like I am - for a change - maybe providing him with some support, someone to talk to. They make me feel like I am actually being useful.

'Well, shall I?'

'God yes OK. That would be wonderful. If you don't mind.'

He doesn't even grace that with a response.

He stays for lunch, and he is still sitting at the table when Chris arrives to take the children to the cinema mid-afternoon. Michael is, miraculously, doing his homework: the project, making some sort of wheeled vehicle, is spread over half of the kitchen table. Ed is helping him; their two dark heads are close together in deep concentration. The rest of the table is strewn with the Saturday papers; we've got the Lord of the Rings playing on the speaker. Rosie and I are decorating sparkly cupcakes. If you were to edit out the terrible mess, we would not look out of place in the pages of one of those glossy supplements called something like Family Life.

Chris says, 'Hello all!' No response. Rosie is far too engrossed in sprinkling pink glitter across the work-surface, and Michael is involved in some serious axle-action. I am ignoring him, just for the hell of it. In fact, only Ed responds; his politeness is too hard-wired.

'Hello Mr Grey.'

Chris doesn't even look at him. He presses on, 'Kids, it's time to go. The film starts in half an hour.'

'Daddy, can't you see we're busy?' says Rosie.

I am fighting the urge to laugh, unpleasantly; this scene was not planned, but honestly, truly, I am enjoying it, just a little. In the end, predictably, the best-behaved, most mature person in the room - by a long way - is Ed.

Ed says, 'Come on guys, we can finish this later. Your Dad's waiting. Come and get your shoes on.'

And at that, the reverie is broken, and Rosie and Michael scuttle into the hall, still a little reluctantly but obediently. I studiously concentrate on the cupcakes, to avoid the conversation that I can sense is brewing.

Chris whispers under this breath, 'Jen, why is that boy here again? He's always here.'

I don't look at him. I can't look at him.

'He's here because he likes to spend time with the children. He enjoys our company.'

'But he's here all the time.'

The anger, when it comes, is white-hot and lightening quick.

'No, Chris. He's not. I'm here all the time, and so are the children. You, however, are not. So I think you'll find that who we spend time with, well, that's our business.'

I sense his gaze over my shoulder. 'Did you mow the lawn? You should have asked me. I would have done that.'

'No. Ed did it. And to be perfectly honest, darling, it has absolutely fuck all to do with you.' And to ensure that this is the last word on this subject, for now at least, I hand him two cupcakes - 'One for you, one for Romily' - and walk out into the hall to help get the children out of the door.

When the children are gone, I help Ed with his history essay and we chat about poetry for a while. Then he does the Sudoku from the paper; he tears out the crossword for me to do. We drink tea. We discuss the merits of our favourite biscuits, at some length. By the time the children return I am so relaxed and so cheerful that I persuade Romily to come in from the car for a cup of tea. I ask polite questions about the film, about her business; we talk about the change in the weather, the commercialisation of Halloween. I can see Chris staring at me. I don't return his gaze. Yes, look all you like Chris. I've nothing to hide, and nothing to be ashamed of. Nothing to apologise for. I shall start to get over it, I shall start to be cheerful and you frankly, will just have to suck it up.

Three days later, my phone buzzes mid-morning.

It's Ed, 'Are you in later? I have news.'

'Sure, come for supper.'

He arrives at 5.30, grinning; I am pretty sure I have never seen him grinning before.

'I have an interview. At Brasenose.'

I am squealing and jumping around with excitement. I hastily hustle him inside the hall, suddenly conscious of the neighbours.

'I wanted you to be the first to know. I wanted to say thank you.' He hands me a bottle of champagne. 'This isn't to celebrate, it's too early for celebration. It's for all the help you gave me with my application. And the essay. And the test. My test. I would never have had the cojones to apply if it wasn't for you.' He laughs, completely joyous.

'And I want to ask if you will help me to get ready for my interview. Would you? I am completely terrified.' In this mood he seems very young.

'I'll put it in the fridge. For when we can celebrate.' I let the idea of opening a bottle of champagne and drinking it with Ed percolate around in my head for a while and I feel suddenly a little tense. I couldn't be prouder if he was my own son. I wonder if he will tell his mother, and whether she is in any state to be happy for him. I put the kettle on - much safer - and we start to talk about clever things to say about books to impress the admissions tutors at Oxford.

CARRIE DOESN'T GET IT

'Poor lad, wasting his life away in this village. I mean he must be bored out of his mind.'

Carrie is on a roll now. My increasingly desperate attempts to change the subject are getting absolutely nowhere. 'I mean, why on earth does he spend so much time here? It makes no sense.'

Shut up, Carrie, please. I try to keep my face totally neutral. 'Well he isn't here that often, I don't think.'

'He is Jen, he is! He's always here!' Yes, and he's here right now, Carrie, at the front, pushing Rosie on a swing. So shut the hell up. I can hear Rosie's delighted laughter, intermingled with the low rumble of his voice. It is a combination that, on a normal day, is enough to fill me with the kind of warm contentment that, just a few weeks ago, would have seemed impossible. You are bloody ruining it. Shut up. With the sheer force of my mind, I am willing him to stay there. Don't come back here, Ed, please. Please.

She's still waiting for an answer. I try to oblige.

'Well, he says perhaps he wants to be a teacher in the future. This is all good experience for him. You know, for the CV.' Well someone else told me that, months ago. It might even have been true then, who knows? Recently Ed has been talking about becoming a writer, maybe a playwright but I am not about to mention that. These are his inner thoughts and dreams and they leak out in little scraps. I keep them close to my heart.

There is a sceptical silence.

I plough on, 'And you know I'm paying him, sometimes. He needs to earn money and it's not that easy to get a job, is it, if you don't have a car? He wants to pay his way. And he's learning to drive, and that's expensive isn't it? You know the situation with his parents.' I wonder if a little reminder of the operatic-quality of his family life might be enough to knock her off track, but no. Carrie is unstoppable.

'Well yes, but you aren't paying him all the time are you?' Mind your own bloody business Carrie. Wind your bloody neck in.

I'm going to have to raise the stakes further.

I say, 'Maybe he misses his mother. Misses family life. Normal life.'

'Maybe... maybe.' At least that's shut her up for a minute. But it's just the calm before the storm. 'I'm not sure that's healthy is it, really? He has a mother, and if he gets too attached to you, surely that's going to be worse in the long run.'

Ruth says, 'Oh Carrie, that's total crap. I mean, medically speaking.' Wow, Ruth. I owe you. I really owe you. 'Anyway, he's not 10, he's 18. It's up to him how he spends his time.'

But that really sets her off; she's got her second - or is it third? - wind on the subject. 'Yes, exactly! 18! It's not normal. An 18-year-old should be out getting drunk and playing the field.' Jesus, Carrie seems to be advocating binge drinking and promiscuous sex. The world is tilting on its axis. 'With young people his own age, not wasting his youth away with a bunch of kids and middle aged women. He's going to look back on this year and say, what the hell was I thinking?'

'Hello Mrs Stanford, Mrs Malone.' Here he is, the boy I am holding prisoner in my rural hell-hole, against his will. Come on, Ed, answer her! What the hell ARE you thinking? 'I think I'll head home. I've got quite a bit of work to do. Would anyone like some tea or anything before I go?'

This is not a popular move with Rosie, who is holding his hands and has her feet on top of his, like make-shift stilts. 'Don't ggggoooo Eddie, don't ggggoooo. We will MISS YOU,' she wails, giggling.

'No thanks, we're fine.'

Even famously taciturn Michael has emerged, blinking, from the darkened living room to say goodbye. 'Will you come on-line later?'

'Sure Mike.' He touches my son lightly on the top of his head, ruffling his hair, and is rewarded, incredibly, with a warm smile; if I tried a similar stunt, the best I could hope for would be a long-suffering grimace, but more likely a snarl.

'Bye guys, see you later.' How much of Carrie's diatribe, I wonder, did he hear?

For a relieved minute or two after his departure I think the conversation has at last run out of steam, but no, we still have our bunny-boiler-lurches-out-of-the-bath moment to come.

'I just don't understand the attraction, I really don't.'

MILK IN FIRST, OBVIOUSLY

To give Carrie her due, it is a fair point. What is Ed thinking? Well, if you'll indulge me, I've given this some thought and I have a few theories:

1. Well, first and foremost, the boy likes a little conversation, I'll tell you that. Not chit-chat, not small talk, not much personal, but proper, serious conversation. Elvis would probably encourage him to try a little more action, but it's conversation the boy wants. And I will also point out that, with the best will in the world, conversation is probably not high on the agenda at Ruby Becker's house. Hearty walks, heavily-moulting dogs, extreme competitive sports: yes. Talking: no. He is, no doubt, a little bored and a lot lonely. As am I. These are just a few of the topics that we have explored (often at some length) in the last months:
   - The rights and wrongs of picking up hitch-hikers, with particular reference to having children in the car;
   - Books. Quite a lot about books;
   - Whether swimming lessons are a total bloody waste of time and money;
   - Politics, in all its many aspects. Our views are just far apart enough for conversation to be interesting. He's even changed my mind on a few things;
   - The persistence of the patriarchy;
   - Whether France is essentially over-rated and, in particular, how the French have persuaded us that French films are cool and sophisticated when the vast majority of them are, in fact, a bit rubbish;
   - The pornification of our culture (this one went on for days);

- Whether the milk goes in first (well, he's wrong about this one; this conversation is not closed);
- The importance of cake to family life;
- Would you rather be a pirate or a ninja?
- This is not a definitive list.

2. He's a serious young man, for sure, especially about his school-work. And about getting to Oxford. It's clear that he gets little or nothing from his family, or his adopted family, and I can help with his work. I am not even sure that he's told them he's applied to Oxford. I love it, actually; it makes me feel like the relationship is balanced, and I have something to give as well as take.

3. It may be obvious but yes, I guess, he must miss his mother. Although we don't talk about it, he drops enough little snippets for me to know that she is on his mind, all the time. And - this one is a little wince-inducing, but I can take it - he is probably used to looking after his mother, so looking after me feels comforting.

4. He may be 18 but his habits, and his tastes, are pretty middle-aged. He likes listening to Radio 4, drinking tea, doing the crossword, chatting about books and films. All in all, he likes to take life at a fairly slow pace, and I can certainly offer that. I can offer life at a pace that makes glaciers look speedy.

5. Also, he actually has quite a bit in common with Michael - he is, after all, considerably closer in age, and particularly close in temperament, to my son. They like slaying things together, and making fiddly little things with wheels. He helps with piano practice - the fifteen minutes a week before his lesson that is - and recently he's been teaching Michael a few chords on the guitar. And he adores Rosie. If you are feeling a bit gloomy and lonely (and I guess he is, all least most of the time) then Rosie's company can be immensely cheering.

6. He hasn't got a home, not at the moment. He is a guest in his Aunty Ruby's house, and - from what I know of Aunty Ruby - she probably makes a massive fuss. And if there's one thing that boy doesn't like, it's a massive fuss. I think he likes my house because he doesn't really need to talk about anything if he doesn't want to. And, I guess this is quite a crucial one, he likes it because he has a purpose, something to do. I know that feeling. Very well. I recognise that need in him, because I have it myself, in spades.

7. We are, in the end, two of a kind. He's having a shit year; I'm having a shit year. We can both hang out, feeling crap but OK, together. We don't have to talk about it, or pretend. It's a match made, if not in heaven, well certainly somewhere calm and nice and lovely, like the Chelsea Flower Show, or a National Trust Tea Room. We look after each other. We're company for each other, and it saves some other person, or some other people, from having to sit with us while time passes and we start to feel better. Misery needs company, and we have found it in each other. Who could deny us that, really?

SO THIS IS WHAT IT'S LIKE TO BE A NEEDY GIRLFRIEND

Bloody Carrie. The next time I see Ed, her words are still rattling around inside my head. Why have I let her get to me like this? I know, really, that she is clueless. She knows nothing about me, or about Ed. But nevertheless her pointed remarks have pressed all my buttons, hard, and the emotions she's stirred up won't settle.

If only we could have a frank conversation, put our cards on the table, life would be so much easier. I imagine what this might be like, a wild fantasy of openness and clarity:

'Hey, Ed. I like having you here. I enjoy your company and I find you interesting. How about you?'

But honesty is always a rarity in male/female relationships and, with Ed and me, this kind of exchange is laughably unlikely. Instead, we have to hover in the gloom of the half-truth, the ambiguous remark. In my search for confirmation, for comfort that Carrie has it all wrong, I am in danger of driving Ed away. He's becoming exasperated with me, and God knows I am exasperated with myself, but I can't seem to stop.

'Are you sure you're OK to come tomorrow? I mean, do you need to be doing something else? I would absolutely understand.'

This conversation has been going on for a while now, round and round in tedious circles and I can see that Ed, kind, patient Ed, is starting to baulk a little at the idea that it might carry on for a while to come.

'Yes I'm fine to come tomorrow, Jen, you know I am.' His voice is gentle, even tender. I can hardly bear to hear it. I am standing at the sink, clattering the dishes noisily. I am angry, angry with Carrie, angry with the situation and I am taking it out on Ed. The force of my emotion is scaring me. I am carried away on the wave of panic and fear and, now, self-destructiveness.

'I mean I don't want you to feel obliged. I guess you must be very busy.' My tone is cold. Stop, I must stop.

'Yes. Jen, I just said yes. It's fine.'

'But I don't want you to think you can't say no. I mean, you've been in the village for a while now. I am sure there are lots of young people that you should be getting to know. People your own age. Parties or, whatever.'

'Actually, I'm going to a party tonight.'

'Really? Well that's good.'

'Not really. I don't particularly want to go but I've been nagged into it. By people who think they know what's best for me. I gave in to shut them up for a bit.'

Ouch. Will I get this hint? No. It appears not.

'Well, maybe not parties but, I don't know, tennis? There

are lots of people in the village with courts. Everyone plays. You should ask Ruby, get her to set you up with a tennis partner.'

'Tennis?' A note of incredulity, even laughter, in his tone.

'Yes. Tennis. If you don't have a racket, I'm sure Ruby will lend you one.'

Ed says, 'Yes. I might do that.'

I turn to look at him, 'Really?'

He picks up a tea towel and starts to dry up. He sighs, 'No, Jen, not really. I don't play tennis. I don't like tennis. It's also November, so not exactly tennis season. But I am just seeing if there might be a way to stop you talking about this.' He smiles, just with his mouth though, not with his eyes. His eyes are serious, and looking at me, steadily.

He says, 'I don't know where this is coming from. But look, if I have given you the impression that I don't want to come, then I don't know how that happened but I'm sorry. I do, I want to come. So, please,' he smiles, to indicate his regret at what he's about to say, 'would you please shut up about it?'

I laugh, 'Shall we change the subject?'

'God, yes, good idea. Let me tell you about this party, and how little I'm looking forward to it.'

And I wash, and he dries, and I am grateful that one of us, at least, has a grip of themselves this afternoon.

MOMMY DEAREST

My mother says, 'What you need to think about, Jennifer, very carefully, very carefully indeed is what you did wrong. What you could have done to change things, to stop this from happening.'

Yes, what could I have done.

Because, obviously, this is ALL MY FAULT.

I am at my mother's house and it's perhaps worth mentioning that this is the first time since Chris left me that I have been to visit her. This isn't co-incidence. I just wasn't ready to take the emotional beating until now. (I'm not too sure I am ready even now, but still, here I am. I can't really put it off any longer.)

I can hear the children racing around the garden, among the immaculate flower beds and trimmed lawns, with Charlie. Charlie, my gorgeous, feckless, brother, the lucky bastard. Fate (or is it karma?) has played a very cruel trick on my mother. She values intelligence in men and beauty in women; she has a pretty son and a smart-arse daughter. It goes against all laws of nature as far as she's concerned.

I wish my brother Charlie were in here, with me. My mother's presence makes me feel very weary, and it would be very comforting to have Charlie here, to dilute the effect. For a start, she's never so much of a total bitch when he's in the room. Mother adores Charlie, with a passion. But of course there's no reason for Charlie to be in here; my mother has no need to chide him. Charlie can, and does, breeze through life failing to hold down any kind of job, breaking women's hearts pretty much on a monthly basis. All this is met with my mother's equanimity and indulgence.

I don't give a reply to my mother; a response is not expected and would not be welcomed. I sigh and shift on the sofa, and settle in to listen to my mother for a little while longer, before I can escape outside.

But if I was inclined to respond to my mother's question, then what could I say? What could I have done? What kind of stupid bloody question is that? Are we supposed to take marital feedback now? Set targets for our performance, check our progress against agreed, calculable measurements. Go on training courses if we fall short. We must all get thinner, prettier, smarter, younger. Perfection, and nothing short of it, or else we only have ourselves to blame if our husbands bugger off with someone else.

We've all done it. I know I have, although this admission is enough to make me blush in shame. When we hear that some man has been cheating on his wife, we have a need to turn this event into a story, give this situation some wider purpose. We want to give it a sense of narrative; we want to believe that it was predictable, that it was always bound to happen. Why? Because otherwise, this could happen to us. Any of us, at any time. We want to think we are immune, that we know the end of our own story. (Believe me, you don't. Your story hasn't been written yet. And no-one's writing it. Life is random and life is essentially meaningless. Get over it.)

Indulge me for a moment while I explore some of the glib, throwaway, oversimplified storylines that we have all used (yes, even you dear Reader) to explain away the extremely complex business of marital breakdown, and see if we can squeeze my own little tragi-comedy into any of them:

1. 'She's let herself go.' I know this is the one my mother would sign up for but I honestly don't think it's true. For a start, I was never that much to look at. No, this isn't false modesty. I was more or less average. (On the up side, losing your looks is not so much of an issue if they were never much to write home about in the first place.) People did not run screaming from the room, but nor did anyone swoon at my feet. But - here's the thing - I was never short of offers. I am prepared to stick my neck out and say that pretty much all the things that attracted Chris, I still have. You know, my personality, my intellect, my wit (ha), all that kind of trivia.

2. 'She's not the same girl he married.' No of course I'm bloody not. I'm a mother for a start. None of this crap about not letting a baby change you. How could it not? Also I'm a decade older. Nor is he the same man I married. Feel free to criticise me for this but I don't feel any moral responsibility for the passage of time. Whatever the magazines say.

3. 'Since she gave up work, she's got really boring.' Seriously, no. If anything I was miles more boring when I was at work. I used to worry about all sorts of crap that I have no time or inclination to whinge on about now, e.g. my weight, how I should cut my hair, should I buy these shoes? (I know I go on a lot about what to wear, but imagine what I was like

before.) Also I used to bang on for hours about tedious work stuff. Who said what to whom, whether she is shagging him, should I try for this promotion, oh my God her office is definitely bigger than mine! At weekends, we filled our leisure time with long discussions about whether we should paint the spare room primrose-white with turquoise aspects, or rose-white with magenta aspects, and which would go best with these curtains? Honestly, truly, could anything be duller than that?

4. 'There must have been something wrong with the marriage, or he wouldn't have to look outside.' Oh this is my favourite one. And by 'favourite' I mean 'the one that makes me feel the most raging.' Because what this one does, very neatly, is place the blame for the infidelity on the one who isn't shagging someone on the side. (Which, in most cases, is the woman. Not always, of course, but lots of times.) Because, you see, s/he had to look elsewhere because there was something missing. Something not quite perfect. This implies that we all have a responsibility to fulfil our partner's every desire and need, and if we don't, then we only have ourselves to blame if s/he goes off and fills in that gap elsewhere. Not only is this morally indefensible, it also makes no sense, does it, really? Hmm, I am not getting full satisfaction from my partner, therefore I must solve this problem by having sex with someone else. That's a great way to achieve additional intimacy, or fulfilment, or perfection in your marriage, right? Think it through, dear, think it through.

In my observation, the infidelity equation, the real one, is much much simpler. It goes like this:

BOREDOM AND/OR NEED FOR EXCITEMENT + OPPORTUNITY = INFIDELITY.

That's it. Sometimes in a long-term relationship you can get a bit bored. It's natural, and not necessarily a sign that there is

Something Wrong. If at this point the opportunity for sex with someone else arises, that's when infidelity might happen. It doesn't have to, of course. There's still a choice to be made. You make a choice to start down the path, and it's a pretty steep downhill slope. It's a bit slippy. You start picking up momentum and pretty soon you are hurtling downhill. But you don't have to get on the path at all. You can stop, turn round, walk back up. Even when you are hurtling down, you can chuck yourself off the path and into the undergrowth at any time.

Some people get bored very easily. These people probably shouldn't get married in the first place, but they do, and then spend the rest of their lives pelting down various scree-ridden paths looking for a bit of excitement. We all know someone like this. There isn't something wrong with their marriage; there's something wrong with them.

So this is what I think: Chris just got on the path, started skidding, and didn't stop himself. I guess he was just a little bit bored. I sort of understand how that could happen. I don't blame him for getting on the path, even, but I do blame him for not getting off.

We are incredibly ambivalent towards infidelity, as a society. We act all shocked when an unfaithful spouse is revealed, but we couch the activity in cosy, gentle, unthreatening language: bit on the side, bit of extra, fancy man, playing around, shagging about, knocking someone off. These friendly little phrases mask the nasty wounding nature of infidelity but they reflect how shockingly normal it is. I am not sure if it is comforting or depressing to realise that my own technicolour personal tragedy makes me nothing more or less than a walking (stumbling) cliché.

MISTAKES, MISSHAPES, MISFITS

But the thing is, mother, although your approach is a little over-simplistic, I am prepared to concede that you may have a point. I mean, I am not absolving Chris of his responsibilities to keep his thing in his pants but still, I am not saying that I'm not a fuck-up. I have some self-awareness. If I look inside me, I know what's there. And if there's a finger of blame to be pointed for the mess that I am, we know where it's pointing and it's right at you, dearest mama.

I know it's seems a bit feeble to lay your emotional faults at the door of your parents once you're an adult but there's a reason why I avoid talking about my emotions, why I hide behind this carapace of brittle cheerfulness. There's a reason why I avoid difficult and painful situations. That's what happens if you have to keep bouncing back from nasty remarks and vicious criticism. If you put someone down often enough, well if you're lucky they might get robust and strong, but it's more likely they just stay down, right down, way out of sight. If you make a child live with vile moods, unpleasant confrontation and personal onslaughts that come out of the blue, it can't come as any surprise that, when that child grows up, she doesn't stay around, just in case it might happen again. She takes the door marked exit. Over and over. If you keep making flippant remarks long enough, confrontation can be avoided. Believe me. I know. And that's why, 4 months after the worst emotional trauma of my life, I haven't spoken to anyone about it, about how I feel. In fact, I barely mention it. I have filled the void with work and activity and distraction.

Worse, even, than that - I haven't spoken to Chris about it, after the emotional maelstrom of the first few days. And I know he isn't happy, not really. I may lack empathy (cheers again, Mum) but even I can spot that the man is having some serious second thoughts. The grass may well be lushly greener on Romily's rolling lawns but he looks like a man who misses his old scrubby patch. Why aren't I doing something about that? I think it would only take a word from me, just a leap in the dark, that's all. But I don't. Instead, and this is the worst crime of all, I avoid the serious business of salvaging my marriage, rebuilding my family, and distract myself with the short-term comfort and superficial distraction of the emotional cul-de-sac of my friendship with Ed. This safe danger zone, where I while away the days and weeks and months with this sweet kind boy, who offers uncomplicated conversation and friendship. And the months go by, and the chances of a reconciliation get further away. And I'm still hiding in this cul-de-sac, drinking tea and talking about poetry.

What am I hiding from? Oh come on, that's an easy one. I am avoiding the necessity to take a bloody hard look at myself, and change. Why won't I talk to Chris? Because I am afraid. Afraid that I might have to face some pretty devastating truths. Afraid that my emotional fragility will be exposed, tested, shattered. Afraid that the real reason why he found solace with Romily is, well, maybe she has more to offer. Maybe she's a real person, a whole person. Maybe he was tired of trying to have a relationship with a broken biscuit, because all the cream filling in the world can't disguise the fact that I am a shattered person. You can't tell from a distance but, close up, you can see I'll never be whole. I'm just crumbs, squashed and moulded. Who can blame him, mummy, if he popped me back in the biscuit barrel and found himself a nice, whole, glossy Chocolate Hob-Nob?

CHAPTER SEVEN

DECEMBER

TELL ME ABOUT THIS BANANA

'Do you want me to take you to Oxford, on Saturday?'

'I can perfectly well take the bus.'

Ed and I are sitting on the sofa after my class on the Tuesday, watching some appalling late night movie with Jean Claude van Damme in it.

'Alright then. Let me put it another way. I shall take you to Oxford on Saturday. Give me the interview schedule and we can work out when you need dropping off and picking up.'

He seems quite relieved. 'That would be nice actually. I'm feeling a bit nervous.'

'Well, don't be. It's only your entire future at stake. Nothing to worry about, not at all.'

Every evening of that week, we look at the Oxford University website, and we talk about what questions they might ask at interview. We talk through the books he has been reading; we talk about the books he mentioned in his personal statement, about Dylan Thomas and Ernest Hemingway, and he tries to sound clever and original, with some success. He practises rigorously defending his reasons for applying for Oxford. We look through his submitted essay, entitled 'The great safeguard is never to let oneself become abstract', and laugh hysterically about how pretentious he sounds in it.

I say, 'It's a good essay. It's Oxford-pretentious. They will be lucky to have you.'

He says, 'That's what you said when I asked if I should apply.'

'Did I? Well I was right then and I am right now.'

We watch Brideshead Revisited and we debate at length the merits of the different methods of punting.

He is as ready as I can make him for the Oxford experience.

On Friday evening, he phones in a mild panic.

'What shall I wear? I haven't even thought about it till now. And now I'm packing and I don't know what the hell to pack.'

'OK well none of that high-visibility check stuff you usually go in for. You don't want to give them a migraine. What else do you have?'

'Erm, my suit?'

'No, probably not your suit. You'll look like you've come up from Harrow or something, and we need to emphasise your state school credentials. Get their quotas up. What else? Do you have anything that could be described as smart casual?'

There is a silence. 'I am giving you a look. Are you getting it?'

'Yes,' I reply. 'I do believe I am. Alright, what trousers do you have apart from jeans?'

'I have some chinos.'

'Yes, if they're not tatty.'

'No. They're quite new. And I have a stripy shirt and one with quite a small check, in blue and white.'

'Yes, that sounds perfect. And some sort of semi-casual jacket or coat? It might be quite cold. You can take your usual gaudy ones for the rest of the time, but keep it stripy and checky for the interviews.'

'Thanks, I feel much better. Jen?'

'Mmm-hmm?'

'I'm glad you're taking me. It makes me feel calmer. See you in the morning.'

ON BALANCE I PREFER EASTER

By the time the run-up to Christmas is here, this bloody polar bear is starting to get on my nerves. I wouldn't mind parking him somewhere else for Christmas, to be honest, to give me a bit of a break, but who would have him? He's been rotting on this sledge for months now and he's starting to stink a bit. People are crossing the street to avoid me because of the smell, in fact. Well, at least I think that's why.

Let me tell you, when your husband leaves you, there's an immediate flurry of prurient interest but it doesn't take long before you're old news. Not to your friends, of course; Mel and Carrie and Ruth show a fairly consistent amount of concern for my state of mind – rather too much, if I'm honest. In contrast, among my wider circle of acquaintance, the sympathy, and indeed the interest, lasted for about as long as the cheesy mini-series that ITV would make of the whole episode (not including the commercial breaks). They've all moved on, and anyway shouldn't I be over it by now, surely?

Don't get me wrong, I'm not complaining about this. Well, not much. Any sympathy at all is, frankly, too much sympathy for me. On one level, I am delighted that my predicament is no longer the subject of village gossip. What's harder to take, though, is my new-found pariah status: as a single person, my social standing in the village is somewhere just above livestock and marginally below a rag-and-bone man. (With apologies to all rag-and-bone-men; I have every respect for your trade but, if you want my advice, don't move to Lower Worthington if you are looking for a lively evening scene.) Again, as a general rule, I don't yearn for a mantelpiece crammed with gilt-edged embossed invitations (not that I have a mantelpiece, but you get the idea). I wouldn't mind a couple of entries in the diary at Christmas, though. I mean, I have a nice new sparkly top and I might even countenance buying a new lipstick to match, like they tell you in the magazines, if only I had somewhere to wear them. But this is my Christmas social calendar, as it currently stands:

Wednesday 14th – School Carol Concert (may involve poor rendition of Little Donkey, that one about Christmas in Waikiki, and possible weeping.) Standing room only; novelty festive earrings technically optional but practically de rigeur.
Tuesday 20th – Pot Luck supper with a group from Silken Ties and Lasso the Muse (not including Barry) at my house.
Friday 23rd – Chinese with Mel, Ruth and Carrie.
And that's it.

Chris and I have, after weeks of stalling (me) and avoidance (him) finally resolved our Christmas plans. What we have agreed so far is that the children will be at home Christmas Eve. (The idea that this is even in question, that one day – maybe even one short year away – this will not be the case, makes me queasy with anticipated misery.) Chris will come round for a bit on Christmas morning, and we will all attempt to be festive and not at all awkward. Then on Boxing Day morning, he will take the children to his mother's overnight, maybe even for a couple of days. (Is Romily going with them? I don't know; I haven't asked. Why ask questions to which you don't want to know the answers?)

So it is with mixed feelings that I receive an invitation to Ruby Becker's Boxing Day Bash. That's how it's being sold to me: The Becker's Boxing Day Bash!!!!' Obviously the breathless punctuation and the excessive alliteration are making me a little weary, but on the other hand the idea of having somewhere to go on Boxing Day evening, somewhere with other people, and quite a large amount of drink, sounds very tempting. In particular, somewhere where I don't have to face the piles of newly-opened toys, silent and significant, is exactly where I need to be.

What makes my feelings about the invitation somewhat ambivalent, however, is the inscription. In shiny gold ink, in a sprawling, almost unreadable hand, Ruby has written, 'Looking forward to seeing you and having the opportunity to thank you SOOOOO much for looking after Edgar! You are a saint!!!'

I am already rehearsing my casual response to this as I jam the invitation, with its jaunty snowman border, onto the fridge with a chunky toucan-shaped magnet. 'Yeah, he's a good kid. No, really it's been a pleasure.' Christ, I mustn't start learning my lines too early, otherwise I am never going to convince anyone; I know Ruby seems pretty sweet, but you never know, she might be terrifically shrewd and observant, and spot it if I'm too glib, too smooth.

I've pulled the 'Yeah he's a good kid' line a few times now, and I am quite proud of it. It sounds comfortably in the right register, nicely casual, and - best of all - that use of the word 'kid' leaves the listener in no doubt as to the nature of the relationship, where the power lies. I even managed to say it in Ed's presence once, without even a flinch. It helped that I didn't look him in the eye. Of course it isn't a lie, not completely: he is a good kid, that's undeniable. He's also my friend, a kind and understanding friend, who not only understands my moods, but knows, instinctively, how to help improve them. His presence is calming, reassuring and soothing. By this time in my catastrophic year, Ed knows more about my real state of mind, more about me, than absolutely anyone else. For everyone else in my circle, I keep up the appearance of coping. It's important to me that they don't suspect just how bad it is; if they noticed that I was struggling, then Carrie and Mel and Polly - and to a lesser extent Ruth - would find the concept disturbing. Not Jen, she's a strong one! No, she's fine I'm sure. I tell Chris nothing, of course, and my mother less than nothing. As for Charlie, well I suspect I would not see him for some months if I sought his support. I would have to go into some major meltdown to shift their comfortable view of me as a woman in control. I'm the one giving support, not the one who needs it. To upset that balance would be disturbing for everyone, me included.

But it's not like I'm spilling my guts out to Ed, either; I'm not. Even if I could, even if my natural cowardice and reluctance could be overcome, and I could theoretically screw my courage to the place where I could manage to open up and tell him my neuroses and pain, to show him my darkest corners, I still wouldn't. I would be too inhibited, too held back by everything about him, and me, and our circumstances, that would make that kind of intimacy wildly inappropriate and reckless. But I don't have to spill my guts - Ed knows me, because he just listens, just pays attention. Sounds simple doesn't it? Well, why does no-one else do it then? Maybe because his calm, serene, non-judgmental presence makes me feel safe enough drop the act: all of the acts, in fact. Whoever the hell 'Jen' is, she is closest to the real me, closest to what's inside me, when Ed is around, because I feel so incredibly safe in his company. And I am not too far gone to recognise, that's the most dangerous thing of all.

I wake up on Boxing Day with a dread so heavy, so monstrously large that I fear I won't be able to shift off the mattress. I think of the many other things that I would rather do today, rather than face getting my children ready to spend a few days with my estranged husband and - I suspect, although I don't know for certain - his new girlfriend, leaving me to spend the fag-end of the festive season all alone.

It's a long list.

1. Take my driving test again. I am not a bad driver, now, but - as Polly would say - they probably shouldn't let squirrels learn to drive, on balance. I finally managed it on the 6th attempt, with the help of a good slosh of Bach's Flower Remedies and a fair bit of luck.
2. Cycling proficiency. I think we can safely say that squirrels are no better at cycling than driving.
3. My finals. Actually I don't mind exams. Exams I can manage. You can work at exams, and concentrate, and it can all be under control. No-one is scrutinizing my

face to see if I am holding it together. They leave you alone in exams.

4. My Dad's funeral. No, really. At least I could cry then; at least I wasn't obliged to keep this gap, this distance, between what everyone knew I was feeling, and what I was permitted to show. It's perfectly OK to weep at a funeral, but if you grab the bumper of the car departing to take your children away, well people judge you for that kind of thing. I need to find some dignity and self-control; I wish I'd asked for some for Christmas.

When the time comes, though, I manage to keep it together, just about. The presence of the children helps, of course; although I struggle with being the grown-up in theory, in practice I can just about pull it off. I manage to speak to Romily with a suitably cheery manner; of course she was going with them, of course. I didn't really need to ask, after all. I fuss a little over the children, making sure they have everything they need for the journey, and for their stay. I even manage to smile and hope that they all have a delightful time, and I manage this with the barest minimum of sarcasm, too. Not that Romily would notice; her kind of serene calm drives out any notions of sarcasm. It can make conversation with her rather awkward, her otherwise-perfect brow wrinkling with incomprehension.

And then they're off, and I wave, and I wave, and I wave. And then I crumple.

And then here I am again, choosing clothes, finding the right costume. I am trying them on, slowly at first, but then with increasing panic. I can't think what role I am supposed to be playing. And the more I think about it, the more ambiguous my role seems. I'm not going as anyone's wife, nor indeed as anyone's mother. But I'm not actually anyone's friend either; I barely know the Beckers. I think Carrie will be there, and some other people I know too, but they will be there in couples, with children.

I'm there because of Ed, is the truth. So, what role am I playing? Saint Jen, selflessly giving up her time for the poor damaged boy? My conscience prickles - quite apart from the fact that Ed is, frankly, more or less better at taking care of my children than I am, well I don't have any clothes that could make me look like a Saint. I could probably manage Respectable Middle-Aged Soon to be Divorced Woman, but who the hell is she going to talk to, and about what? She isn't going to have a good party, and frankly I really need a good party.

In the end I choose an outfit of Ambiguity: just young enough to make me feel like, well, me, but sexual allure kept to a minimum. It's a sort of chiffonny long sleeved dress with a lace trim in some sort of pale brown. (Mink? Shrew? Actually I think the colour is closest to Roadkill Bunny. Pick your rodent, choose your connotations.)

By the time I knock on the door, I am wishing I had had a quick drink before leaving. Jim Becker greets me politely but with no real enthusiasm, although I am not exactly gushing myself. Once inside the living room, I am wishing I hadn't come. My eyes are sliding, scanning the room; looking for someone to talk to, ostensibly, but if I'm honest, looking for Ed. I want to know where he is. Is he even here? I wish I'd pinned him down, but as usual I was too inhibited to just ask him straight out.

I join a group by the food table - would it help to have a plate of food? I'm not sure. It would give me something to hold onto, and of course line the stomach because in a minute I'm going to get a massive drink and see if that makes me feel more in a party bloody mood. But, on the other hand, my reputation and history with party food is not very distinguished. Party food can be so slidey, I find, and often fairly slippy too. My contact with food at parties often ends with kitchen roll and apologies. I thought I wanted to come, thought I wanted company, but now I'm here, you know what I would really like to do? Put down my drink, get my coat and run out of the door and just keep running until I get into my house and into my bed and close my eyes and let the tears come.

I decide to forego the food for a while. I recognise a couple of faces from the playground and though I don't know these people well, I know them well enough to stand, smiling and listening. The topic seems to be - my perfect Christmas so far. Tales of amazing presents, joyful children and all-round blissfulness are swapped, cooed over and developed into glistening epic tales. Who could have imagined that listening, simple listening, could be so incredibly difficult?

I decide to give it a go with the food after all.

I am struggling with the couscous, already spilling a little on the tablecloth, when I see Ed across the room. I focus hard on the salad bowl, trying not look like the simple task of spooning out some food onto my plate is completely beyond me. I sense, rather than see him, making his way across to me. I feel suddenly incredibly self-conscious.

He says, 'Would you like me to get that for you?'

I say, 'Christ yes, and then you can get me a drink because frankly if I can't manage a grain based salad, I am not risking any form of liquid.'

He says, 'Sit down, I'll be back in a minute.'

I sit down, in a corner seat with some friendly familiar faces. He is indeed back in a minute, with a plate of food, and a large gin and tonic. He holds them both for me until I am settled, then perches next to me, on the arm of the chair. I can't remember anyone ever taking care of me like this, and yet it feels incredibly natural. I feel the now-familiar mixture of emotions: calm, warm, cared-for. I relax, and - aided by the gin - start to join in the conversation. The presence of Ed by my side is comforting. We aren't talking to each other; we aren't even looking at each other. But he's there, and I feel safe. I relax and start to laugh, then start to contribute, even make the others laugh. Before I know it, I seem to be accidentally enjoying myself.

'Would you like me to get you another drink?' he asks quietly, during a lull in the conversation. 'And maybe some pudding?'

'Yes, please, you're very kind.'

'No really, it's good to be able to do something for you for a change, to be the host.' Wow, nice big fat comforting lie there, Ed. Good work.

But kind as his offer is, it's a mistake, because the vacated arm doesn't stay empty for long. I see Imogen approaching, and I am tempted to stick my arm across it in a pointed fashion, but luckily (perhaps) I am not quite drunk enough yet.

'Jenny darling, here you are! I've been looking for you! How are things, my darling?' Concerned tilt of the head. Laying on of the hand of comfort onto the forearm. Jesus, can I stand this? Ed returns with the drink, a dish of some sort of meringuey pudding and an apologetic smile; he mouths 'sorry' and backs away. And I'm stuck.

'How has Christmas been for you darling? Must have been awful. But the first time's the worst, eh? Where are the girls?'

Nice one, Imogen. Not so good with the deets, as Carrie would say.

'They're off staying at their grandma's. Chris took them earlier. They were really looking forward to it.'

'Yes I'm sure. I guess they don't see too much of their Dad any more. Sad, very sad.' Imogen does her best sad face. Oh very good Imo, very convincing.

'Well they see a fair amount of him. Every other weekend, and often during the week, if he's not working away.' Why am I justifying this, to this woman? Why? I look around for a refuge, an escape route, but I am trapped here. This corner seat, so cosy and safe until a few minutes ago, suddenly feels like a rat-trap. Where the hell is Carrie? She's at the party, I know. But she would never work out that I needed a friend and ally here; good old Jen, life and soul of the party. Do her the world of good. The Becker's party, such fun!

'It's so hard on the children isn't it? I mean people always say that children are resilient. But it's not true is it? They are so fragile. So easily damaged, and the damage is hard to fix. Impossible really.' She shakes her head, with the infinite sadness of a woman contemplating all the horror of the world.

Why are you doing this, Imogen? Are you really an evil woman, or just a bored one? Can you really imagine how much this conversation is taking out of me? What have I ever done to you, to make you want to wound me like this?

I so, so want to run away, to make an excuse and exit, but no, I grip the seat and force myself to a reply.

'Actually no-one really talks about the positives. It's been so good for them to get to know Romily. Such an educational experience for them, to see a range of social lives. Without Romily, they would never have ridden in a Mercedes. Well definitely not a convertible.' I smile, what I hope is a beatific smile.

Imogen looks a little confused, hesitates just a beat, then smiles.

'Will you excuse me? Must just go and....' She trails off, and I try to look regretful.

'Jen!' Oh dear God, no, give me a minute to recover, please. But no: there's no respite and I'm straight out of the shallow fat and into the licking flames. Ruby Becker bounces over and perches on the arm; Ed's arm. Ed, where the HELL are you?

'Oh I am so glad to get to talk to you at last! I am sure you know how grateful we all are to you.'

Around me, I can sense that my companions are pricking up their ears, trying to catch the details about Ed and the Bonkers Mother, without looking obvious about it. It's just the sort of juicy stuff that they find fascinating from the comfort and cosiness of their rural bliss. I am judging their prurience but really, would I act any differently? Village life brings out the worst in us all.

'Really, it's a pleasure, no trouble at all.' Here we go, press one to hear a pre-recorded banality: 'He's a great kid.' Nice, very good. An award winning performance. Applause, applause. Thanks I'll be here all week.

Ruby leans forward, lowers her voice to a whisper. Our sofa companions lean forward too, almost imperceptibly. 'We've been so worried about him. Such a difficult year for him. I mean, poor Liberty, I am not sure that she'll ever be..... and as for Dave.' She shakes her head. 'I know I shouldn't really talk to you about this, but I feel I know you. You have been so kind. I haven't seen Ed so happy in a long time.'

'No, me neither.' What? What am I saying? Shut up Jen. Luckily, Ruby is in full flow and misses this rather ambiguous comment. 'I really appreciate everything you're doing for him. Helping him with his work. Helping with his Oxford application, we're really grateful. Really. But it isn't just that. He loves your children, loves spending time with them. He's such a lovely boy.'

'Yes, he's a good kid.'

No! Not twice! Don't say it twice! Oh God, I need some fresh air.

'Honestly, I enjoy his company. We all do.' Leave Jen, leave. You are hitting an honesty seam here. You need to get away. But I needn't worry, Ruby is a sweet person but she's a hostess and she is moving on. She airkisses me vigorously and backs away, leaving me with an escape route. I take it.

On the way out, I grab my drink and my cardigan, and a handful of some sort of chocolate crispie cakes. I may be gone for some time. Slipping out through the kitchen door, the shock of the cold winter air sobers me up a little. I wish I smoked; this would be a good time for a cigarette. Shrugging the cardigan around my shoulders, I mainline the chocolate crispies and sip the white wine.

'Party going well then.' I don't turn round, but my

anxieties settle at the sound of Ed's voice, and I smile.

'Actually I prefer a party from this distance. Anyway I have chocolate crispies. Do you want one?'

'Sure,' Ed replies and drags a chair, scraping along the ground next to mine. I want to tell him to shhhh, quiet down. Don't attract attention. Quiet, like a mouse; I really don't anyone to disturb us now.

He says, 'So how's this party been for you, so far?'

'Oh swell. Really swell. The couscous are lovely, for a start.'

'Yes Aunty Ruby's couscous, it's legendary.' He laughs.

'And these chocolate crispies, want another?'

'Sure. Why not, it's Christmas.'

'My favourite bit was hearing about everyone's amazing Christmas.'

'Yeah well let's compete. My Christmas has been more shit than yours. You can go first.'

I laugh, 'Sorry. I am feeling sorry for myself, as usual.'

'Yeah, obviously your shattered marriage and utter humiliation is nothing. Get over it, that's what I say.'

'I will get over it, if you could only stop whining on about yourself for once.' We are both laughing now; I am more than a little drunk, and I wonder if he is too. 'Honestly, blah blah blah, my terrible childhood, oh isn't it sad about my crazy mother, whatever.'

Oh shit, too far? No, thank God, not too far. He is smiling, leaning forward onto the table. 'I know, I know, what a wuss, eh? All a big play for sympathy. Nothing like a motherless child to get the girls, you know?'

Girls? Girls? 'So where are these girls, Ed?' Yes I am drunk. Really drunk. I should shut up, go home.

But I feel the layers of ambiguity, the barriers between us, falling away. 'Well, just one girl. There's one girl.'

'What's her name?'

'Charlotte. Char. I have been chasing her, and catching her, and then losing her, and then chasing her again. God, for years.'

Years? How can you have been chasing her for years?

'And right now? Is she caught?'

'No, she's not caught. She found the whole thing with my mother, it was too much for her. It was too much for me too, but I don't get to run away. Lettie ran away. And Becker. Even Dad. But I have to stay and face it.' He glances at me, sideways. 'I guess you know how that feels.'

I nod, but don't risk any words.

He goes on, 'I mean she's young, she's just enjoying her life.' That sounds like a direct quote. 'She's not a strong person. I was always the one supporting her, looking after her. It wasn't really fair to expect her to look after me. That's not how things were between us.' I nod again, force myself to look at him, to show that I understand the words, the sentiment, the pain that this represents. 'I mean, it wasn't fair. We're still friends, but right now we can't be together. Not yet.'

I say, banally, 'Well time will pass, and I am sure it will all work itself out.'

He shakes himself, 'Sorry, this must seem all so trivial to you, in your situation. You know, there's no comparison is there?'

'I definitely wouldn't say that. Definitely not. Love, well, it's hard when it's doesn't go right. It isn't really to do with age or the time of life.'

'That's why I haven't said anything before about this, I mean, because I can see what you're going through. I don't want you to think I think it's anything like the same thing.' A moment passes. We both look out across the lawns, to where the mist is rising off the river. The night is clear and crisp, and the stars sparkle in the inky blackness like twinkling fairy lights. 'I wish you could meet my mother.'

Christ. 'Yes. I wish I could too.'

'You would like her, very much. Although she's not much like you.' He laughs. 'Mel reminds me of her, sometimes. Though she isn't as together as Mel.' We both laugh quietly at this rather ironic idea.

'When did you see her last?'

A silence stretches. I want to fill it; to stop myself I start to count the stars. I have reached 145 when he replies, 'Not since Easter. It hasn't been .... possible.'

'Yes.' I think of my own mother, and try to imagine having the kind of relationship that would render such a lengthy separation so obviously painful. I am finding it impossible to bridge that gap of imagining; it's too wide.

'I am going to see her tomorrow.' Another pause, a pause during which I try to will myself sober. 'Maybe. I hope it will be possible. This time.'

'Have you tried, then?' Is that intrusive? I don't know.

He replies, 'Yes, a few times. Many. Some. It might help if Dad was with me, but I don't even know where he is at the moment. I haven't heard from him in weeks. Months.'

Instinctively, I place my hand on his arm, gently, firmly. I want to ask, why? Why hasn't it been possible? But this seems prurient. I don't really need to know. I have nothing much to say, so I just say his name. 'Ed.'

'Jen.'

'You know, I think this is definitely going to be our year.'

It is only later, when Ed has walked me home and we have said a slightly awkward goodbye on the doorstep, when I've cleared a space to lie on the bed by tipping the huge pile of abandoned clothes onto the floor, that the restless ambiguity of that sentence hits me. I wrap the duvet around me against the chill of the night, the chill of the past, present and future, and try to sleep.

CHAPTER EIGHT

JANUARY

THE FOREST

I open my eyes.

We step closer.

Your words stop, as suddenly as they began. And now I can feel what's inside you. The precious centre of you.

Closer.

And this is the point I feel the change in me. In the eye of this paradox, I have slowed down enough, for long enough. My breath is slow, regular, incredibly deep. I start to feel the sweet warmth of your love, shimmering on my skin, penetrating the surface. I feel the wounds knitting, the scars smoothing over, pulling together, the gaps closing all over. I feel, with every minute that passes, more whole, more full, more safe. And stronger. Strong enough to stop the thoughts, the jangling fears, about the power of this feeling. This love is working miracles, making me heal. What potential to harm does it hold, to rip open those healing wounds, wider and wider and -

But no. I stop thinking like that. You step closer and the fears are driven out. Your steady liquid gaze on me. I am close enough to see myself reflected there, right there in your chromatic eyes. I can look, I can see myself, without flinching, without blinking.

And just for a moment, I look beautiful.

And I feel you step closer.

LET IT SNOW

The new year begins with a massive fall of snow. I find another entry on the (extremely long) list of Reasons Why It's Crap To Live In A Village: when it snows, you get snowed in.

Snowed in! It sounds terrifically romantic but it really isn't. The first day isn't too bad. It's still possible to get out to civilisation, if you have a four- wheeled drive (and I do, I do, to my shame) or on foot, if you're careful.

I have resolved, in the post-Christmas time of reflection (read: self-flagellation) to stop fretting so much about my friendship with Ed and how it's being perceived, and just enjoy his company. We have nothing to be ashamed of, and nothing to hide.

All of these good intentions last about the standard length for the New Year's Resolution: until that first snowy morning, January 6th. I am woken up by the buzzing of the phone; I reach across to check the time. 6.37. Shit, bad news – no-one phones at that time with the good kind.

Ed mobile calling

SHIT.

I drop the phone on my face trying to answer it.

'What's up? Is everything OK?'

He says, 'God I'm so sorry to phone you so early, but I'm in a panic.'

Yeah and so am I, now.

'That's OK, what is it?'

'I have a French oral exam this morning and it looks like the roads are all blocked. I know it's a lot to ask, but could you take me in the jeep. The jeep thing. Four by four. Whatever it is.'

'Of course it's not too much to ask. Come round, and I'll find someone to look after the children.'

I try to stick to my resolutions, and not to sound guilty or suspicious when I phone Carrie to ask her, but when I drop the children off, still in their pyjamas, I can see her squinting at me narrowly, and at Ed. Is she suspicious? Is she judging? It's hard to say, but I suspect so.

'Exam, can't be missed. He needs it for university.' Oh stop gabbling Jen. If this was ten years in the future, and it was Connor, Mel's son, in that front seat, I wouldn't be getting these significant looks. Or am I imagining it? My paranoia is running wild now. I glance back at the jeep. Ed looks so incredibly tense and anxious, that I can hardly bear to be away from him. I am drawn back, magnetically. I am counting the seconds until I can leave Carrie and get back to him, without looking like I've dumped the children. I give it ten more seconds, I think to myself; I am counting them in my head. At least I hope it's just in my head.

The other thing I can see from Carrie's doorstep, Carrie's line of vision, is how incredibly young he looks. Despite his elevated position in the jeep's passenger seat, he looks vulnerable. His hair is fluffy and unstyled - no time for gel this morning, I guess - and his fringe is falling into his eyes, making him blink a little. He obviously hasn't had too much sleep, and the painful contrast between the pale skin and the bruised eyes make me want to stroke his hair, to push it out of his eyes, to soothe away his worries. I use up the final three seconds of my polite doorstep pause lingering on this morally-ambiguous idea.

Yes, New Year's Resolution going well.

The snow holds off for the morning, and I collect a relieved looking Ed - it went 'fine thanks', oh do stop your endless wittering about yourself, Ed - and we plunder the supermarket together for supplies before returning to Narnia. But as the afternoon wears on, the snow clouds return and it snows, it snows and snows some more. By nightfall, when the temperatures fall to -13 according to the fridge thermometer, we are properly snowed in, and likely to stay snowed in for a few days.

'I saw Charlotte at New Year.'

We are walking back from a massive snowball fight on the Downs. The children are all absolutely soaked. (I include Ed in this definition, because his enthusiasm for the fight was surprisingly, charmingly juvenile.) I have managed to avoid the snowballing by strategically taking photos of the action. Rosie and Michael have run on ahead, and Ed and I are following behind. We are so wrapped up in padded jackets and hats and scarves that our faces are not really visible. This brings a sort of intimate anonymity, a feeling of the confessional to our walk home.

'Was she well? I mean, how was it? Did it go OK?'

'It depends what you mean by OK.'

The sound of our boots crunching on the snow is rhythmic, even hypnotic.

'She was at a party I went to. God I hate parties, especially New Year parties.'

'Yes. Me too. Always far too much heavy drinking and forced jollity. I'd rather stay at home.'

'Well lucky for you that you can stay at home. At my age, everyone nags you till you go out.'

'I always tried to work at New Year, when I was your age. That at least gives you an excuse. Or be the designated driver.'

'She's seeing someone else. Dan. His name's Dan. Someone from her course. She says it's nice to be with someone who is not afraid to show his feelings. Who she can really talk to.'

Now come on Jen. Don't judge her. She's young and inexperienced.

'He was at the party too. She left us alone together for a bit, to get to know each other.'

Well, that might have been with the best intentions. You just can't tell, from that. You don't know what it's like to be in her shoes.

'Then when he'd left, she asked me to take her home. And she told me she's still in love with me.'

Fuck. Ing. Bitch.

'And what did you say?'

Trudge, trudge. Silent minutes pass.

'I told her, I don't know what to feel. I think I still feel the same but then I can't remember how I used to feel. It's hard, when she's with someone else, to pin it down. Hard. I don't know.'

Trudge, trudge, trudge. Silence. Minutes tick by. Bloody hell, conversation with Ed can be a very trying experience, patience-wise. Actually, Charlotte, you may have a point. Just saying.

'I think I am meant to be with her. To marry her..'

'Yes.'

Trudge trudge trudge. Trudgy trudge trudge.

I say, 'And did you tell her that?'

'No. Well yes, I hinted at it. I mean I said that I thought we would end up together. I didn't say marry. But, we've known each other so long. I think she is the one. I mean I thought she was, is. I can't imagine being with anyone else.'

Trudge, trudge. Over the stile. More trudging.

'Anyway, she's been messaging me ever since. So at least the lines of communication are open, which is a good thing. I suppose.'

Oh God. I just want to bundle him up and hold him, tightly, until this moment passes. If I could find him in the middle of all that goose-down and padding. And when I've done that, I want to go and find this girl and bop her on the nose. I swear I never used to have these violent thoughts. I blame you, Chris, for this. Among many other things I blame you for.

Ed says, 'Can I ask you something?'

Well I'd rather you didn't, to be honest.

'Yes of course. Anything you like.'

'Is that how you felt about Chris? That he was the one? Is that too personal?'

Yes. Yes, it's massively too personal.

'No. No it's fine. Well I am a very different person to you. I don't really go for the whole 'The One' thing.'

'Well I don't have much experience I guess. Probably you think I'm young and stupid.'

'No I don't think that's it, necessarily. I think that you're a romantic, in way that I'm not. But I wasn't a romantic at your age either. It's a state of mind, I think, an approach, a way of looking at the world. I don't see the world that way. But I know plenty of people my age who still believe that, that's there's one person for you.'

(Yes, and they're the single ones. The luckless losers. I don't say this; probably not massively helpful.)

I carry on, 'I don't buy the whole 'The One' idea because, well, that implies that someone is up there, looking after and controlling us. That there is some sort of design. And I really don't think there is a design, a plan. I think life is random. I think when people say that things happen for a reason, I think they're deluding themselves. I think people look for narrative, for meaning, when it really isn't there. We want to think there's a story, so we can work out the ending. But that's not how I see the world.

'I think, I always thought, that many people could make me happy. Potentially. And I could make lots of people happy. Love, it's not like a jigsaw. I wasn't looking for the missing piece. It's like, I don't know, a dance floor. A big crowded dance floor. You could pick any number of people to dance with, and still have a great time. Not the same great time, but a great time nonetheless.'

'And Chris?'

'Chris is a great dancer.'

We laugh, in a slightly embarrassed way, at the mild innuendo.

'No. I never thought Chris was the one. But I did think he

was a wonderful person and that he could make me happy. I never had any doubt about that. I know that probably sounds too pragmatic, not very romantic. To you.'

'No, it sounds romantic. Is this too hard to talk about?'

'It's fine.' Actually it is fine, now I've started. 'The thing is, it's still true. He did make me happy. I don't have any regrets. I'm not looking back and thinking how stupid I was. My judgment was right, at the time. But times change, things move things on. You just have to do your best to respond to it. You can't control it. You can't guarantee your relationship will work out, just because you picked your partner really really carefully. And marriage, it's not like a pension. You can't just keep paying into it and be guaranteed to get it all back later. You have to take a risk. Sometimes you just don't get back what you paid in. That doesn't mean you shouldn't have had a shot at it.'

'Just like a pension then.'

'God I can't believe you're making a pension joke. I swear you're 60 years old.'

We have almost caught up with the children now, nearly home.

Ed says, 'It's hard, being in love with someone, having those feelings, and not being able to do anything with them. Sometimes I find it hard to process it. It, well, it starts to drag me down.'

'Don't give into it, Ed. Being in love with someone when you can't be with them, it isn't a tragedy. It isn't necessarily a comedy either, but you can just live with the feelings. Just let yourself feel love, without getting bitter.'

'Really? You think that's possible?'

'Yes I really do. It's not easy but you have the choice. You can make that choice. I still feel love for Chris, of course I do. I just let it lie, just feel it and don't try and twist it. Maybe it'll always be there, maybe it will fade away. I don't know. But you can't really control the way you feel, at least I never have been able to. I'd say the only thing you can control is what you do with that feeling.

On impulse I link my arm into his. 'This is what I think. If you still feel something for Charlotte, if you love her, then don't give up. I mean don't invest everything in her either, but if you love each other, who's to say what will happen? Life's a long game. You can't tell yet how it's going to end.'

'A long game.'

'Yes, a long game. Like golf.'

'Like cricket.'

'Yes like cricket. Or Scrabble.'

'Yes. Loads of tiles still in the bag. Like Monopoly?'

'Yes. Exactly. Like Monopoly. Long and very boring and you have to keep buying houses.'

'Or Top Trumps. God no, silly me, nothing's as boring as Top Trumps.'

'No, hold on, I have it: life's like a game of I-Spy with Rosie. Long, boring, often surreal and almost completely incomprehensible.'

'Mummy why are you laughing so much? And why are you saying my name? Tell me!' Rosie demands.

Did I ever laugh like this with Chris? It's hard to remember. Memory plays tricks. Maybe it's the long periods of misery that I have had to face since the summer, but there is something about these moments of connection with Ed that seem incredibly powerful and precious. When I can't tell where my thoughts end and his begin. Speaking to him makes it incredibly easy to think. Sometimes, when I'm in a fanciful mood, I can almost feel our thoughts coming together with a satisfying click, like two pieces of jigsaw. Which may not be my definition of love, or marriage, but is certainly an extremely pleasant way to spend a long, snowy afternoon.

TELL ME THE TRUTH ABOUT LOVE

It's only later that I start to mull over what I have said to Ed, and wonder if I stand by it. Is that what I think about love?

Actually, what the hell do I know about love? I used to think I knew nothing, but now I know that for certain. I loved Chris, I really did. I didn't doubt it, didn't experience any second thoughts. I never once, in all the years we were together, looked at him and thought - I wish I'd married someone else.

And where did it get me? All this certainty of feeling and sincerity of emotion? Nowhere. Or, rather, maybe it led me up the garden path. It didn't stop anything, it didn't prevent him from hurting me and breaking my heart. What is love, if it isn't a way to sleepwalk into misery? To leave yourself vulnerable to being broken on the wheel of betrayal.

So, when I told Ed to stick it out and not to give up on love, that was massively bad advice, wasn't it? My only consolation is he won't pay the slightest attention to me anyway. Love will go its own way. Ed will keep ploughing that same furrow for as long as he can't help himself. He won't stop because it's the logical, the sensible thing to do, because love is not subject to logic or sense. He will keep on, trying to make it work, long after he should have given up and long, long after he has stopped behaving with any dignity. He is a romantic fool, like many of us. Like all of us. His need for love is greater than his fear of being hurt. And thank God for that; thank God for the triumph of hope. It's hard to watch the young make the mistakes we made, to put their hearts out there on the line, ready to be stamped on. But really, we all know, we would do the same, every time. That's what being human, and being alive, is all about.

The four days we spend snowed into Lower Worthington are among the most magical of my life. Reality seems a million miles away, and all routine goes out of the window. No-one goes to school and hardly anyone goes to work. In this affluent, fancy-pants village, we all have well stocked freezers and no-one is in any danger of running out of food. (The nearest we get to an emergency food shortage is when the Red Lion runs out of olives.)

Being trapped in this village has a number of interesting effects. It makes people much friendlier. There are impromptu parties. People stop and chat in the street, look over fences to admire each other's snowmen. In fact, after the second day, snow sculpture becomes something of a competitive sport. Soon, whole families of snow-people appear, as well as igloos, cars, a whole menagerie of animals and, on the green, a whole model village.

On the green, I observe village life teeming like a wintry petri dish. There is quite a bit of loudly competitive parenting; a whole lot of conspicuously-worn ski gear, to prove slope credentials. High-powered Dads, giddy and unused to long periods of parenting, start vicious games of snow-balling, with the sole intention of winning - not just winning but beating their opponents into humiliating and public defeat. The teenagers court each other, flirting with the whole snow-down-the-back routine and there's quite a bit of giggly chasing about. A couple of startlingly-blonde teenage girls, rigid with self-conscious beauty, hover and circle around Ed, laughing and flashing their perfect teeth. They look ravishing, their faces glowing with youth and the flush of exercise in the chilly air.

Michael attempts to build a dragon in the back garden with lots of help from Ed and absolutely none from me. I see more of Michael in these four days than I have for months, certainly since Chris moved out. The snow holds more attraction than the screen; he and Ed spend hours with their intricate feats of engineering and snow sculpture. He doesn't say much, but I see him smile, and I hear him laugh, and it's a wonderful sight and sound. He straps on skis, lent to him by Ed from Ruby's massive outdoor equipment cupboard, and I don't see them for hours; just as I start to get a little anxious, they come swishing back into the garden.

Rosie is less thrilled with the reality of the snow than with the idea of it; she spends hours getting ready to go out into the snow, and then lasts about ten minutes before scuttling inside to demand hot chocolate and a blanket. But she loves it that she has my full attention during these long, slow-paced days and we engage in long bouts of colouring in, making and do-ing, followed by afternoons watching DVDs and eating biscuits. When the biscuits run out, we send the boys on a skiing mission across the fields to the Spar, for emergency Jammie Dodgers. This enterprise brings with it all the glamour and excitement of the start of a Bond film.

As for me, I take a lot of photos. I find the play of light on the snow endlessly fascinating; at different times of day I capture blues, purples, oranges, yellows and reds. The slow pace of life reminds me of that canal boat trip last summer; the memory is both painful and hopeful, because although the pain hasn't passed, it is comforting to recognise how far I have come since those first excruciating days and weeks. I am still low, but I won't be that low again. The dead polar bear is still around, but in this snowy landscape he slips into the background, and once or twice almost disappears from view.

Chris misses the beauty and joy of these precious days. With killing irony, he is on a skiing trip with Romily in Zell Am See; although there is not enough snow there to ski, he can't get home because all the UK airports are snow-bound. By the time he gets home, all the snow is gone, apart from a few greying, gritty snowmen-stumps, and the magical snowy interlude starts to seem like a dream.

AN OFFER YOU CAN'T REFUSE

The extended fall of snow means that the college system for making offers is delayed. Ed gets a message saying not to expect an answer just yet. The waiting is excruciating. Three days after the snow has cleared, it still hasn't arrived. He messages me Friday morning.

I've got the email in my inbox.... I haven't opened it
WHY???? Are you crazy????
Because I want to open it when you're there - not here when I have to

see everyone

My heart lurches.

Shall I come and get you? After school? I can come now?
Yes, as long as you hoover out the car first - I just had this suit dry cleaned ... jk!

I understand that this abbreviation means 'joke'. I understand that it isn't a joke, not quite, but a tiny little hint that my car might just be a health hazard. I don't quite get the Hoover out but I do scoop out the worst of the debris and clean the seats with a baby wipe. It actually looks quite respectable.

As I pull into the drive of Ed's college he is waiting out the front, sitting on the edge of the flower-bed, with a tall, striking-looking girl carrying an instrument case.

I wind down the window, 'Hello! How are you?'

'God don't even talk to me, I am so nervous. I have been a nightmare all morning. Haven't I?' The girl laughs and nods, 'Even more than usual,' she says.

'Jen, this is Heather. Heather is sarcastic to me during the daytime when you're busy elsewhere. You two have a sort of relay thing going on, so that no-one ever drops that particular baton.'

Heather leans into the jeep, extending a hand; she shakes mine warmly.

'Thank you Heather, I appreciate it.'

She grins, 'That's OK, I've got your back. Anyway, it's pretty much an open goal most of the time.'

'Can I give you a lift somewhere?' As soon as I say this, I start to worry if this is the sort of offer that could be misconstrued these days. Is it still OK to give sixth formers lifts if you don't know them? God I've no idea. Twenty-first century living is very complicated.

'Oh that's kind, thank you, but my Mum's on her way. I

have to go to my lesson.' She indicates the instrument case. 'Good luck Ed, although obviously it's all over now anyway!' she says, cheerfully.

'Thanks. It's been a great comfort to talk to you, as always.'

'See you Monday.'

'Yeah you too.'

'She seems very nice,' I say as we pull away. 'Is she.... ?' I turn to him, questioningly.

He raises his eyebrows back, 'Into me?'

'Yes, is she into you. God I sound about a hundred years old saying that.'

He laughs, 'No she isn't into me, I don't think. She's just a friend. She's extremely entertaining. Anyway she thinks I'm a bit lightweight. She has an offer to read Music at Cambridge. Clare I think. And some sort of choral scholarship.'

'Oh yeah, out of your league then. Why don't you ask her for tea sometime, she can be a role model for Rosie.'

'Great idea, then you can both be sarcastic to me simultaneously.'

'Oh you'd love it.'

'I'd love it right up until I started to cry.'

We laugh, and then he is quiet for a while, looking out of the window.

'So are you going to look now, or what?' I say.

He bites down on his thumb, 'No I am going to wait until we're home. Sorry.'

'Don't apologise. It's up to you.' I'm about to open my mouth to tell him about how I left my offer letter lying on the doorstep for the whole day until I could bring myself to open it, but I change my mind.

After a few minutes, he says, 'Will you be disappointed, if I don't get an offer?'

'Yes,' I say, deadpan. 'I will never speak to you again.'

He smiles, weakly, 'You know what I mean.'

'I don't, really, no. Of course I won't be disappointed. I think you might be, but I won't be. Just put that out of your mind. You are very smart, you work incredibly hard, and whatever happens you are going to get a place at a great university, have a marvellous time and an amazing life. And that's my honest prediction.' We are pulling into the drive. 'Why don't you go into the living room and read the email there. Do you want some lunch?'

'That depends on what it says, I think,' he grimaces again.

I start make some sandwiches anyway, to pass away the tense minutes while I wait. And wait. And wait.

After what seems like several hours, he flings the door of the kitchen open so hard that it bangs against the fridge. His face is triumphant, exultant, jubilant.

'A* and two bloody As!'

I jump around in uncontained excitement; he doesn't quite join me in this - he has a little dignity - but he does laugh out loud in a pretty excited way. Then, he stops, suddenly, and sits down, his face contorted with terror.

'Shit, Jen,' he says, worriedly. 'A* and two bloody As!'

'Ha,' I say. 'Yeah, you'd better start doing some bloody work.'

CHAPTER NINE
FEBRUARY

MY FUNNY BLOODY VALENTINE

The year after you carelessly lose your husband in that great poker game we call life is tricky in many ways. For example, it's full of firsts. Doing things for the first time on your own, feeling the strangeness of your lonely state, or feeling conspicuously single. I had struggled through the first child's birthday party, the first weekend apart from the children, the first Christmas. Now in February I had to face a pretty towering hurdle - my birthday. Quite bad, yes? Your first birthday as a separated woman. But no! We're not done yet. Because my birthday coincides with the Feast Day of St Valentine, the patron saint of hearts, flowers, excruciating pain and suicidal desperation. But wait! You think we're finished? No. For there is one more punch to take on the chin. For it was on this day, of all days, that Chris asked me to marry him, thirteen years ago.

So how does one cope with this level of horror? I mean, how can I reasonably be expected to live through a day like that? And yet, incredibly, there doesn't seem to be a choice. Apparently there isn't an upper limit on the amount of horrible misery that one person is obliged to deal with at any one time. No alarms go off. No-one is sent to rescue you. There isn't an ombudsman (OfSob?) that you can appeal to, if you think you are being subjected to inhuman levels of emotional torture. You can't complain that your human rights are being breached. The only option, apparently, is to get on with it. Endure. Make plans for your birthday/Valentine's day/anniversary of proposal with a cheerful smile, and make like you aren't dying inside. And better make it convincing, because if you think people aren't watching to see how you're coping, and judging you, then you're wrong.

So I make plans. I make plans for a night out with the girls on the Saturday following the Big Day. Then I change my mind because I can't book a table, and I realise that's because the restaurants will be jammed to the rafters with loving couples. So I suggest a takeaway and cocktails and a DVD for the Saturday following my birthday. A nice gangster DVD, preferably, with only slaughter and no love. Perfect.

My birthday is on a Tuesday, which would normally be my evening for Silken Ties, my poetry appreciation class. (By this stage in the year, I am rather regretting the decision to call the class Silken Ties, although it is somewhat less cheesy than the name of the creative writing group, Lasso the Muse. Both of them have a mildly sado-masochistic connotation that I hadn't really noticed until it was too late. The students have become very attached to the names, though, and have taken to tying up their notes and books with real silken ties, in a disappointingly literal interpretation of the metaphor.)

But my birthday falls in half term, so I am free that evening instead. Ed calls to offer to babysit, so that I can go out.

'I can't tell you how much I don't want to go out,' I say. 'Going out on Valentine's Day is bad enough when you actually have a Valentine. I think it is best avoided.'

'Oh, OK.' Is it my imagination, or does he sound a little disappointed? 'Well I have something for you. Would you mind if I brought it round in the evening?'

'No, that would be lovely. You shouldn't have, but thank you.'

He arrives with a beautifully wrapped parcel, white with purple stripes and tied with lilac silk ribbon, and also a card and a bottle of wine from Ruby.

'Are you sure you won't change your mind about going out? It seems a shame to be in on your birthday.'

'Really, I can assure you it isn't a shame, in any way.'

'Well, then,' he hesitates a little. 'Do you have any plans?'

I am turning the present over in my hands, unsure whether to open it now or wait until the children are in bed. 'I was planning to order a curry for delivery and slump on the sofa. Why?'

'Would it be OK if I cooked something for you? I could go and get something now, and then come back?'

It's my turn to hesitate, but really, how could I say no? And, more importantly, why? Because other people wouldn't like it? Who? And anyway, who would know? Sod it, yes. Ed is always here anyway, why should it bother anyone if he's here on my birthday? Or on Valentine's Day? That's just details. Well, more or less. These details are not significant unless we make them so. To send him away because of what other people might think is just ludicrous. Isn't it?

'That sounds lovely, thank you. Let me give you some money.'

As he's leaving, he adds, a little anxiously, 'I'm not really that great a cook. I mean I can only cook a few things.'

'Don't worry really, I have very low expectations.'

That makes him laugh, 'Shall I get a takeaway? Would you prefer that?'

'No, not really Ed. I don't really care about the food. It's nice to have someone else take care of it, mostly.'

'But would a takeaway be better? It's your birthday, and that's what you had planned.'

'It will be lovely just to have the evening to chat with you. Now, just go. You're making me crazy with this dithering, go.'

When he's gone, I wonder if that was a little too far in the way of truth and honesty. Well, too late now. I go into the kitchen to open the gift and card, before he comes back. Easier when he isn't here. Card first: a hand made one, on the front a picture of me and the children in the garden with the snow dragon, from that week we were snowed in. We look ruddy-cheeked and happy; it's a beautiful picture. I slot it at the front of the stack of cards on the dresser. Next, the gift. I carefully unravel the silk ribbons. Inside, a beautifully bound edition of Shakespeare's sonnets in a peacock blue cloth cover with golden lettering, and inside an inscription in Ed's scrawling hand that reads 'Happy Birthday Jen, and thanks for all the rhythm and rhyme, and for helping me to unravel the silken ties (see what I did there?) all my love EBx.'

I am extremely glad that I opened that in his absence, because I am shaking pretty obviously.

I hear the doorbell ring. I drop the book guiltily; it can't be Ed, that was too quick and anyway, these days he just knocks and enters if he's expected. I think about shoving the book in a drawer but in the end I grab the newspaper and rest that on top of it to cover it up.

It's Ruth and Mel, with a bottle of wine. 'We were worried you might be alone. I know we're going out on Saturday, but we thought we would just pop round make sure you're OK.'

I have one eye on the door, waiting for Ed to return. I feel the awkward crunch of the two halves of my life coming together.' Oh Christ, now I appear to be living in a French farce.

They both look startled when, about thirty minutes later, there is a knock at the front door and the sound of someone entering.

'Is that Chris?' says Mel, confused.

I am blushing, at my own stupidity more than anything else, 'No it's Ed. He's bringing some food.' This piece of information would have seemed a great deal less suspicious if it had been passed on before his arrival, I see now. Thankfully,

Ed has social skills to spare and he handles this situation, the one that is making me squirm with guilt and awkwardness, with calm and nonchalance. Of course, it helps that isn't feeling guilty. I take a step back, and let him set the mood of the evening.

'Shall I make enough for all of us? There's plenty. I always buy too much.'

'Why not?' says Ruth. She is charmed, and so is Mel. He sits us round the table, pours Aunty Ruby's white wine into generous glasses, and leaves us to chat. He lights a few tealights, and puts on a nineties playlist to suit the old folk. Then he starts dinner, leaves it to simmer while he makes sure that Rosie is settled, takes some snacks to Michael, who's allowed to stay up gaming a little longer as it's half term. I watch him, feeling both proud and taken care of. He really is a very good friend.

He makes sure our glasses are topped up; I fret about offering him wine; the idea of offering him alcohol is, somehow, just a step too far. Thankfully, he is drinking coke: 'Too much work to do tomorrow.'

He serves us a chilli, Greek salad and garlic bread, followed by cookies and ice cream. 'I apologise for the student food,' he laughs. 'I know I cook like a man. It's been mentioned before.' If Mel and Ruth have something to say about Ed being here, cooking me dinner on my birthday, on Valentine's Day, well they can say it on their way home. I notice them exchange glances, but I can live with that. I can live with a lot if I could have another birthday like this.

After dinner, we put on Singstar on the X-box and sing so loud that Rosie wakes up and comes downstairs to see what the noise is. We swap to Singstar Disney; Ed sings a duet of 'The Bare Necessities' with her before taking her back upstairs to settle her with a story. By the time he comes back down, we have pretty much finished the washing up. Ed offers to walk Mel and Ruth home; they are giggly and behaving very badly, and I don't envy him the task of getting them through the streets without waking the whole village.

I lay in bed half an hour later with my phone resting on my chest, waiting for the buzz. I am trying to read but I am feeling too distracted. As always, the vibration makes me jump.

Message Chris
Hope you had a great birthday. Was thinking of you today. Chris x

I test out my reactions to that; I open up a few of those closed doors in my head and my heart. I can feel only numbness. The places where that used to hurt, are they dead? While I am contemplating whether I should reply to this message, and what I could possibly say, my phone buzzes again.

Message Ed
Thanks for a lovely evening

No need to think about what to reply to that.

No, I should be thanking you - It was, I promise you, the best possible birthday I could have hoped for in all the circumstances... you make a demon chilli

Thanks, it has been said before x Did you open your present?

Bugger, in all the excitement, I forgot to retrieve the poetry book from the pile of newspapers. I scuttle downstairs to recover it.

I am so sorry! How rude of me not to have said thank you! The card was perfect, and I am so pleased with the book! It was so kind of you

I am so glad you liked it - was worried because you hadn't mentioned it. I had 116 running through my head tonight, it will always remind me of you now. Good night, and happy birthday EBx

My hands are shaking as I turn to the sonnet 116, but I already know what I will find. I know that sonnet, but I scan the familiar words until I find this line, the one I am looking for, and roll the delicious words around my mouth, savouring every syllable:

'Love's not time's fool.'

An appropriate thought with which to end Valentine's Day. I turn off the light, and fall quickly to sleep.

PUSH PINEAPPLE, SHAKE THE TREE

It's possible to get used to anything. As the months pass, what previously seems unbearable, becomes the new normal. Even dragging the polar bear around is no longer surprising, just tiring and occasionally irritating. I think my strength is building; in any event, he doesn't seem quite so heavy any more.

It's even possible to start looking on the bright side about a few things. Living with Chris wasn't hell or anything, but there are one or two things I don't miss so much as all that. Having the cricket on all day for example - on the TV with the sound turned down and the radio as the soundtrack, for some reason - I don't miss that. Nor am I sorry that Sunday afternoons are now free of the white-noise screech of Formula One cars.

Chris had a tendency to take extremely long and extremely deep baths at all times of the day or night, in particular when he had just returned from a plane journey, waking up the house with the banging pipes and using up all the hot water, leaving me to grit my teeth over a lukewarm sink and a flannel in the morning. Not having to endure the icy, polite disapproval of the in-laws, that's also quite a plus. Oh, there's a whole other story right there, in that last sentence, if only I could bring myself to tell it. One day. Maybe.

These upsides don't amount to much, I grant you, when you've written them down in black and white. Certainly not enough for a divorce petition. (Don't worry though, we have the A word for that purpose. That's all very straightforward, thank goodness. No wrangling over whether his behaviour - or mine - was unreasonable. Shagging another woman, that's officially, categorically, legally unreasonable for these purposes. I suppose that might even count as another blessing to be thankful for, if you can stomach the irony.) But put them together, these random bits of 'good' news, and maybe, just maybe, you could have enough to weave together some sort of fragile, flimsy silver lining.

Then, just when you're enjoying your new-found freedom to eat chips in the car without being tutted at, and to leave your CDs naked and scattered about the living room then - WHAM - along comes a fresh, unexpected broadside to take you by surprise. In this case, I couldn't have been more surprised if Imogen had popped round to tell me she was joining the Socialist Worker's Party.

'Mum,' says Michael, 'Can I go to the school disco?'

A silent hush descends on the assembled party. Mel, Carrie and Ruth all stop their conversations, drop their cutlery with a clatter and turn towards him in slow motion.

'What???' they all chorus, in unison. (I may have lapsed into exaggeration here, but not much.)

'It's Friday night. Everyone's going.'

'Yes of course you can. This Friday? Sure.'

'Can I go? Can I go?' Rosie is leaping up and down, already mentally planning her outfit in her head.

'No, juniors only,' says Michael. 'No infants.' He sounds somewhat regretful. I guess he wouldn't mind having Rosie there. I don't blame him. Rosie would be a good person to have at your side at a disco. She's a natural at any social occasion but a disco is right up her street.

Wailing, Rosie throws herself to the ground. 'Oh that is so unfair! I really want to go. Why can't I go?'

'Because you're too young. That's just the way it is, Rose.' She runs, distraught, from the room, no doubt to throw herself on the bed in deep melancholy. This is almost a daily occurrence at the moment. I can't wait till the teenage years. I may move into the shed for the duration, let Michael take over for a bit.

I am still slightly boggled at the idea of Michael at a disco. It seems so unlikely. I wait till he's out of the room before I share my wide-eyed surprise with the others.

'Is Connor going?' I ask Mel.

'I guess so,' she says, vaguely. 'He hasn't mentioned it.'

'Molly and Maisie are,' says Ruth.

'Well Molly and Maisie is one thing,' I say. 'They've probably planned their outfits and filled their dance cards already. But Michael? Really?'

'Maybe there's a girl,' says Ruth.

I scoff at the idea. 'Hardly, Ruth. He's only eight.'

But of course, she's right. There's a girl. He tells Ed, over some mutual orc-slaying. How the hell they concentrate on the serious business of slaughter and talk at the same time is quite beyond me. Such a lot of buttons to press simultaneously. I find even watching them to be far too confusing.

Oh Lord. A girl.

My baby boy wants to go to a disco, with a girl.

I am flummoxed, lost at sea, totally broad-sided. What should he wear? I never know what to wear, so how can I advise an eight-year-old boy? What should I tell him about this girl? Christ, I'm barely able to manage being a mother, I can hardly start pretending to be a functional father-figure too. I just can't pull it off. People will start to notice.

'Her name's Georgia and she's beautiful,' Ed reports back. 'Apparently, according to Michael,' he adds hurriedly, suddenly very uncomfortable with having commented on the physical qualities of a nine-year-old girl.

'And is it mutual?' I am not sure what answer I want here. Requited, in which case, my son will have a girlfriend. Unrequited, in which case I will have a broken hearted eight-year-old on my hands. Neither of these prospects is filling me with delight.

'Mutual, I think. But she is making him work for it.' He smiles. 'She sounds a bit like Charlotte.'

Oh dear God, that's not exactly what I need to hear. Luckily my head is in the fridge, and I can pull a face privately, with only the Dairylea to see.

'What did you say to him?' I am trying to keep the anxiety out of my voice.

'I told him to treat 'em mean, keep 'em keen.'

I turn round, appalled.

'Relax, I didn't tell him that. I've just always wanted to say it. I told him to keep his head, be himself and be kind to her. If she doesn't like that, then don't change to please her. Was that OK?' He is a little anxious himself now, looking for reassurance that he has done the right thing.

'Yes, thanks. God sorry to put this on you.'

'No, it was kind of interesting to have that conversation. Although it made me nervous, having someone listening to my advice, all attentive, hanging on my every word, like I was wise or something.' He snorts, 'It made me think how much easier it is to give advice rather than follow it.'

I laugh at this. 'Ain't that the truth.'

'I also told him something my Mum said, that I think makes a lot of sense. I said, treat her like you would want your sister to be treated.'

'Yes, that's nice. I like that.' I am chopping the peppers, a little too vigorously.

'Would you like me to take over? You seem a little agitated.' He's smiling, but has his hand out for me to pass him the knife. He may be right; squirrels shouldn't really chop peppers when they are contemplating their son's first encounter with love. It's fraught with potential danger. 'Have a cup of tea, calm yourself down a bit.'

'Is this normal, Ed? I mean isn't he a little young?'

He squints at me, quizzically. 'Don't you remember? When you were that age?'

I try to give it some thought. 'Well we used to chase each other in the playground I guess. God it's a long time ago. I was friends with boys at that age, but there wasn't any pairing off. There certainly weren't any discos.'

'I don't think you should worry. Really. Michael's pretty sensible. He's well-balanced. And it's all quite innocent. I mean, I don't think you're going to be getting a phone call from social services any day soon.'

'You can sell it to Take a Break. 'My pre-teen Dad shame.' Yeah that would get them talking in the village.'

'No-one in the village reads Take a Break surely?' says Ed.

'No, good point.'

Ed throws the peppers in the wok, making the oil sizzle and spit.

'He was worried about what to wear,' Ed says, stirring the vegetables.

'Really? That's something I thought I'd never hear.'

'What would you think if I took him to buy something? I mean I don't think he has anything suitable.'

I roll my eyes, 'Is this the point at which my son starts dressing in your migraine-inducing style? Is it all logos and orange checks and flip flops from now on?'

'I shall try and rein it in a bit. Limit the amount of orange. I'm not sure Michael could carry it off with my flair, anyway,' he smiles. 'And, what about the hair? Could I take him to the barbers?'

'A real male bonding session, right?'

'Yes, the bathroom is going to be a different place from now on. Gel, wax, putty, body spray, deodorant .... More gel.'

'Are you going to teach him to do that guinea-pig thing you do with your hair, when it goes in all directions at once?'

'Yes, but I am going to make sure you and Rosie are out of the house. That stuff, it's a secret. Boys only.'

He's cutting up the chicken now, wielding the scissors carefully, sliding the pink flesh into the pan. He stirs, with infinite care.

'Ed I really appreciate this. Thank you.'

'It's fine, really. Becker sort of did this for me, although I knew enough even then to ignore most of what he said. Shall I come and sit on Friday while he goes?'

I'm confused, 'Why? I wasn't thinking of going.'

'No, but you will need to take him and collect him and you don't want to have to take Rosie too.'

God he's right, I hadn't even thought that through. That's what's so complicated about my life; the logistics just don't work most of the time.

'If I take Rosie, she'll crash it. She's desperate to go.'

He laughs, 'I bet she is. She's the ultimate disco queen. Shame she can't, she'd be able to help him.'

'That's exactly what I said! She's much better at this stuff than I ever was. School discos. My idea of hell.'

And yet, somehow, by the next morning, I am signed up to attend my first school disco in 25 years. Imogen pounces on me, with her Rota-Firm expression and wielding her clipboard like a sharpened spear. My head spins, the room spins, and then before I know it, it's all over and I am on lemonade and sherbet Dib-Dab duty. I can't imagine what Michael is going to say when he finds out that I am going to be observing his courtship of Georgia. I shall attempt to keep a low profile.

I'm on my way back from the school drop-off when a thought pops into my head of such vivid horror that I am stopped dead in my tracks.

I get out my phone:

To: Ed

Can you dance? And if so, can you teach Michael? Please?

Yes I can dance and yes of course. What did you have in mind? The foxtrot? The Charleston? The hokey cokey?

This is no time for joking, sunshine. This is serious. This is my son's street cred on the line. He needs to be cool. Just teach him what the young people do on the dance floor, shaking their stuff. OK?

Well to be clear the young people don't say 'street cred', 'cool' or 'shaking their stuff.' But yes, I'll come and shake my stuff. Now, could I possibly get back to learning about Dr Faustus, if you don't mind?

You are messaging in lesson :-o I am shocked. You rebel.

Yeah get me. I'm, like, so cool

Thanks Ed you are my saviour xx

Don't worry, I like it when you owe me ;-) EBxx

Ed comes round that evening, and the boys lock themselves in the living room. There is the sound of pounding music, and quite a bit of laughter, and half an hour later they emerge sweaty and mysterious-looking. It all reminds me of some arcane coming-of-age ritual. A disco-mitzvah, maybe.

Friday tea-time is a very tense affair, between Michael's jittery nerves and Rosie's heavy-duty sulking. The unfairness of her exclusion from the dance floor is pretty much the sole topic of conversation. I have never been so relieved to hear Ed in the hall.

'Eddie, they won't let me go to the disco, can you believe it?' she whines.

'No, I can't believe it. It's totally unfair. I need to go and help Michael get ready. But after that, I have a plan. A plan to bring the disco here to you, if you can't get to the disco. OK?' She nods, appeased.

Half an hour later, the boys reappear from the bathroom. Michael is barely recognisable, his hair beautifully tousled. He is wearing jeans and a white t-shirt, with a fairly discreet logo. At first I can't quite work out what looks so different, but then I realise: he's smiling.

'Ready?' I ask. He nods, still smiling.

By the time we get to the playground, it's swarming. Boys on scooters zoom dangerously around the climbing frame, with one eye on the groups of girls. The girls' part in this ritual is to engage in loud, animated conversation with each other, tossing their hair and pretending not to notice the boys. I feel like I am watching a wildlife film; I also feel very very old indeed. Michael leaves me at the gate to join his posse; even his walk is more confident as he lopes across the tarmac.

The school hall is dark, dank and sweaty; a heavy fog of hairspray and Lynx lingers and catches in the throat. I feel very conspicuous as I cross the dance floor to install myself behind the counter. Imogen gives me a whole list of instructions, and I pretend to concentrate. The music is so loud that I have to guess what the children would like to drink, but in the darkness one stubby bottle of Polar-pop is pretty much like another.

I try to observe Michael without being noticed. He dances with a nonchalance that is studied, but none-the-less effective. God, he actually looks cool! Well, to my eye he does anyway. He certainly isn't alarmingly awkward. Thank God for Chris's genes in the mix, because I have no cool to pass on. It seems the squirrel genes are recessive after all. I am almost looking forward to his teenage years now, and start to fantasise about Michael as rugby captain, Head Boy, dream-boat. Oh yes, this could all end well. I am snapped out of this pleasant reverie by the sight of Michael holding hands with Georgia, who is looking gorgeous in a silver strappy dress, whirling her round the dance floor, laughing. Holding hands?! No, no I don't think so. I fight a sudden urge to vault over the counter and stand in between them. Maybe I had better lurk behind this pillar, so they are safely out of my line of vision.

The curious thing about this school disco is not that so much has changed from my school days, but that so much has remained the same. Granted, the clothes are much nicer than we used to wear, and these days the boys wear more hair product than the girls. But the drinks and snacks are little different – cheap cola, Monster Munch and Twixes – and there is a huge overlap with the music too. There is something almost surreal about watching a room full of twenty-first century pre-teens scrabbling on the floor doing 'Oops Upside Your Head' or making the approximate shapes of the letters YMCA. I try to make a punning joke to Imogen about The Village People, but it's all rather lost in translation.

The evening reaches its bizarre climax with Agadoo by Black Lace. I am delighted to note that Michael isn't deigning to dance to this; that's my boy. But hold on, where is he? Nowhere to be seen. And, scanning the dance floor frantically, no sign of Georgia either. Oh Lord. Please tell me he hasn't taken her outside! I am in a panic now, imagining the scene: Georgia's parents calling the police and my son being led away in handcuffs. I bring to mind, in a rush, Imogen's face, then Romily's, then my mother in law's, when they see this scandal on the news. I abandon the sugary snacks and lift open the hatch; I scuttle across the dance floor and through the open double doors to where the children are congregating on the steps.

'Have you seen Michael?' I ask Connor, who is doing some complicated skateboard flipping.

'He's in the music room.'

I turn the corner, still panicking, when I hear the all too familiar sound of Beethoven's Für Elise. I stop in my tracks and listen.

OMG, as the young people have probably stopped saying by now. My son is wooing a girl by playing the piano. Really rather well, as it turns out. I am impressed and let's hope she is too. Thank goodness for all those expensive lessons, the nagging to practice. It's all worth it for this moment. Is this

Ed's suggestion? I smile to myself as I wonder if this is a trick that Ed has played in the past too, and whether he has had any degree of success.

Back home, a sweaty and triumphant Michael makes straight for the fridge for some juice and food. He has worked up quite an appetite on the dance floor. I open the door of the living room. Inside, all is dark apart from a flashing lights ball, throwing multi-coloured shapes onto the walls. Abba's Dancing Queen is playing from Ed's phone, and Ed and Rosie are throwing some pretty impressive shapes themselves.

'Mummy, Michael! Come and join our disco?' Rosie grabs my hand and pulls me into the room, closely followed by Michael clutching a half-eaten Babybel. The four of us dance with wild enthusiasm and varying degrees of elegance to 'Rosie's Special Disco Mix Playlist' until way after bedtime has come and gone.

CHAPTER TEN

MARCH

MARS AND VENUS

'Dad and I went to see Mum yesterday.'

We are in the garden, attempting to clear some of the winter debris from the flower beds. Well, Ed is. I am floating in and out of the garden with cups of tea and half-hearted excuses about having to supervise the children. Anything to avoid the actual kneeling down and grappling with undergrowth. I always thought that I would grow into gardening. It hasn't happened yet. I think I am far too short term in my habits to get anything out of it. Right now, I am - a little belatedly, some might say - chopping up the Christmas tree that has been rotting at the side of the shed since Twelfth Night, and trying not to think about last Christmas and how bloody miserable I was.

'Oh?' I say, carefully and deliberately matching his casual tone.

Having a close male friend is something that I am finding it tricky to get used to. I am just about able, after eight months of hanging out with Ed several times a week, to predict his behaviour with some degree of success. I am, at least some of the time, able to respond to these little bombshells without falling over, startled or shouting 'WHY DIDN'T YOU SAY SOMETHING BEFORE NOW??'

With female friends, you know where you are. If Mel, for example, had some news to report of this magnitude, I would get quite a bit of prior warning. There would be a big old build up. She would sit drinking tea and eating biscuits round my table while we talked about the different possible outcomes, how she felt about it now, how she might feel about it afterwards. There would be a detailed analysis of similar situations in her life, in my life, and how this is fitted into the bigger picture. We would rehearse what she might say. Advice would be sought, and given. I would call or message her just before the significant event, to let her know I was thinking of her. Then she would call or message me straight afterward, to report back on how it went. Later, she would come around to talk it over; the arrival of her car onto the drive, the sound of her steps on the gravel would give me clues as to her state of mind. Does the gravel fly? Does she pound up the path, or is she dragging her feet? And then there would be a long post mortem, with tissues and cake. More advice would be shared, tears would be shed, fresh perspectives would be sought. Even Polly, probably the most masculine of my female friends, does this too, although her emotional highs and lows tend to be accessorised with vodka shots and kebabs.

Emotional sharing with Ed is quite a different experience. There's no early warning, no run up. One minute you're minding your own business, doing the crossword, maybe contemplating a trip to the shops to buy more ham and then WHAM suddenly you're parachuted without warning into the wilderness. Or a battlefield. Or, possibly, a meadow of flowers. Right now it's hard to tell. You just have to wait. Oh yes, waiting; there's quite a bit of waiting.

'Yes,' replies Ed after a few minutes.

I keep my gaze focused on the brown and crispy conifer. Why didn't I do this earlier? Why can't I sort my bloody life out? The heavy symbolism of the rotten tree rips painfully into my hands. I wish I'd worn gloves.

'How was it?' Come on Ed, come on. You must know I am desperate to hear this. Don't make me beg for details.

'Well, it was OK. She looked not as bad as I thought she might. Of course she is on some pretty strong drugs. She managed to talk to us for a bit. I mean she knew who we were.'

'Is she...I mean will you be able to see her again?'

'I hope so. I hope I might be able to go more often.'

God I wish I had more empathy. Should I ask more? Does he want to talk more? He clearly wants to talk about it, to some extent, otherwise he wouldn't have brought it up. But, how much more? If this was Carrie or Mel or Polly or even Ruth, this would be such an easy question to answer. But it is agonizingly difficult to judge. OK, this is one thing he might want to talk about:

'And what about your Dad, how is he?'

I haven't heard Ed mention his Dad since December; in this case I don't think that we can assume no news is good news.

'Yeah. I think he was relieved to see Mum a bit better. I think he knows it's a long road. He still can't face staying in the house, so he's been kipping with some friends. You will never guess where he's been till now. In Goa. Cliché or what?'

Goa? He's been in bloody Goa? Jesus. I take out my sudden burst of fury on the crumbling branches of the Tannenbaum. Nice one Mr Becker. Bugger off to lie on a beach staring at the sunset and contemplating the meaning of life. Don't you worry. I'll be here trying to keep your son together with Sellotape, digestive biscuits and tea. Nice work. I appreciate that this thought is probably unfair but still, the righteous anger feels good, while it lasts.

'He's staying with some friends in London now. He says he will look for a flat in Oxford once the house sale goes through.'

I look up for the first time, startled. 'What? I didn't know you had to sell the house. God, when?'

'Well the mortgage wasn't getting paid so yeah, it went on the market last week. Becker says he'll sort it out, though I expect it'll be me in the end.'

The tone of this last comment is hard to identify. It's not like Ed to show any bitterness but there is a touch of bile, just a touch, if you listen hard.

'I asked if we could maybe rent it out for a while but Dad said no, he wanted a clean break. Start again, somewhere new. I think it'll kill Mum to know the house is gone. She loves that house. Especially the garden.' And so do you, I can tell; I think this, but I decide not to say.

'Did you say that to your Dad?'

'I tried but he doesn't listen much. At all.' There's the bitterness again.

'Is it likely to be sold quickly? Do you know?'

'That's what the agents said. Shouldn't take too long. Very popular area and they've priced it for a quick sale.' Ed is hacking away at a shrub with alarming violence. Look at both of us, taking out our frustrations on the foliage. We'd better stop before we decimate the garden.

'But it was good to see your Mum, I guess.' God, very banal, but just testing to see if there's anything else, any more in this tank that needs to leak out before the tap gets turned off again.

'Yes, and no. She looked better than my worst fears, but, well. I guess I can't comfort myself with the idea she's doing fine. I know the truth now, and sometimes I could do without the truth.'

I laugh, 'How I bloody agree with you. The truth can go hang, for all I care. I much prefer fiction.'

'In a way, and this is going to sound pathetic, but in a way it was easier not to see her. Now I have to find the strength to go and see her every week. I can't say I'm looking forward to it.'

'Yes. No it doesn't sound pathetic. It sounds like you're

human. You are doing the best you possibly can. I am sure she's proud of you. I would be.'

Ed squints at me, over his shoulder. 'Thanks. Really. I don't know if it's true but it's a nice thing to say.'

'Ed if there's anything I can do, you must just say, you know?'

'It helps to be here.' Silence for a moment, then, 'Actually there is something. It's a lot to ask, feel free to say no.'

'Sure, ask away.'

'Would you come and help me clear out the house? Becker's coming to sort out the furniture, put it into storage, but I need to sort all the personal stuff. Would you mind? God you should definitely say no.' He's laughing, 'I wish I could say no.'

'Of course. Yes, of course.' I can't say I am delighted at the idea, but I am touched he has asked me.

MY LIFE, IN BOXES

We go to the house the very next weekend, when the kids are at Chris's. The agents think the house will sell more quickly if it is cleared, and suddenly everyone is very keen to get moving. Becker is going to come up during the week, when the surf school is quieter. Our job is to clear out everything we can, throwing out what isn't worth salvaging and putting into storage what could be useful. His dad is going to buy a much smaller house or more likely a flat with the proceeds, so a lot of the house contents will need to go, one way or another. All in all, it's shaping up to be another grimly traumatic weekend in our perfect year.

Ed is more than a little agitated on the drive to the house, reaching over and fiddling with the music system. He can't listen to more than one song at a time before he changes channel or fast-forwards to a new track. He alternates this irritating fiddling with similar, but slightly different, fiddling with the air conditioning. In between, he is flicking through some property details, exclaiming at the ridiculous prices of property close to Oxford city centre, like this is some sort of surprising news to me. (Me, looking on the bright side: 'It'll be handy, though, if you do get into Oxford.' Him, looking on the gloomy side: 'Not so handy for Durham, though.') Thankfully the journey is not much more than half an hour, otherwise I might end up opening the passenger door and shoving him out at some traffic lights.

I am not too sure what I am expecting of the house, but it isn't this very normal, if slightly run down, 1930s semi. As we pull into the drive, I can see that Ed can't take his eyes off the skip on the front lawn. This was my idea, and seemed a practical one. (I was trying to avoid too many soul-destroying trips to the tip.) But now it seems like a glaring symbol of what's to come, and Ed is finding it hard to take.

Once inside the door, the smell of damp and neglect lowers Ed's mood even further. 'I should have come back before now.' We open some windows and leave the doors ajar to let in the spring air.

The living room is full of packing boxes, and we dump our bags on the dusty sofa. In the kitchen, I start to unpack the cleaning equipment, and the food we have brought for the weekend's stay.

'Shall I make some tea, or shall we make a start?' I ask, hoping for tea. I am not sure I am ready to face the task ahead quite yet.

'No, come into the garden, I want to show you something.'

The garden is enormous, not much more than the width of the house but incredibly long, probably 100 feet, mostly grass with lots of shrubs and mature trees.

'This must have been amazing to play in,' I say, thinking of my back garden, tiny by comparison.

'It was. I always thought I would bring my own children here. Come on, the thing I need to show you, it's just a bit further.'

At the far end of the garden, behind a bank of hedges, is a beautifully constructed climbing frame underneath a huge tree. I am not great with trees, but I am pretty sure it's a sycamore. Ed walks me underneath it, and tells me to look up; about 15 feet up is the most amazing tree house I have ever seen, with a sloping roof, and a platform with a fence around it. I am almost speechless. 'Wow,' is the most I can manage.

'Isn't it amazing? Dad built it, but Becker and I helped him. It took weeks.'

'Your Dad made it? Really?'

'Yeah he's an engineer. Frustrated architect. I wish I could have brought Michael and Rosie to see this. They would have loved it, although it's probably not entirely safe.'

'Can I go up?'

He laughs, 'I hoped you'd say that. You climb up, I'll bring us some tea.'

Inside, it's amazing. Really solidly built, with opening windows, and furniture - chairs and tables, a dresser. This isn't some child's playhouse, it's a proper structure, built to last. I stand on the balcony, admiring the view: from here you can see right down the valley. Ed leaps up the ladder, without the tea; his eyes are sparkling.

'Watch this,' and he turns a handle to work the dumbwaiter to bring the tea and packet of HobNobs to our level. I am genuinely impressed.

'That was me and Becker, we did that.' He laughs. 'The proudest achievement of my life.' I haven't seen him like this since snow day, and the snow-ball fight on the Downs: full of child-like enthusiasm.

Ed looks over the balcony and says, 'I really should mow the lawn.'

I laugh, 'This is incredible, really. You must have had such a good time out here.'

'Yeah. I am ruining my sob-story now, aren't I? "My terrible childhood." Not quite so convincing now, is it?' He stands up, leans against the edge of the fence, 'Good place to hide out here. Becker would bring girls here, of course. And Lettie,' he laughs, 'Well, I won't ruin your Enid Blyton fantasies by telling you what Lettie probably did out here.'

'And you?'

'Nice quiet place to do my homework of course.'

I say, 'I wouldn't mind hiding out here for a bit. Say, decade or so?'

He holds up the packet, 'Hmm, I think we might need a few more HobNobs.'

We look out at the view for a while, in silence. 'Ten more minutes, then back to reality.'

'Sod reality,' says Ed. 'Bollocks to sodding reality.'

But sodding reality can't be ignored for much longer. We have a lot to get through. Everything needs to be packed up and sorted by tomorrow. And it seems that Liberty, at least, was not one to throw things away. I start with the kitchen, a fairly neutral zone. We have a post it note system: T for throw, S for store, C for Charity shop. Ed works on his room, and his parents', before coming downstairs to help me with the living room. I can tell he has been crying, but I don't say anything. I make more tea, and put the radio on while we tackle the living room. We talk, we chuck, we wrestle with bubble wrap.

By six, we are flagging a little, and stop to sit on the sofa.

'Shall I cook something?' I say. 'I brought some pasta.'

'No I've got a better idea,' he says. 'I want to take you out, to say thank you. There's a nice Chinese place in town, the Lotus Flower. We used to go there a lot. Nothing smart or anything. Is that OK?'

'Sure, that would be great. Thank you. I need to go and get a shower though. Get all dolled up.' I laugh. One good thing about being here, I won't have my usual wardrobe indecision. I have one more pair of jeans and another top. Perfect.

It's a beautiful sunny spring evening; we park by the river and then take a detour to throw some bread to the ducks. Ed gets intimidated by the swans. 'They scare me. You should be scared too. They can break a man's arm you know.'

The Lotus Flower is almost full, the tables filled with family parties. It's quite a relief to be in a strange town, with no chance of bumping into anyone we know.

'Ed! Eddie! God, where have you been hiding!'

The table just to the left of the door is packed with a group of teenagers, the boys mostly dressed in an approximation of Ed's vibrant surfer-style, the girls with long manes of hair, heavily sprayed, and little floral dresses.

One of the girls has leapt up from her chair so energetically that she has knocked her tiny bag flying. She flings her arms around Ed, hugging him tightly and kissing his cheeks, exclaiming with delight. I experience a sharp stab of jealousy to the stomach; if only I could be as relaxed with him as that. A cuddle every now and again would be incredibly useful. Dream on, Jen, and put that thought right out of your mind.

Now the others are standing too, and there is much hearty greeting. I can barely see Ed now, he has been enveloped in a tsunami of arms and hair. I stand to the side, slightly awkwardly. I sense that a consensus is building: Ed must join them, he simply must! We have only been in the restaurant for less than five minutes, but my mood has taken a nose-dive.

Ed manages to extricate himself from the crowd, and turns to me. 'I am sorry, everyone, this is....'

'Is this your Mum?' says the over-excited girl, turning her face to me. 'Is it OK to join us? Do you mind? We have missed Ed; you can't imagine how much.'

There is a palpable sense of discomfort around the table now. Those who know I am not Ed's mother, those who know that particular back-story, are bristling with the knowledge, and trying to share it with the others, quietly and discreetly.

'No,' says Ed, slightly too loudly. 'This is Jen. She's been helping me clear out the house.' He turns to me, trying to communicate with me without words - is this OK? I am sorry, but I don't think I have a choice.

I nod and smile, as broadly and convincingly as I can - Yes. It's fine. Don't worry.

He is convinced, or he is prepared to take it on face value. We join them at the table, squishing onto an already-full bench. I am jammed between Lucy, the over-enthusiastic girl, and Ed. It is such a squeeze that I can feel the heat of his thigh against mine, as well as Lucy's on the other side. I try to ignore the feeling.

Ed does some quick introductions; it goes something like this: 'Lucy, Jack, Josh, Tom, Dan, Holly, Becky, Jools, Jonny, Josh, Alex, Tash, Hannah.' (I may be paraphrasing.) Oh dear God, can we do name tags? No matter, just smile and listen. More food is ordered; prawn crackers are handed round.

Ed is the centre of attention; he has been much missed with this crowd. He fills them in on the last year (heavily edited version). It's quite interesting to hear how Ed creates a narrative for this audience. Cheerful, happy, relaxed. Yes, college is fine. No, moving to another college in year 13 was fine. Living with his aunt is fine. Village life is fine. Things with Charlotte are, well if not quite fine, just taking a break before they are fine again. This is a whole new side of Ed that I haven't seen before - Ed plays normal teenager. It looks reassuringly convincing. I am fascinated by it, actually. Will the real Ed please stand up? I would like to talk to him about it later, this role he is playing, but I wonder if that would be too sensitive a topic.

I have quite a bit of time to muse about the nature of appearance, the slippery nature of truth and reality, and the different roles we play in different circumstances, because I am an observer at the table. This is a really nice group of kids, but of course none of them have any real interest in me. And Ed is fully occupied with catching up with their news, and filling out his role of Ed-Doing-Fine with appropriate detail. From time to time, Ed speaks to me at a volume that only I can catch, just to reassure himself that I am OK and that I have enough food and drinks.

As the main courses are being cleared away, Lucy's neighbour (Jack? Josh?) levers himself off the bench. We all shift gratefully for a moment, and my thigh is no longer pressed against Ed's, leaving me feeling mostly relieved and little disappointed. Lucy says, 'Oh that's better! Sorry I've been so crammed against you; you must be so squashed.'

'Don't worry I'm fine, really.'

'So, how do you know Ed?'

I try not to look too shifty.

'He's been staying with my friend Ruby, and he's been doing some babysitting for me.'

'Oh that's nice. How old are your children?'

'Five, and nine. They're called Rosie and Michael.'

'Oh, did you have them quite late then?'

Hmmm. 'I had Michael when I was 32.'

'I think it's good to have children when you're still young enough to enjoy them. Otherwise it's not fair on them because you're too exhausted to run around after them and then you leave them orphaned if you die.'

'Well, I wasn't planning to die just yet. I expect I shall last a bit longer yet. I'm feeling pretty well, actually,' I say, trying to make a joke, but I fear I may be whistling in the wind here.

'No,' she persists, 'But if you have them when you're older, then you won't get to see them get married or have children. And your children will be taking care of you when you're old and sick, when they're still young.' Her brow is furrowed at this terribly sad prospect. 'Which is very wrong, I think.'

Do you now? Well thank you for your opinion, missy, it's been fascinating. I decide that a non-committal 'mmmm' is probably the best way forward.

Pudding arrives; I have ordered a coffee, and Lucy tucks into a banana fritter. Jack/Josh has returned and we are crammed together again.

She eyes my coffee and smiles. 'It's hard to keep the weight off when you get older, I bet.'

'Yes, I guess so,' I smile, fixedly.

'So, if Ed's your sitter, where are your children tonight?' she asks.

'They are with their father.'

She looks up from her fritter, interested. 'Oh? And you're out with Ed?'

I wonder if she has spotted the crucial use of 'their father' rather than 'my husband.' Probably not, she doesn't seem that bright. (Meow.)

'Yes, that's right. I am helping Ed pack up the house. We are here for the weekend.' Ah, slightly too much information there, Jen. I have given too much away, because I want to give this girl a little hint that yes, we are close and so butt out, sister. She blinks a little as she tries to process this idea.

'You're staying for the weekend?'

'Yes,' I say, coolly and levelly.

A further silence, while this idea ticks through her brain.

'What does your husband think about that, if you don't mind me asking?'

Yes, I do mind you asking, you nosy cow.

'Ed needs a bit of help, and what are friends for?'

Does that answer your question, dear? No, it clearly doesn't. Ha. I should become a politician. I'm a natural at dodging the issue.

'You're friends with Ed?' She's incredulous at this idea. 'Really?'

I can't help but laugh. 'Yes, really. Why?'

'Well, you're so much older than him. It's not very usual is it?'

'Don't you have any friends who are older than you?'

'No. Only my parents and my parents' friends. And I wouldn't say they are my friends, no. Well, I think that your husband must be very understanding.'

All right, I give in. I'll tell you.

'Actually, we're separated.'

'Oh I see. Well that's a shame. For your children I mean.

I'm so glad my parents are still together. So many of my friends have divorced parents. It's horrible for them, having to live in two places. And then when new children come along,' she glances at me, 'not that you have that to worry about.'

It's curious this, because I honestly can't tell if this girl is being deliberately unpleasant, or just crass and insensitive. I think probably the latter, but perhaps I am being naïve. I just don't get this instinct that some people have to be deliberately nasty; how do they get the energy and why don't they feel embarrassed while they're doing it? I know I would. I get all flushed and shifty even when I am trying a bit of well-deserved bitchy retaliation.

It suddenly occurs to me - who Lucy reminds me of: Imogen. Watch out Lucy. Don't be a bitch all your life. Take a day off.

Lucy is thankfully distracted from the exciting pastime of making me feel shit by the arrival of the bill. There is the usual bartering and palaver; I note with some pride that Ed seems to have taken charge. That's my boy, I think, entirely illogically. Ed bats away my attempts to pay with a firm shake of the head.

The discussion turns to - where next? The pub? Some dodgy nightclub above a furniture shop? The sofa with a nice cup of tea? No, I am imagining that last one.

And yet....

I say, as quietly as I can, 'Ed, would you mind if I ditched out and went home? Don't let me stop you going out.'

Not quietly enough. Lucy says, 'I can drive you home Ed.'

'Is that OK? Do you mind?' he asks, a little anxiously.

'Yes, of course. Good night all!' I say louder and more cheerily, to general indifference.

'I'll walk you to the car,' he says, but I shake my head, no, and scoot thankfully out of the door.

Jealousy: it's a bastard, if you want my opinion. The most illogical, the most soul-destroying, the most knee-buckling, the most undignified of all the emotions. Right now I can feel it gnawing away at me. I try to treat it with disdain, but still, there it is. Making my stomach turn over and over. Maybe I shouldn't have eaten all that crispy duck.

If you suggested he went out without you, then it makes no logical sense to be all grumpy when he does what you suggest. You may have been looking forward to a quiet evening together, but you can't blame him for bumping into friends; that was an accident. You can't blame him for wanting to spend time with his friends. That's normal, of course it is. So why are you lying here on the sofa, failing to read your book, watching the clock in a bit of a childish sulk?

I should probably go to bed.

I hear a car engine outside. A glance at the clock – 12.39. Well don't blame me if you're tired tomorrow Ed; we have a lot to do, I humph to myself. But minutes tick past and the car engine noise is still there. 12.46. The temptation to twitch the curtain is almost irresistible.

It's 12.52 before I hear the car door slam and the car drive off. I arrange myself casually on the sofa, pretend to read my book.

'God I am so sorry. That was not the evening I had in mind,' he calls from the hall.

'Don't worry, it was fine. It was nice to meet your friends,' I yell back.

'Do you want a cup of tea, or are you ready for bed?'

'Tea would be nice. I brought some camomile.'

A few minutes later, he brings in the mugs and I move my legs to let him sit down. He begins again, 'Seriously, I can't tell you how sorry I am.' He is flushed - is he drunk? Embarrassed? Guilty? Some combination of the three?

'Stop it, it's fine.' I can tell my voice has a little edge, so to cover this up I carry on, quickly, 'Did you go dancing?'

He grimaces, 'Yes, so I had to knock back a few beers to catch up. I had forgotten how dodgy it was in there, and it was full of everyone I went to school with. It was weird. Like I had just stepped out of the room two years ago and then I stepped back in and everyone was still there, wearing the same clothes and saying the same things. Freaky. Do you want to put the TV on? Watch a film maybe?'

'Nice idea, but someone's packed it.'

'Oh yeah. Sorry. That wasn't smart.'

I settle back, flinging my feet over the side of the sofa. 'I should go to bed in a minute.' I feel much better now he's here. Just the same old Ed, just the same old chat. I feel comforted.

'I still owe you dinner, you know. Next week? We'll go somewhere miles away, so there's no chance of being disturbed.'

I hear his phone buzzing, and I feel the now-familiar twinge of jealousy. He ignores it.

'So how did it feel to see them again?'

'Oh I don't know. Weird, normal, weirdly normal.'

'Did you miss them?' I ask, trying to make my tone as casual as possible.

'No,' he says, straight away. He pauses, and I hear his phone buzzing again. 'But, hold on, I can't quite get my head around this. I need to sober up.' He laughs, and drinks his tea. 'I guess I miss being the person I am with them. Does that make any sense?'

I nod, 'Yes of course. It makes perfect sense.'

'But it also makes me realise I can't be that person any more. I can't be normal. I can't even pretend to be normal for more than an evening. It was starting to wear off by midnight, and I was worried I was going to turn into a pumpkin in front of their eyes. I was going to get a taxi then but Lucy insisted on bringing me home. She is hard to say no to.'

'I think she likes you,' I say, as casually as I can.

He laughs, 'You don't say? Is that why she tried to grapple with me in the car just now?'

I laugh over-heartily, through gritted teeth, 'Could be!'

'Luckily I had my wits about me and I was able to fend her

off. I blame you, buggering off early and leaving me to her clutches.'

'She slipped me a fiver,' I say, laughing genuinely now, with relief.

'Traitor,' he says.

'She seemed a very nice girl, Ed. You could do worse,' I adopt my best mumsy tone.

'Er, Jen. Hardly. Listen to this.' He leans forward conspiratorially. I can smell his citrusy scent, the smell of his fresh sweat, a little hint of beer. 'We watched The Importance of Being Earnest once, in class.' Whispering in an exaggerated tone, 'She didn't find it funny.' He leans back again, with a look of "SEE? I told you so!" on his face.

'Oh dear God! The poor girl,' I shake my head. 'I can only pity her.'

It is weird to be in Becker's room, in Becker's bed, under the gaze of several impossibly beautiful surfer babes. I am just drifting off to sleep when I hear Ed on the landing; his phone is buzzing again, and this time he answers it. 'Hello? Hi, yeah just give me a minute.'

He goes into his bedroom and closes the door. My traitorous, illogical stomach twists.

Jealousy, it's a bastard.

CHAPTER ELEVEN
APRIL

ROLL AWAY THE STONE

As the Easter holidays approach, the empty date-squares on the family wall-calendar loom blankly, like a row of gleaming tombstones. Faced with the idea of a week in the house alone while the children frolic in the South of France in Romily's villa, I make no plans at all. So, a week before the schools break up, I start to get a tiny bit panicked.

Ed listens patiently as I start to talk, with a sort of vague fervour, about my plans to decorate the downstairs bathroom, take up watercolour painting, learn Italian, do a week-long detox. In fact what I dream of is a week in bed, with a pile of books and Radio 4 in the background.

In the end, he cracks. He's only human.

'Jen. Shut up a minute. I know you don't like it when people tell you what to do, but, well I'm going to.'

God, is that true? It sounds sort of convincing, the kind of thing that might be true, about a woman like me. But I don't think it's quite on the button. For sure, I don't like it when people tell me what to do, when I don't want to do it. That's quite different. I don't like it when people boss me around with their own agenda, for their own reasons. If someone were, theoretically, to tell me what to do with my best interests at heart, with a good solid knowledge of what I needed, well that would be quite a different scenario. All terribly theoretical of course, because that kind of thing never happens to a seemingly-capable woman like me.

Ed hands me some sheets of paper, a computer print-out; the top panel is turquoise with stylised waves and leaping dolphins, and the sunshine-yellow logo reads 'Becker's Surf School', the uprights picked out in silver surf-boards. His hands are actually shaking a little, I notice, but I don't point this out.

'I've arranged everything. You're going to Pennack Sands, to stay with Becker.'

Wow, am I? What? Sorry? I'm going where, to stay with whom?

'I mean, if you want,' he hedges, rather meaninglessly.

'On my own?'

'Well, Becker will be there. He's going to look after you.' Meaning, Ed won't be there. Ed's Easter plans involve a great deal of revision and, this latter aspect discussed with studious casualness, he's going to see Charlotte for a couple of days, 'just to see how things go.'

I am staring at the sheet of paper, trying to make some sort of sense of this conversation.

'Do you think surfing, well is it really my thing? Won't I be massively out of place?'

'You don't have to go surfing, not if you don't want to. Becker has a room that you can stay in and it's right on the beach. It's a lovely place, honestly. You can just hang out, read some books, look at the sea. Get some rest. You can see dolphins from his window. Char and I stayed there last Easter. It was lovely. I've even booked a train, so you don't have the drive. Becker will pick you from the station.'

'Really? God you've gone to a lot of trouble.' The whole idea seems incredibly tempting. Almost too good to be true. There must be a catch, a reason I can't.

Ed says, 'Sorry. I know this is a bit out of the blue. But I have been thinking about it for ages. I don't want you to be here on your own at Easter. I think you could do with a break. And I think this would be just what you need. That sounds really bossy, I know, but this is the perfect solution, honestly.' His tone is a little apologetic; now I have got over my initial shock, I am feeling a bit teary. 'You have been really good to me, these past months. Helping me with my work, the Oxford thing, sorting out the house. Let me do this for you, please. Just let me sort this out for you, that's all.'

'God, this is really kind, but I am sure your brother won't want me hanging around.'

Ed laughs, 'Oh don't worry, Becker won't let you cramp his style. He wouldn't have said yes if he didn't want to. Becker never does anything he doesn't want to.' Ed's tone is mostly admiring, with just a hint of resentment. 'He gets away with murder.'

'Yeah, I've got a brother like that.'

'Well, will you go? Please?' He is looking at me with intense concern. 'Otherwise I will just worry, and I won't be able to relax.'

It's impossible to say no, when he puts it like that. 'Yes, OK. Thank you, yes. It sounds perfect. But I'll just go for a couple of days. I don't want to be a nuisance.'

Ed laughs, 'You sound like my grandmother. You won't be a nuisance; Becker will love to have you around. Honestly.' And I may be imagining it, but I see just a hint, just a flicker, of worry pass across his face.

CAN I CALL YOU HEATHCLIFF?

In the end I stay for the whole week. In fact, would like to stay for longer. I would like to stay forever to be honest, and forever might be about how long it would take for me to learn to surf. Actually, that's not quite true. I am perfectly good at surfing, as long as I stay exactly horizontal. It's when the vertical is attempted that things start to get messy.

Becker's Surf School is set on a sloping beach at one end of the Pennack Sands, a picture-perfect little bay. It is a beautifully warm Easter, but the beach never gets too crowded. Becker himself is pretty picture-perfect too, almost startlingly good-looking. Ed's description of him as 'skinny and five-two' turns out to be something of an understatement; he is gorgeous, and blond, and tanned, and muscular. He has the tendency to walk around with his top off as much as possible; by the end of the week, I could probably draw a pretty accurate sketch of his nipples, which is not something I can say about any of my closest friends. Though if I had his torso, I might keep it in the foreground too. Becker lives in some sort of parallel universe, where all the women are young and good looking, with amazingly perky breasts, work involves walking about on beaches looking buff, and every night is party night.

I sit on the fringes of this charmed life, and observe. I settle quickly into a restful little routine. In the mornings, the sunlight wakes me up about 8; I lie in bed reading, until Becker brings me a cup of tea about 8.30am. (Although Becker is out until the early hours drinking, and doing whatever impossibly-cute surfer boys do in the early hours, he is up and ready to open the school bright and early.) Then I get dressed and take a walk to the harbour, buy a paper and have coffee. I have lunch on the beach with Becker, then in the afternoon attempt some sort of water-based activity: in the hopefulness of the early part of the week, some surfing tuition, and then towards the end just lolling on body-boards or going for long swims.

I love my new wet-suit; I like the way it holds everything in for start. I also love the way I can swim and swim for hours, and not get cold. When I was a teenager I loved to swim out for miles, around bays, finding out hidden places. Now, I feel liberated, really free, with my head laying back in the water, staring at the robin's egg blue of the late-spring sky, tracing the foamy cloud patterns and listening to the sound of the ocean in my ears.

It's on one of these long afternoons that I realise, floating out in the bay on my back looking at the sky, in the middle of a long train of thought about nothing in particular, that I have no idea where the dead polar bear is. Is he on the beach? I can't remember bringing him, in fact; maybe he's still back in Lower Worthington. This idea makes me smile; I roll over onto my front, and swim for shore.

In the late afternoons, after I have showered away the salt-water and plaited my hair, Becker cooks dinner – normally some sort of burnt slab of meat, with chips. (Becker is not a friend of the salad; he's more of a protein and carbs man.) We chat, and drink a beer or two. Then, while Becker finds something to cover up, but not disguise, his ravishing torso, and goes out with his friends, I sit on the deck and read a book until it's dark and I go to bed.

By the third day, I am starting to think that this is the best holiday I have ever had. By the fourth day, I am filled with the sincerest hope that Chris and Romily are having a wonderful holiday too.

Becker's company plays a big part in this; talking to Becker is an incredibly uncomplicated experience. He shares Ed's laid-back inner calm. But I see in Becker absolutely nothing of Ed's intense seriousness, even earnestness; Becker doesn't appear to take anything seriously at all, except perhaps surfing. And the state of his torso. When Ed enters a room, he tries not to attract attention; he carries the weight and seriousness of the world in his shoulders, in his face, and in his hands. In contrast, Becker fills the room with his casual, expansive presence; in fact, he dominates the whole beach with his ever-present laughter, and his compacted energy. There's no wonder that the girls flock, and God do they ever flock. Becker doesn't sprawl like Ed; he's too conscious of the impression he's making, whether the women are looking, whether the men are admiring. Like Ed, though, Becker is an incredibly relaxing person to be around; talking to him is extraordinarily straightforward. Becker tells you stuff, asks you questions, nods, smiles, leaves.

Despite his undeniable beauty, I have never found anyone less sexually alluring in my life. I think it's because he is enough like Ed to bring him to mind, and then immediately, vividly and obviously the absolute opposite of his brother. It makes me remember Ed, and then it makes me yearn for his seriousness, for a little substance, for solid intellect: a little meaningful conversation beyond the state of the surf and the temperature of the beer. Being with Becker reminds me just enough of Ed to make me miss Ed's company, so very much. (Sorry Becker.)

'So, what exactly do you want with my brother then.'

He does an excellent line in straight talk, though. I'll give him that.

This opening gambit comes on my last night; by this time I am relaxed enough to be able to laugh, but not quite relaxed, or stupid, enough to give a quick answer.

'I know that you might find it hard to believe, but sometimes men and women can, you know, be friends. With conversation and all that.'

'Yes, I heard that. Not something I want to try, but I did hear about it.'

We drink our beer. I am staring out across the bay, feverishly searching for any movement on the surface. I leave tomorrow and I am determined to see a dolphin. I was promised dolphins. I absolutely insist on seeing one.

'I thought it was pretty bloody weird, when he asked if you could stay. It didn't make any sense. But now you're here, it's obvious really.'

'Is it? Give me the benefit of your wisdom.'

I open another beer.

'Yeah, since you've been here, well it's like having Eddie around. You have the same little habits. The same way of just padding around doing fuck all, all day.'

I am more than a little affronted. 'Well, to be fair, I am on holiday. Normally I am really busy.'

'That's what I mean. Normal people don't come on holiday to sit around doing nothing, reading and looking at the sea and, I don't know, going to bed early and doing the crossword. Not young people anyway. But that's what Eddie would have done, just what you did this week. I can just imagine the two of you, moseying around, listening to the bloody radio, discussing politics and talking about what just happened in your book. I bet you have a whale of a time.'

I laugh, 'Yes you have it right, that's our perfect weekend.'

'I bet. He always was a boring little fucker. No offence. Always doing his homework, saving his money. Going to bed early. Not that he disapproved of me and Lettie, but he didn't want to join in, either.'

'Surely your parents wouldn't have wanted him joining in anyway.'

This makes Becker laugh out loud. 'I take it Eddie hasn't told you much about our home life, then? No, our parents wouldn't have much noticed. Eddie is pretty much the white sheep of the family. A disappointment all round.'

He laughs again, and I wonder if there is an edge to it, or am I imagining it? Maybe Becker isn't quite as chilled out as he would like everyone to think.

'So, you two aren't fucking then?'

I have been waiting for this question to come for months now, from all sorts of directions, preparing my response. And when it does come, my well-rehearsed responses of outrage and disbelief just aren't appropriate.

'No,' I say, 'we aren't fucking. No.'

'Sorry to ask, but I am a nosy fucker.'

'That's OK.'

'I think I trust you to look after him. I'm glad. He comes off like he's all mature but he's a kid, really, underneath. And his life hasn't been easy. But he's also very protective of you. He was pretty clear that I was supposed to watch out for you. I think maybe he likes to take care of you. And maybe you like that too. Do you?'

I reply, before I can edit my response, 'Yes, he takes care of me. Yes, I like it. I like it a lot. But.'

Where's this going? But?

'But, there's nothing else. Nothing more.'

It actually feels quite good to say it out loud. I have one more thing, before I'm done. I am a long way from home, a long way from my usual reality and I feel the need to speak something out loud, something that I think might be, if not completely true, then certainly very close to the truth. What happens in Pennack, stays in Pennack.

'It's not going to happen, not ever. If circumstances were different, radically different, then we could make each other very happy. But circumstances would have to be incredibly different. It's impossible. It can't be done. It's never going to happen.'

Yes. That feels like the truth. Now it's out there, I want to cover it up, quickly, with a distraction. 'Anyway he's off with Charlotte this week.'

'Yeah, I know. Stupid bastard. I have told him to leave it but he won't take advice about his love life from me, for some reason.'

'Can't think why. With your track record.'

'Yeah exactly.' He drains the last of the beer from his bottle. 'Though as it happens, I'm right about this. He thinks if it's hard work, you just have to try harder. That love isn't real unless you're miserable. He just wants to save her. Even though she's not really worth saving.'

'That's a bit harsh, isn't it?'

'No take my word for it, it's fair. More than fair. For years, she's run him around, made him think he's not good enough. She drops him, picks him up again, just because she can. She treats him like shit, but he lets her. He looks after her, all the time. She sulks, gets her own way. Then, the very first time he needs her, where is she? Nowhere. Bloody nowhere.' He's really angry now; there is a dangerous edge to his voice that makes me feel a little nervous.

'If he takes her back after this, then I will have something to say about it.'

'You can't help who you love, though.'

He looks me right in the eye. I feel the full force of his disdain at this trite comment.

'That's bullshit. If someone treats you like shit, doesn't care about you, doesn't watch out for you, that's not love. If you let yourself be treated like that, if you start to like it, well you better sort yourself out. He'd better sort himself out.'

We sit in silence for a while, looking out at the sea; I think about the damage caused to these boys, under their charming, laid-back facade. Ed, needing to be needed. Desperate for love. Blinded by romance. And Becker... well I'm not sure about Becker, but I suspect that his anger about Charlotte might just be rooted in his own guilt about leaving Ed to cope with the aftermath of the last year on his own. Why, if Ed is the youngest, is he behaving like the eldest in this family?

'Come on, get dressed, you're coming out with me.'

I start to protest, but the Becker boys don't take no for an answer. Another shared family trait, and one that works quite well for me.

'I'm not asking you. I'm telling you. There must be something you can wear in your suitcase. Go, now.'

It's a long time since I faced a train journey while hungover; I have to rest my forehead against the murky window a few times until the queasiness passes. I have my book on my lap, but reading is not a possibility.

When I close my eyes, I keep getting flashbacks of the evening. They make me smile. Those surfer boys know how to party, and if the surfer girls were a little bemused by the appearance of their Mum on the dance floor, they were too polite to say so.

My phone buzzes, making me jump.

Message Ed

Good week? Becker show you a good time?
Yeah, far far too good. May need week in rehab to recover.
Glad to hear it. Hope he took care of you.

(I stare at that one, trying to read through the subtext filter, but I am too hungover.)

Yes, he was wonderful, thanks for asking. Becker was really kind, although he couldn't manage to teach me to surf. I have asked him to come and stay.
That would be lovely
How was your week?
Terrible thanks for asking

And a little smiley emoji. Becker won't need to give him that talking-to after all.

THERAPY, MARK II – POLLY'S IDEA

Polly bounces onto the train platform, closely followed by an attentive ruddy-faced tweedy young farmer type, carrying her two enormous bags (bare minimum for an overnight stay, darling).

'Sweetie I can't thank you enough,' and once he has stowed the luggage in my boot, she air-kisses him, making his ruddy cheeks blush even deeper, before dismissing him with a decisive turn of her back. 'So, my luvvveerrrr, here we are in Netherington Wallop! Are you ready to show me a GOOD TIME!'

'Polly, stop talking in that ridiculous accent, this isn't sodding Devon. We're still in the Home Counties for God's sake.'

'Whatever, Jen, you know I can't face the country without a drink in my hand. Let's get the fuck home.'

Many years ago, when we lived in Gower Street (which we liked to think of as Upper Bloomsbury), Polly made me promise that we would never live anywhere outside of the

London Underground Zone 1. This vow, and my breaking of it, remains an area of some tension. Polly experienced my move to the country first as a personal affront, but latterly as utterly hilarious.

Polly treats the country with disdain; in contrast her arrival is always greeted with great feasting and rejoicing. Rosie finds her endlessly fascinating; Michael is equally captivated by her. He can barely take his eyes off her; her sinewy, shiny glamour providing a glimpse of a world of femininity that is a million miles away from the mumsy frumpiness he is used to seeing at school and among my friends. (Chris always found her rather intimidating, but that's very much by the by. Chris is with Romily right now, I guess, and he can bloody stay there.)

Even Polly, self-obsessed Polly, has noticed that I'm a bit cheerier than I have been in a while. She has her own theory about this. Which she is very keen to share, of course.

'Thank God I made you go back to work. That's been the making of you.'

'Yes Poll, all your idea. Of course.'

'Seriously, though. You are much better now you have something to do.'

'I always had something to do.' I am feeling a little combative. I love Polly, and she has been supportive in her own way, but I can't help be a little irritated when she floats in and claims the credit for my improved mood. I mean, she's not been the one carrying me along this beach on her back. She's off again; I'm seething a little, but quietly.

'You know what I mean. Real work. You weren't ever happy when you weren't working. You were all fucking pigeon-toed. I mean even more than usual. I come and see you in this village, and you don't know what to say, what to do. You were never like that with me. And you're blaming yourself, that you don't fit in. Well the answer's simpler than that. It's not you, it's them.'

I am still seething, but I am thinking about what she's

saying. I think she may have a point, but I need some time to process this.

'Why didn't you say something before? This is all hindsight, Poll. I could have done with this advice a few years ago.'

'No, I always thought it, and I did say it, but you didn't want to hear it. You were in the wrong role, in the wrong play. It was painful to see. It was weird for me, and it must have been weird for Chris.'

Christ, that stings.

'Are you saying you think I drove him away because I was a crap village Mum? Really?'

'No, that's not what I mean. It's just, well, you've slipped inside yourself these last few years. It wasn't relaxing to be around you. Well, anyway I think you got your groove back, now you're writing again. And the teaching. But you're just not cut out for being a village Mum. That's not your fault. But just fucking get over it, and move on. Don't think if you try harder you will manage it. You won't. This is not your place. Just, fucking move on.'

At seven, Ed arrives to sit with the children. I hope my natural act is enough to fool her, and it certainly seems to be. We have dinner at Retro and she flirts aggressively with the waiter, persuades me to drink some very strong cocktails. There is no mention of him all evening, no significant sideways glances or pointed remarks. I think I have got away with it, until we are back home on the sofa.

'So how long have you been shagging the babysitter?'

I can't help but laugh. 'Polly, he's 18!'

She rolls her eyes, 'And? Come on, Jen, it would do you the world of good.'

She chooses a film – *In Bruges*, just up Polly's street. Swearing, violence and sleazy drug-taking – your basic busman's holiday. 'A little meaningless sex with someone young and gorgeous. Honestly, perk you up a treat.'

Despite my better judgment, I can't resist saying, 'Well I am not sure he'd be up for it.' But Polly has already moved on from this conversation. No, I really have got away with it. That was just Polly's usual bullshit. She didn't spot a thing. She doesn't know that meaningless sex with Ed would be utterly impossible.

CHAPTER TWELVE

MAY

WIRES

The land-line hardly ever rings any more; the only people who bother to ring that one, rather than my mobile, are generally trying to sell me something. But no-one is trying to sell me something at 05.33.

I race downstairs, trying to find the phone amid the piles of random family debris. I scatter the stacks of post, hairbrushes and Kinder toys to find what I'm looking for; I am relieved, and surprised, to note that it isn't making that low battery beep.

'Mrs Grey?'

Fuck.

'Speaking.'

'This is The Davies Infirmary. Mrs Grey, I'm afraid I have some bad news.'

It's at times like this, times of extreme stress, that we give away our darkest fears and imaginings. In the grey gloom of dawn, half-awake, just about to receive the promised bad-news, my imagination prepares a set of holes to drop this bad news in. In the short seconds before I hear the truth, my sub-conscious tells me, brutally, clearly, how deep these different holes need to be.

It's quite informative.

'I am afraid your mother has had a bad fall. She is really quite poorly.'

No, that's not the worst possible news. A pretty deep hole, but not the deepest.

'She is with the doctors now. She has been asking for you. I think you should try to come as soon as you can. Is there anyone there with you?'

Mum had been found in the early hours by a young neighbour, who had noticed an unusual light in the hall when returning from a night out. (I imagine my mother's sneering judgement on this neighbour's behaviour; I hope that she was polite enough not to make some comment on the appearance of this Good Samaritan. Or failing that, I hope she was unconscious when he arrived.) The neighbour called an ambulance and the police had broken the door down. (Again, let's sincerely hope she was unconscious for this bit, because otherwise I can't imagine how she would have coped with the terrible shame of this sort of scene.) She has a broken arm, hip and some sort of head injury, and also what the nurse describes as 'complications'. It wasn't clear how long she had been lying there, but long enough to be in the kind of state that needed me to go to her, right now.

It's the May half term holidays, and - of course - Chris is away working. I am not even sure where he is, but thankfully he picks up his phone.

'Christ Jen I'm so sorry.'

Latvia. He's in bloody Latvia. Of course he is. He wouldn't be in Paris, or Margate. I am not even terrifically sure where Latvia is either.

'I'll get back as soon as I can. I'll message you when I know what flight I am on. Jen.' His voice is hesitant. 'Would you leave them with Romily? Until I get back? She's at home this week. I know you might not want to, but she wouldn't mind and you know, they know her pretty well by now.'

Do I mind? I know I am pretty strung out and this is an emergency but, you know, I really don't mind. I am not sure whether this is progress or a sign of terrible damage.

I think of the depth (or, more accurately, the shallowness) of the hole I dug in case the bad news was about Chris, and I feel a twinge of guilt, and a jolt of liberation.

'No, that would be fine. Will you phone her, or shall I?'

That's the spirit, Jen.

After Romily, Ed. I try not to think about the hole I dug for him; I keep well away from the edge, in case I fall right into it.

'I'm going to drive you.'

'No really, you aren't. I'll be fine.'

'It's not a question. Is there someone to look after Mike and Rosie? I can ask Ruby.'

'Romily's coming. She said she'd be here by seven.'

'OK. I'll be round then. Be ready. Go and pack a bag.'

Romily is, in fact, incredibly sweet. 'Please, don't worry about a thing. I'll stay here with them. Or,' she hesitates, 'I could take them to mine for a while?'

'Really, whatever is best for you. Just... they were very upset. Michael wanted to come but I don't know, I don't think it would be good for him. I don't know if I will be able to look after him. I might come back and get him. I'll see what she's like, if she can have visitors. I just don't know what to expect.' I'm gabbling, not really making much sense.

Romily nods, sympathetically. 'You'll just have to play it by ear.'

I am grateful for her coolness, her formality, actually; if this was Mel, or Carrie, the atmosphere would be a little overwrought by now, and I am not sure that I could cope with that.

'I think Chris will be back by this evening. But...'

Horrifically, and for the first time since receiving the news, I start to cry. My legs buckle and I have to sit down. I can't let it out, not yet. I need to get there; I just need to get there.

'I'm really sorry, Jen.'

I look up; Romily is biting her thumb absently, but looking at me intently, seriously. 'Really sorry, you know?'

'Yes,' I reply. 'Yes. I know. Me too.'

And then I hug my husband's lover, the woman whose name I dictated, sobbing, onto the divorce petition, just a few weeks ago. The woman who colluded in horrible deceit for months, right on my doorstep. The woman who took my husband away from me, the father away from my children. The woman whose name filled me for months with anger, and now I give her comfort, and she gives it back to me.

We are still hugging each other when Ed arrives.

I have never been more grateful for Ed's taciturnity. He fills up with petrol and brings back a Danish pastry and coffee, and the Guardian, wordlessly passing them to me. He asks no questions, beyond the practicalities. He doesn't ask how I'm feeling, and he certainly doesn't ask why I was hanging onto Romily's neck when he arrived.

We leave the M4 and the streets start to take on that repetitive suburban quality; Home Sweet Home. I am glad of the pastry and coffee to settle my stomach, because I guess that I won't be able to eat much for a while. The hospital looms, a vile concrete monolith; I am very pleased that I don't have to negotiate the double-parked streets around the hospital. We finally find a space in the car park; Ed manages to make manoeuvring the car into the incredibly tight space look easy. He sorts out change for the extortionate parking ticket, while I stand around, mute and numb. Thank God, thank God he's here.

Once through the stained grey entrance, he checks the map and I follow him to the lifts. I think, for a moment, about how we might appear, and the huge gap between that appearance and reality. This boy, young enough to be my son, is taking care of me, leaving me to just be in the moment. I think about the hospital corridors he must have walked down, with dread in his heart, as I am right now. We look so different, so far apart, but our lives, like our thoughts, as so often, are overlapping. As we walk into the hospital, towards this uncertain present and future, I can feel that he is ready, waiting, to catch me if I slip. I am on his territory, and his familiarity with these parameters feels hugely comforting.

Time seems to have taken on an elastic quality; I feel like I am in one of those dreams where I am trying to get somewhere really important, and the more I try to approach it, the further away it seems. The corridors stretch endlessly, and every corner I turn seems exactly like the last. We trudge, like we trudged back from the snowball fight in January; I think of everything that's happened since then. I deliberately don't think about what lies ahead, about what I might find when I finally reach the ward. I read the notices as we pass - Room for Rent, Do you like to sing?, Just had a baby?, Take Care of Your Heart - and let the words drift into my consciousness until they lose all their meaning. I make the sounds of the words buzz in my brain, to drown out the thoughts lurking there, to push them beneath the surface.

Lister Ward. I buzz the door and speak my name, and Mum's name, into the intercom. The door is released and we walk through.

'Jen, do you want me to come, or shall I stay here?'

'Come, for a bit, please?'

After the oppressive subterranean gloom of the corridors, the ward is airy and filled with warm light. There is an expectant quality to the hush that makes me feel like I should hold my breath. I wait at the nurses' station, scanning the beds to see if I can find the familiar figure of my mother, but it's hard to distinguish any individual features. The sister smiles warmly, but her expression changes when I say my name; her expression says, expect the worst.

'Is this your son, Mrs Grey?'

'No.' Maybe I should just say yes, that would be easier in

the short term but I don't even know if Mum is conscious, and the arrival of a fake, adult grandson at her bedside might not be good for her in her current state of health. I struggle for a label for Ed, something socially acceptable in this circumstance. This is Ed, my quasi-au-pair? Semi-nephew? My life-belt? This is Ed, we have a deeply ambiguous relationship. As to its specific nature, leave that one with me. I'll get back to you.

'Well, could you both follow me.' She doesn't care, really. Why would she? She just wants to get us in the room, get this crappy news over with, and move onto the next thing on her list.

About an hour later, we are able to see Mum. She has returned from theatre, and we have spoken to the doctors. The prognosis is vague but not great. My mother is elderly and frail. (Frail! I try to resist lifting an inappropriately sceptical eyebrow.) It seems she was lying in the hall for so long that a number of complications have arisen. The list is long and resonant: kidneys, UTI, thrombosis, hypothermia, chest infection. Some of these may be 'suspected'; it was hard to focus on the details. It's the chest infection that stands out though. I know enough to know that's what kills old ladies, even stroppy, hard-edged old ladies like my Mum. Her heart may be hard but her lungs are as soft as the rest of us.

I must stop thinking like this.

'We are giving her the best possible treatment, but your mother has been left very weak by what has happened to her. At her age, well, recovery won't necessarily be straightforward. I am very sorry, Mrs Grey. We will do all we can, and we will keep you informed. We are taking good care of her.'

By her bedside, though, this description of my mother suddenly seems more convincing. She looks old, and frail. Her skin is papery and almost transparent. I can hardly see her face, obscured by the oxygen mask. Around her, machines beep and click; the sound makes me anxious, but is simultaneously strangely comforting. She looks tiny, the angles of her body under the sheets making her look like an injured bird. She looks, frankly, like she might die. Oh God, she might die. She might really die.

I start to cry. Ed sits beside me, and holds my hand. I cry some more.

I sit by her, not touching, not speaking, for what seems like hours. Ed sits with me; he reads, and I do too, when I can concentrate. Nurses come, doctors too; drugs are administered, my mother's lifeless body is shifted around in what seems like an unnecessarily violent way. From time to time, the machines start to beep alarmingly, making my heart pound. Once, we are ushered away and the curtains are drawn, but the emergency – whatever it is – passes, and we are back to this tedious vigil.

Around us, crises and emergencies ebb and flow. Each family faces their own moments of high drama in isolation; we don't comfort each other, we don't try to overlap. This ward is the very opposite of a community. So far from trying to connect with each other, we try not even to look or to listen. We pretend we can't see the crying, the pain, the intimations of love and mortality, just a few feet away. It's an alienating experience.

I have Ed, though. And Charlie. Charlie arrives just after lunchtime, with grapes and flowers, both of which are confiscated. I guess it's a long time since Charlie has been at a bedside, and he doesn't realise these Carry On symbols of hospital visiting are now just infection hazards. He stays for half an hour - he's 'in the middle of something crucial' - but he does give us a key to Mum's. He promises to return later.

I try to leave it as late as possible to phone home, so that I can pass on some sort of news, but by 5pm Mum still hasn't woken up. Although I haven't been in the hospital long, the normal world seems so far away as to be almost fictional; the background sounds – cooking, television – jangle my nerves with their brutal reality and chaos. I am longing to end the conversation and return to the hypnotic artificiality and order of the bedside, where everything is controlled, everything is monitored.

Ed goes to eat dinner in the early evening; when he returns, I suggest he might want to go home.

He says, 'Do you want to go home?'

'No, I couldn't settle. I want to be here, in case.'

In case? In case she dies? In case she wakes up? Both I guess. I shut these thoughts down.

'Then I'll stay.'

He returns with a case of revision from the car. The piles of textbooks and revision notes give the bedside a surreal quality. We spend most of the next few hours whispering about the texts he's studying for his literature exam; if Mum can hear, this must be a strange experience for her. I imagine the plot of Frankenstein winding into her dreams.

Just after midnight, Ed goes to sleep for a few hours at Mum's house, leaving strict instructions to call if anything changes. I am too strung out to sleep yet.

As dawn arrives, Mum starts to murmur. By the time the nurses' shift changes, she has her eyes open for a while, but it's not clear what she can see or understand. She begins to get a little distressed; more drugs are administered, monitors checked, but I can't get any more from the staff than 'we just need to wait and see.'

Ed is back at the bed-side by mid-morning, and we walk around the hospital corridors, just for a change of scenery. We buy a take-out coffee, and then we sit on some uncomfortable chairs just outside the ward. But not even the coffee, and the plastic clamminess of the seating, can hold off the inevitable, and I find myself drifting into a fretful sleep. It isn't restful though; my dreams are vivid and disturbing. I wake up with a start, to find myself resting against Ed's shoulder.

'Are you OK?' His voice is low and soothing.

'Yes. Just a really horrible dream.'

'What was it? Can you remember?'

'No, I can't quite. It's already slipping away.'

'That's the beauty of dreams. That we forget them.'

Now it may be my fragile, sleep-deprived state but I think that is the beautiful and profound thing that anyone has ever said to me. I think about saying this, but change my mind. I rest my head against his shoulder again, and try to drift back into sleep, just for a few more minutes of oblivion.

That afternoon, I feel like something to eat. We walk down the stairs to the Horizons Café. I realise I haven't eaten anything for more than twenty-four hours; even the smell of cheap food, deep-fried, makes my stomach rumble.

The piles of puckered sausages, flabby grey burgers and sunshine-orange fried fish reminds me of school dinners. I am not sure when I'll be able to face food again, though, so I pile my plate high. With my hands full of ketchup sachets and salt in paper squares, I feel - just for a moment - a little festive, like we are on holiday; this seems like the kind of meal for an early morning ferry journey. I'm just about to share this with Ed, to see if it makes him smile, when I realise he's crying, silently but very, very hard.

I hand him a serviette, cheap and thin. I think about looking in my handbag for something more substantial, but then remember that tissue supplies ran out late last night. We came ill-prepared, clearly, for the amount of crying that might occur on this trip. I consider going to fetch toilet paper, but I don't want to leave him, not now. I sit by him, tentatively leaning into him; he responds, leans back. It isn't quite a hug, but I can feel him relax against me. His face is hidden, turned away from me.

'Shit I'm so sorry Jen.' Ed rarely swears, and the sound is quite shocking. 'I know this isn't the right time. I should be... I'm sorry.'

He is really sobbing now. I wonder if I have ever seen him

cry in front of me; I don't think so. Not even that bloody awful weekend when we cleared out his mother's house. It feels surprisingly OK though. Sitting in these red plastic seats, in the glaring electric light, these extreme emotions feel very normal. I think of all the weeping that has taken place here in this building, in this room. I pass my arm around his shuddering back, and grip his arm.

'It's Mum. I just started thinking about Mum.'

'Yes. Of course, I guessed that was it.'

He looks at me sideways, guiltily.

'I am sorry; I know you have all this to deal with. You don't need me in this state. I am supposed to be looking after you. Not the other way round.'

'Shut up Ed. It doesn't matter. You are looking after me, better than anyone else could. Honestly. It has saved my life, you being here.' Clichéd, hyperbolic, true.

I say, 'I mean it. I am only too happy that I can actually help you for once. To support you. It makes me feel better about all the weeping I have done on your shoulder over the last days.' Weeks. Months.

Guiltily, I wonder if I could start to eat, or if that would be horribly rude.

'Why don't you start? I am going to be a minute, to pull myself together.'

'Would that be OK? I wouldn't mind.' Thank God. I shove some bacon between slices of toast, in the undignified manner of one who has been wandering, starving, through the barren wilderness for many months. 'I want you to talk, though, if you want to, I mean... I've wanted to ask about your Mum, for a long time. She's been on my mind since we got here. Since I got the news.'

He says, 'Yes. I know. Me too. Give me a minute.'

He gets up to get us both a coffee; when he returns, he positions himself next to me, facing in the same direction, to avoid - I guess - eye contact. I glance at his swollen face, surreptitiously; I hand him another serviette.

'No, I'm OK. I've got a grip.'

'You don't need to. I mean it's fine to not have a grip.'

'Yes I know, but I need to keep it in control. Otherwise I am afraid of where it will take me. If I start to let it out, I am scared I won't get it back. You know?'

'Oh God, yes. You know I know.'

He turns, just for a moment, and looks directly into my eyes. For a moment, just a moment, he lets me in. I feel the full force of his pain, of his vulnerability, staring back at me. It is incredibly hard to see; the strength of his feeling, of the feeling it stirs in me, and I am struggling to absorb it. I know that this is a compliment to me. I know this shows his trust in me. I hold his gaze, difficult as it is. And return it. I try to show him, too. To return the compliment by showing him what's inside me too, although I am horribly afraid of where that might lead. You open up a crack, and the full force of what's behind might split it all wide open.

He looks away first, back down to his coffee. I wonder if he is going to change his mind, change the subject. I wait, running the steaming mug back and forth between my hands, the heat of it forming a keen distraction.

'I can't remember a time when she wasn't ill. Even before I went to school, I would never know how she would react to things. She was.... unpredictable. Some days she would be cheerful, making us go out for long walks, talking to me about her childhood, talking to me about everything. Laughing her head off. It was often just the two of us. Becker would be off playing with his friends and Lettie, well, God knows where Lettie was but it wasn't at home.

'Then some days, I couldn't persuade her out of bed. I would try, bringing her tea and chatting to her, telling her stories about what we could do - well, sometimes that would work. But then I would sometimes regret it. She could get so angry.' He adds, hurriedly, 'I mean, not in a bad way.'

He leans back in his chair, hand over one eye, twisting away from me now. I think, that's it. That's all I'm getting;

that's all he can manage. Poor kid. I wish, suddenly, that we weren't here. I wish we were in my living room. I wish he was lying on my sofa and he could take all day, all night if he wanted, and I could stroke his hair and he could let all this out and I could make it better.

As if I could make it all better. As if.

'I would sit with her and I would watch the force of her emotions racking her. It was painful to watch. Obviously it was more painful for her. Incredibly painful. She used to say that she hoped that her children wouldn't inherit her ability to feel. That it was a curse. It looked like it, from where I stood.

'I was thinking, when you came over with the food, about the first time I came to see her in a hospital. There have been many times since of course.' He laughs. I can't quite pin down the emotion. Bitterness? Misery? Exhaustion? But the sound makes me wince. 'And the last time. I started thinking about the last time. If it is the last time. If she'll ever come out again. Jesus.'

I hold him again, lightly, just with one arm, and wait for the tears to come and the words to flow again.

'This café, it's just like a million hospital canteens I have been in over the years. It made me remember. The ward, that's really different. The places she goes, they're not much like the ward your Mum's on. They are usually much much louder. Always someone screaming or crying. Doors banging. Your Mum's ward, it seems so quiet. Almost peaceful. Have you ever been on a psychiatric ward?'

I shake my head, no.

'This is going to sound horrible, I am sorry, but this is what's honestly been going through my mind. I mean, what's happened to your Mum is so straightforward, compared to my Mum and her, I don't know what you'd call it, her illness. Her condition. Mum, she's never going to be better is she? She might be able to come home for a bit, maybe. But she's never going to be free of these places. I'm never going to be free of these places. I am going to be eating bad food in hospital canteens, for the rest of my life.'

'I'm sorry. I'm really really sorry.' And that's it, that's all I have for him. For a moment, he leans into me, rests his dark head against my shoulder, and I feel him relax. And then he sits up again, turns to me and says, 'Shall I go and get a paper? I fancy doing a crossword. I might get the Telegraph, if you can stand it.'

I laugh, 'If you must. And some more tissues? A man-size box, maybe?' He smiles, and then he's gone, striding purposefully away from the table and from the conversation.

Mum seems 'stable' and 'comfortable' - we are bilingual in hospital-speak now - so Ed and I decide to spend the evening and night at Mum's to get some rest. If she's better in the morning, or no worse, we are considering going home tomorrow. As we approach Mum's house, Ed says, 'It was a bit of a mess, you know?'

I look at him, startled. 'Really?'

Mum is the most house-proud woman I have ever met; the idea of her house being 'a bit of a mess' is almost beyond comprehension. I start to worry – has she been ill for a while? Started to let her standards slip?

When I open the front door, the smell hits me. I look at Ed, and he nods.

'I think maybe she was in the hall for a while. I tried to clean it up just with a scrubbing brush, but I think it might need a professional clean. I'll have another go in a minute. We should just leave the door open, though. Let the air through.'

The thought of Ed, on his hands and knees, scrubbing up the mess left by my mother on her hall carpet, has a curious dignity. I hope for her sake that she was too far gone to realise that she had caused such a mess.

'Thank you, you didn't have to.'

'It's OK. I've done it before. I don't mind.'

Christ. A little, narrow chink into a pretty dark place. As quickly as it's opened, it's shut again, and he's in the kitchen. I follow him; he's tidied in here too, piles of clean, dried dishes arranged neatly and respectfully on the side.

'Are you hungry? I put most of the stuff from the fridge in the dustbin. It was bin day. But I could find something?'

'No, let's get take out. I'm starving. I fancy a really big dirty curry.'

The relief that the immediate danger of the last few days has passed makes me light-headed with relief. The evening has quite a surreal quality - Ed in my Mum's house, for a start. Eating masala and dhal out of foil packets, scattering poppadum crumbs over my mother's John Lewis décor. Mum would be truly appalled. 'I'll Hoover tomorrow,' I say, only mildly guilty. I keep expecting to see Mum stride through the door and have something - many things - to say about our behaviour. Ed is sprawled across the sofa; his revision notes - now lightly splattered with mango chutney - are fanned around him in total disorder. I have my feet resting on - horrors! - a footstool. I am reading and eating at the same time and we are watching some trashy TV. If my mother came in right now, she would be adding cardiac arrest to her list of problems.

'I feel like a naughty child.'

Ed squints at me, 'You look like one.'

'If my mother saw me now, she would come over and give me a good smack.'

'What, now? Or when you were a child?'

'Both. Although she's perhaps too weak at the moment. I am probably safe until she gets her strength back a bit.'

'Your mother used to hit you?' Ed is staring at me curiously. 'Really?'

'God Ed you're so young. Yes, of course. And Dad. It was perfectly normal, although to be fair my mother relished it more than most. She used to keep a tally and deliver the verdict at the end of the week.'

Ed looks horrified. 'God I hope you're joking.'

'No I'm not joking. Honestly, that's what used to happen. But yes, if she caught me eating in the lounge, there would have been swift and painful retribution.'

I can see him thinking about the frail, half-dead woman in the hospital bed, and re-appraising her.

'Don't worry, this isn't my cue for the story of my painful childhood.' I laugh, 'You have the monopoly on that.'

'Yeah, don't go stealing my thunder with your pathetic attention seeking abuse nonsense. Like one of those books. "Mummy, Put Down the Poker!",' he mimics in a high-pitched sing song voice.

'Exactly.' I go back to my book. 'Of course you'll be sorry later when I show you the dungeon.'

'Would you ever hit your own children?'

'God no, can you imagine? Michael giving me his 'I'm so disappointed in you' look. And Rosie, well I reckon she'd just hit me back. With a big stick. Now, get back to your Russian Revolution.'

'Actually, I'm conjugating. Want to help with the French?'

'Sure, although it's not one of my main languages.'

'Yeah, whatever.' He thrusts a sheet of vocabulary in my lap, and I reach for the remote control, to turn off the TV.

Ed sleeps in Charlie's old room, and me in mine; being back in my narrow single bed makes it feels a little like Christmas, although I try very hard not to spend Christmas here: festive cheer is not high on the agenda, especially since Dad died, and Mum doesn't encourage overnight visitors. The next morning is Saturday; while Ed pops out for a paper and breakfast supplies, I phone the ward.

Mum has had a very good night, and definitely seems to be improving. In fact, the nurse starts to talk about plans for discharge. 'Is there someone she can stay with?' Christ, I don't know. I call Charlie, and he promises to come round at 10 to talk about it.

He arrives around 40 minutes late, tousled and

unapologetic. We discuss a number of options, for the short and long term. Mum's sister and brother in law are close by and will help; realistically, though, Mum would prefer some professional help. She won't want to be grateful to relatives; she will prefer to pay someone. The servant dynamic is one she will be much more comfortable with.

'Jen, I really can't commit to helping too much, you know? I have a lot on.'

'And I don't? Charlie, I am an hour and a half away. I will come when I can, but you know how things are with me.'

'But you know I am no good at this sort of thing. You need to be the one doing the arranging. That's just how I am. I can't keep this stuff in my head. Please, Jen, say you'll take care of it? Otherwise I'll just worry.'

I look at him across the table. My beautiful brother. The face staring back at me has changed little from the 15-year-old asking me to help his 18-year-old girlfriend get an abortion. Or from the 17-year-old needing me to persuade the school not to expel him after he was caught with a joint in his blazer-pocket. Or from the homeless 20-year-old, thrown out for bringing back not one, but two, girls from the pub when his girlfriend was working a night shift. This is the way it would always be. Any anger has long been used up.

'Alright. Look I'll go to the hospital now, take her a few things, talk to them. Will you wait here with Ed until I get back? Is that OK? Then we'll head off. Ed, is that OK?'

'Sure.' Ed is at the sink, washing up and wiping down the surfaces. Charlie hasn't mentioned Ed's presence. The good thing about having an extraordinarily self-centred brother is that he's far too wrapped up in his own life to think about commenting on mine.

I have been sitting at the bedside for about half an hour; I am just about to give up and go and get a cup of tea when my mother starts to shift in her bed, and opens her eyes. She is breathing by herself now, the oxygen mask next to her in case she needs it. This morning, before I arrived, she ate some breakfast - 'said it was cold and tasteless' reported the nurse ruefully; just you wait, I thought, till she gets her full strength back. You ain't seen nothing yet. It is a huge relief to see her looking close to normal; her face has lost its papery pallor and she has regained a little colour in her cheeks.

She moves towards me; it takes a great effort but she leans towards me and starts to speak.

'Jennifer, you look terrible. Now, did you bring my make-up bag?'

I laugh, 'Yes, of course I did. What do you think I am?'

She leans back in relief. 'Well in a minute you can help me with it.'

'I'm not sure if you'll be allowed, though?'

She looks at me, incredulously. 'Allowed? What are you talking about?'

Actually, I'm not sure what I am talking about. I try, feebly, to explain my thought processes. 'Well I don't know, health and safety?' But she isn't really listening, and I can't blame her.

We discuss the practicalities of her discharge; she rattles off a list of instructions, which I dutifully write down. She implores me to 'make sure the house is presentable (by which she means, immaculate) before anyone goes in.' By the time I leave, my head is reeling and I am starting to wish she might slip into unconsciousness again, just to give me a break. Just kidding. Well, mostly.

A nurse approaches the bed. 'You should try and get some rest, Pat.' Mum rolls her eyes at me, significantly. I am slightly amused; I have never heard anyone call her Pat, and she would certainly prefer to be Mrs Dottridge. Or failing that, madam. Well, I'll leave her to sort out appropriate terms of address by herself; she's more than capable.

I kiss her cheek, arrange her belongings so they are in easy reach, and start to leave. Just as I am about to turn away, Mum says in an urgent tone, 'Jennifer, you will look after Charles won't you? I mean, I don't want him worried about anything.

He's not a strong person.' Worry deeply furrows her brow.

'Yes Mum, you can trust me to do the right thing by Charles. Don't worry.'

I kiss her again, and as I turn to leave for the final time I realise that during the entire conversation she has not asked one question about me or my children.

When I get back from the hospital, Ed is mowing the lawn. (The boy is obsessed with mowing.) Charlie and I sit on Mum's uncomfortable patio furniture and talk over the practicalities.

'Look, Binky, I was thinking when you were out, you know I will help you. I mean, you can leave things to me. Just give me a list, and I will do it. I promise I will do it.'

I stare at him, a little startled. 'OK, well that would be a relief. Thank you.'

'I was being selfish. I know you have a lot on, at the moment. A lot to deal with.'

Bloody hell. Well, I'm not one to look a gift horse in the mouth or indeed in any direction, so we make two lists - one headed 'Jen', and one headed 'Charlie'. Will he actually do anything on this list? Well, time will tell but for now, it's a comforting sight.

'How was she?'

'Well, I think she was OK. Not chatty, but definitely better. I said I'd come back tomorrow evening, for visiting. Ed will look after the children.' Charlie looks across at Ed's back, mowing the lawn with studied energy.

'He's a great help to you, isn't he?'

'Yes, he really is. I've needed help. Especially this year.'

Charlie is silent, staring out of the window, as if contemplating for the first time my year, my life, how it might have been for me.

I carry on, 'If she's still improving, they're hoping she'll be home by the middle of next week.' I hold the list in my hand, 'if we can get this all sorted by then. Talk to social services, all of that.'

'Yeah, don't worry, you can rely on me.'

I almost laugh at the irony of this statement, but I decide it would be rather unkind.

Later, in the car, I start to work down my list, making phone calls to anyone I can raise on a Saturday afternoon. As I hang up the third call, Ed says, 'Make sure you don't do it all. Make sure Charlie does his fair share.' It suddenly occurs to me, far later than it should have: Ed told Charlie to help. Ed had a go at my brother while I was at the hospital, told him to grow up, pull his finger out.

'Did you talk to him, while I was out?'

Ed says, 'Yes. Why?'

I look at his profile. Not a flicker.

'No reason. I was just wondering.'

Ed says, 'I made him do the vacuuming.'

He turns to me, briefly, and gives me a broad, knowing smile, before turning back to the road ahead.

God I bet that went down well. I would have liked to witness that.

I say, 'Thanks. I mean, for everything, these past days.'

'You're welcome.'

I look at him with new-found respect. A man who can not only make my brother feel guilty enough to think about other people, but also get the Hoover out? The force is certainly strong with this one.

Charlie is, contrary to any reasonable expectations, surprisingly helpful over the next few weeks. He doesn't do everything on his list, but when I tell him to wait in at Mum's for deliveries, to transfer money, to organise a hospital bed to be placed in Mum's dining room – all these things actually happen, with a minimum of fuss and reminders.

In a few days Mum is settled at home, healing well and pretty much back to her old self. When she phones me one afternoon to tell me that she has found a bit of crisp (read, poppadum) down the side of the sofa, it's all I can do to stop laughing; she's definitely better. I think about Ed scrubbing her hall carpet, and consider telling her that story for a moment, before deciding against it. I promise to come and Hoover inside the sofa the very next weekend.

The curious thing is, when I look back at those few days, it isn't with any sense of sorrow or remembrance of misery. Having Ed there made the week seem, if not quite a pleasure trip, then at least bearable, companionable and, at times, fun.

CHAPTER THIRTEEN

JUNE

THE FOREST

Closer, closer still.

I can smell your breath, sense the radiating heat of your skin. And the sweet gentle love, the soft strings of love are drowned out by the pounding bass beat of desire. I am trembling with it, weak and faint with it.

I can hear your thoughts now. Your thoughts pour out of you. Golden glimmering threads connecting with mine, interweaving, running over and under and around and through and between. Such beauty and purity and power in those thoughts, I am dazzled by them.

I am heady and dizzy and intoxicated with them, and the ravishing beauty of this moment is so right and natural and perfect and I feel so alive and full of love and I feel like it will go on and on forever.

A FUNNY FEELING INSIDE OF ME

'Come to town tomorrow, Mare, it's been ages.'

'Hello Polly, yes I'm fine thanks how are you?'

'Yeah whatever Mare, I don't have time for your provincial chit chat. I need to know if you're coming to town?'

There's a launch, and a party, and I'm needed for some reason.

Tomorrow. I am not sure why I'm needed so desperately, but all will no doubt become clear. I glance in my wardrobe, hopefully but not expectantly, for clothes suitable for a launch.

Hmmm, no. Not so much in the way of clothes suitable for a launch. It's a long time since I've been to a launch, so I am not entirely sure what such clothes would look like, but I certainly can't see them.

'Come in the afternoon, and we'll go shopping.'

Nice idea but no. Polly's idea of shopping is some edgy little boutique where the assistants will glare and sneer at me; they will spot me for the dowdy country bumpkin I clearly am. Also, the clothes in such shops do not accommodate hip and bosom, and I have both.

'No that's alright, I'll find something in the outlet.' Silence. 'Look, I can manage to buy clothes, now get off my case. Yes, I would love to come. This is my weekend with the children, so I need to get a sitter.'

'That gorgeous little pup from last time? Shame, you could have brought him. I have a few people I would like him to meet.' Evil cackle.

'Polly you sound like a dirty old woman. Stop it. Anyway he has exams.'

'Jen, you sound like his mother.'

'Well I am more or less. I feel very motherly towards him.' Liar. Pants on fire. 'I'm just saying, this is not the time to be getting him drunk on cocktails and letting middle-aged women trap in cupboards, to teach him a thing or two.'

'No fair enough. Let's do that in August, right?' We both laugh, Polly lasciviously, me slightly guiltily.

'Well wear something sexy. No cropped trousers.'

I am horrified, 'When have you ever seen me in cropped trousers?'

Polly laughs, 'Well, just making sure. Keep it funky, is all I'm saying. See you at seven? Outside Agony?'

I laugh, as I always do, at the name of Polly's favourite bar. Who would have thought a bar called Agony would be so popular? That's urban taste for you. Unpredictable.

I call Ed. 'You know how you were coming round tomorrow for a takeaway and a DVD and some History revision?'

'I have rarely looked forward to an evening more.'

'Sorry but Polly's insisting I go to London. For a launch. Do you mind?'

'No, of course not. I'm not entirely sure what a launch is. Nothing to do with a ship?'

I laugh, 'It's a party for something. Like a coming out party. I didn't ask actually; a book, probably.'

'And this book needs you there? Otherwise it will be all nervous without you?'

I reply, 'Yes, exactly. Actually I'll tell you why Polly needs me. She'll want to impress someone at this launch, someone she's liked for a while and I will be there as her sidekick. She likes to look witty, and she likes my help.'

'What are friends for?'

'Do you mind? Is it OK?'

'No, it's fine. You go and watch this book coming out. Be my guest. Do you want me to sit for you?'

'Would you? The kids will be disappointed otherwise. Also,' I add, feeling a little embarrassed now, 'would you come and help me shop for clothes? This afternoon? If you can take a break from revision. I'll cook you dinner, in recompense. I need a little help.'

Ed is a lively and opinionated shopping partner. 'God no. Too long. Way too long,' he shouts across as I appear at the door of the changing room. 'Makes your hips look enormous. Which they aren't,' he adds hastily, although clearly it's a little late for pussy-footing around.

Next, 'Draining colour. No.'

'But I like this colour. Sort of pistachio?'

'Well it doesn't like you. No. Next.'

When I next appear, he hands me a bundle of clothes.

'You clearly need a bit of help here.' And so I buy his first suggestion, a short-sleeved shirt-dress in khaki canvas 'to go with those espadrilles'. It's perfect; not too muttony - my worst fear - but simple, sophisticated and it doesn't look like I'm trying too hard.

We are out of the shop and in Starbucks within 15 minutes.

'God I feel a bit shell-shocked.'

'To be honest, I would have been even quicker without you. Next time, I'll just install you in here with the paper and go by myself.'

'Did you learn that shopping technique with Charlotte?'

He laughs, 'God, no. Charlotte and I wouldn't go shopping together. Well, not for clothes. Shopping is more like a hobby for her. A vocation. She likes to take a good run at it. A minimum of six to eight hours.'

I am not sure if he's joking. 'Really?'

'Yes, really. She didn't appreciate my style of decision-making. We stopped in the end.'

'Have you heard from her? I mean, is she doing OK?'

'Yes, we've been messaging. I am going to see her when the exams are over.'

I let that filter through for a while.

'I was thinking of taking her down to see Becker.'

Ha, I think, unpleasantly. Becker will be thrilled.

'I would love to meet her.'

WHAT? WHAT ARE YOU SAYING JEN? WHAT?

'Really? Would you?' he's surprised, though perhaps not as surprised as I am.

'Yes, of course.' I sip my coffee. 'I mean, you are such a big part of our lives now. I hope that won't change next year. I hope you'll feel that you can come and stay whenever you like, and bring Charlotte. If things are working out. Or by yourself. Well, you know what I mean.'

'Yes, I would like that too. I suppose I haven't thought that far ahead.' He hands me a Red Velvet Whoopee pie; stupid name, but utterly gorgeous in the mouth. 'But yes, of course, I'd want to see you all next year. If I get the grades, I won't be too far away.'

'There's no reason why you shouldn't get the grades.' I allow myself a little fantasy moment of visiting Ed at Oxford, proudly taking pictures at graduation.

'I can't quite imagine bringing Char to see you.'

'Why? Would I scare her?' I laugh, but then realise he is looking at me seriously.

'Well, kind of.'

'God really? I was only joking. I'm not scary. Am I?'

'No, not scary but, well, Char doesn't much like spending time with people older than her. She doesn't really have anything in common with them. She never really spends any time talking to Dad. Or Mum.'

'Oh, I see.' Do I? I am not sure.

'And she doesn't really like children. She is awkward with them, doesn't know what to say. She is quite a shy person.'

'Right. OK.'

'I'm not saying you're scary, it's just... well if it was the three of us, or even with the children, it would be awkward, I think.'

OK, well this has been interesting.

'When I tell her about you, you can tell she doesn't really understand. She thinks it's weird, that we get on.'

Right, more than interesting. Very enlightening. If Charlotte and Ed do get back together, she won't want me around. She'll put her foot down. And, I see now, he'll be off. Why wouldn't he? He loves her, he wants it to work. Hmmm.

The friendship that we have, built up over months, hardened in the crucible of the last year, suddenly seems incredibly fragile. What's that gripping at my heart? That would be fear. The cold, dread, fingers of fear. What the hell I am going to do when Ed goes? What will I do without him?

I sip my coffee, and try to close the thought down. I push

it inside a box, and sit firmly on the lid.

ACTUALLY, MORE LIKE TURQUOISE

I hear them before I see them: like a swarm of buzzing flies. Continental flies, with matching rucksacks and brightly coloured raincoats. Many years of close contact with the foreign language student have made me an expert in their habits. They flock to the tourist traps of Britain for a few weeks in the summer, ostensibly to learn English (and try to kill themselves by riding their hired bicycles the wrong way down one-way streets). They travel in packs and spend much of their leisure time snogging each other in the street and, when they are forced to come up for air, blocking the pavements looking paradoxically both geeky and cool.

Spanish, this lot, I reckon. Not cool enough to be Italians, too tanned to be French, too well dressed to be German. Not always easy to tell though; there is a hint of Fraulein-fashion about the girls, and quite a few heads of madly frizzy hair. I make my way down the platform to a quiet seat near the trainspotters, clutching my polystyrene cup and paper.

Even when I used to commute every day, travelling to London never felt like a chore. It felt, and feels, like a homecoming. I love to drive to London, to feel the green fields whizzing past and then thinning, fading, the buildings getting taller and the traffic heavier. The part of the journey when my heart lifts is when I enter Chiswick; Chiswick, where the streets are paved with over-priced little delis. By the time I'm sailing over the Hammersmith Flyover, surrounded by winking, flashing billboards and fields of plate glass, my heart is soaring. Ah, London. God bless you, you filthy, messy, noisy merry-go-round. How I've missed you.

The train journey is pretty bloody good too, and still fills me with a rising excitement; close to miraculous considering I've travelled this same route hundreds of times already. I sip my coffee carefully, so as not to spill any on my new dress. I check my phone for instructions: Agony at 7pm, followed by the launch, ending up at karaoke, then the last train.

I can't quite settle on the train though; I'm feeling a bit jittery. I spoke to Mum this morning; it was hard to tell, but she sounded teary and a bit fuddled. I wonder if she is getting the proper care from the agency we've employed. I feel a stab of guilt that I am not there to look after her. Maybe I should have gone there tonight? Instead of indulging myself out on the lash and at a launch. I tried to speak to Charlie about it, to try and get some reassurance that Mum was OK and that I could justify putting her out of my mind for a while. Of course that was laughably optimistic. Charlie wasn't really listening; he couldn't really give me any details because although he sorts out the practicalities, assessing Mum's emotional and psychological state is rather beyond his capabilities or indeed his interest.

And yesterday's conversation with Ed has been playing through my mind over and over, too. Up until this point in the year - stupidly, I guess - I hadn't really thought about what was going to happen once Ed had finished his exams. I know, I know, it was pretty obvious but I guess this year I haven't had the energy to do more than exist from day to day, stumbling along dragging the polar bear behind me. But now the idea of Ed disappearing from our lives, from my life, suddenly seems terrifyingly close and real. Of course, if I was a good person, and a decent friend, this prospect would be a cause for great rejoicing. Because it would indicate that Ed's shit year was coming to an end, that he was in a better place emotionally speaking, and that he no longer needed my support. No longer needed to hide out in my kitchen, drinking tea and waiting for the violent storms to pass over.

Secretly, shamefully, I want him to stay in my kitchen forever, laughing with me at The News Quiz and playing board games with the children when I can't be bothered and reading out clues to the crossword. The anticipated pain of his departure, into the real world and the arms of the woman he loves, is excruciating and terrifying. How will I bear the loneliness without him?

No, I am not a good person.

The final complication in my already deeply complicated week is the message I received earlier:

Jen, I am sorry to spring this on you, but I really really want to talk. I know it's been a long time but please – will you call me? All love, Chris xxx

The longer I look at it, the less it makes sense. I sit and stare at it now, with my head resting against the train window, the blurred and lush green of the early summer countryside flashing past.

Polly's already fairly far gone by the time I arrive at Agony; she is keen to move on, and urges me to knock back the Bellini and get going. She waves down a cab - predictably, Poll doesn't do the tube. Or walking. The launch is for a book written by Polly's friend, another barrister who - I imagine - wants to get off the treadmill. I remember the type from my publishing days; they stank of world-weariness, and of desperation. Maybe I am being harsh, but I am not holding out great hopes for the merits of the book. I have read far too many bad books; finding a good one always comes as a welcome surprise.

The venue though, I'm not complaining about. We are in Painters' Hall, just down the road from the Old Bailey. We hop out of the cab and I admire the elegant white building front and the contrast of the bright blue front door.

'What colour would you call that, Poll? Turquoise? Azure? Cerulean?'

'Dear fucking Jesus, Jen. What are you on about?'

'I'm just trying to get better at this colour naming stuff. I am really bad at it.'

'I swear if you come off all provincial at this party, I am putting you in a cab and sending you straight back to

Emmerdale. Get a grip. Come on.'

'Azure,' I mouth to myself, and follow her up the steps.

The launch party is in the Livery Hall, a room of ravishing proportions, beautifully lit by chandeliers. I wonder if going over to admire the stained glass windows would count as 'coming off all provincial' and decide to wait until Polly is distracted before I risk it. The room is bustling; the canapés are amazing and the champagne is the real thing. Either this book is actually good, I think, or this author has a lot of vanity money to slosh around. Whatever, I feel very happy to be here, as I roll my third quail's egg in some pinkish celery salt and pop it in my mouth.

I wish I'd asked Polly a bit more about the book, though, because sooner or later I am going to have to have a conversation about it. Sooner, I guess, rather than later. Now she's introducing me to a group of lawyers from her chambers. They have that well-fed, well-read, extremely jaded lawyer look; their conversation is amusing and moves at a galloping pace and in a number of directions at once.

I excuse myself to visit the loo and take the opportunity to check out the crowd. Many have obviously come straight from work; I am relieved that I (or, to be more accurate, Ed) chose something smart to wear, because I would have looked out of place in anything too casual. The thought of Ed brings back a wave of anxiety, that I try to fold up and tuck away. Later, later, not now. In the loo, I get out my phone and look again at the message from Chris. I can't quite get my head around it, let alone frame a reply, so I close it down again. I open a new message, and type Ed's name in the 'to' line.

'What time will you be home?' Ed had been standing behind me as was getting ready earlier this afternoon, making me nervous. 'I mean, what time will you be back?'

'Well the last train gets in at 1.15, so I guess about 1.30. I'll get a taxi from the station.' I was at the mirror in the hall, trying to apply lipstick, although my view was somewhat obscured by the crowd of envelopes and photos stuck into the edge of it.

'Will there be taxis there at that time?' he asked, not quite keeping the anxiety out of his voice.

'Yes, don't worry. I'll phone for one from the train. Will you stay over, or go home then?'

'I'll probably go home, but I might be asleep. If I can manage to sleep. I might be too worried.' I looked in the mirror at his reflection. I wasn't sure he was joking. His face looked a little strange, a little twisted with tension, but that may have been the illusion of the mirror reflection.

'Ed I'll be fine. This may come as a surprise to you but I was managing to stumble around in the world all by myself, well, quite a long time before you were born.' I smiled to let him know that his fretting was rather sweet, but needed to stop, please, before it got irritating.

His brow was still furrowed, but he said no more. I shouted goodbye to the children. He was still hovering on the doorstep.

'Ed, I will have my phone with me all the time. I will message you when I'm on the train. Please, don't worry. You're making me twitchy.' Spontaneously, I leant over and kissed his cheek. The skin felt smooth there. I hugged him, a little awkwardly; I felt, momentarily, the outline of his hard, tense body, and breathed in his sharp-citrus scent.

'Have a good evening!' I slid out of the door, taking care not to make eye contact.

I may be imagining it, but I think I still have that citrus smell in my nostrils, if I breathe deeply enough. I start to type my message:

Am launching book. Champagne flows, but not down me – yet. Have stuffed pockets full of canapés to bring home for you. Hope children are behaving. Thank you and see you later, Jx

It immediately shows 'READ' and 'Ed is typing.....'

Children are locked in cellar. Buried key in garden. Have fun trying to find it later! EBx

I smile and tuck the phone in my pocket.

Back in the Livery Hall, the noise is rising. I see Polly; she is signalling for me to come over with frantic subtlety.

'Jen, this is Alex Forbes. Jen used to be in publishing, but now she writes herself. Alex has been asking to meet you.'

Alex Forbes. Oh dear Lord, Alex Forbes, you are pretty damn good looking. Oh and yes, that smile doesn't hurt either. Gosh, no. Improves the looks if anything.

I say, 'Nice to meet you.'

'You too, always good to meet a fellow writer. Especially one who looks normal, because so many don't, don't you think?'

'I'll go and get you two a drink,' says Polly, and she's off grinning and signalling to me again, but I've no idea what she's trying to communicate.

'Oh absolutely. Being a writer is not a profession that attracts normal people, in my experience. Now I'm pleased to hear that I look normal and all that, but I'm afraid Polly is exaggerating a bit. I'm not really a writer. I teach creative writing and poetry appreciation, and I write a few articles but I am just a bumbling amateur really.' A passing waitress proffers a plate of salmon-y canapés; I take two. You never know when she might be back.

'Oh I'm sure you are just being modest.'

I laugh, 'I promise you I'm not. But I take it you're a writer? What have you written?'

He looks at me a little curiously, 'I just wrote a novel.'

'And do you have a publisher?'

He laughs, 'I do. Quite a good one actually. In fact, they're launching my book tonight and the catering is really very good.'

He is laughing very good-naturedly, but I can only cover my face with my slightly-fishy hands. 'Oh God no, I am so sorry, there's no excuse for me. Please, forgive me. I blame Poll.' We are both laughing now; thank God he is finding my embarrassment amusing. 'I was confused by the fact that you are talking to me. It seems quite unlikely when you think about it. Surely you should be at the centre of the action, signing things. May I say as a former publisher, I wouldn't advise wasting any more time talking to someone who is clearly only here for the canapés.'

'Well, it's my launch and I'll talk to who I like. And you can hoover up as many canapés as you like. Be my guest.'

'Thank you. I can assure you I will do my best. Anyway, I hear your book is really very good. What's it about?' To my relief, Alex doesn't seem to have taken offence at all; my brittle banter seems to be working. We chat a little for a while, and I start to wonder where Polly has got to. Then - der - of course, I realise. How dim can one woman be? Alex is the reason why she wanted me up here so urgently.

God, really? Alex Forbes? Well it's a step up from Barry.

After a while he says, 'Look, you're right of course, I really should go and talk to some people who might be able to do something with my career. Dull I know, but otherwise those lovely people over there are going to get a bit angry. Livery Halls don't come for free, after all.'

'No, I guess not.' I am a little disappointed, and I think it might show.

'But will you be around later? I think Polly said dinner, maybe karaoke?'

'Yes, sure,' I reply, and I watch him return to the centre of the action.

As he departs, Polly appears again, like one of those clocks where the woman pops out as the door closes on the man.

'Ha, cute or what? He's been begging to meet you for months. And he loved you. I knew he would.'

'Polly are you drunk? I can't imagine he's been begging. That's sheer hyperbole.'

'Well maybe not actually begging on his hands and knees. But keen, all the same. I've asked him out to dinner. And karaoke.'

'Yeah he said. Surely he'll have plenty of offers later?'

Polly rolls her eyes, 'Yeah whatever, now come and meet some other people from chambers. Nice frock by the way. Is it new?'

I smile, and nod.

'Ed chose it,' I say. It's an excuse to say his name; as usual Polly is only half-listening so the reference, and its significance, passes her by.

Later, as I watch him signing the books I notice that, from this distance, he seems if anything even more good-looking. Tall, broad with muscular shoulders, his face is all slopes and angles. His mouth is cushiony and almost feminine. His eyes, though, are something else. Edged with a fan of fine lines, his eyes haven't stopped smiling the entire evening. 'Azure,' I think to myself. 'Yes, definitely azure.'

I imagine, just for a moment, kissing that soft mouth, biting the bottom lip. The idea is curiously unexciting. I look harder, longer. I see a very attractive man, clearly interested in me. A writer and a barrister. Honestly, what's wrong with me? Why am I not interested in this extremely interesting man?

There is a voice inside my head answering this question very loudly, very clearly, very forcefully. I decide to ignore it.

By the time we manage to leave the Painters' Hall it is nearly ten; Alex can't really leave before the business of the evening - signing, thanking, schmoozing - is done. Polly, Alex and I are on the pavement with a few others from their chambers. Polly decrees that it is too late for dinner and no-one argues; half an hour later we are installed in a karaoke booth in Soho, knocking back shots, because apparently we are all 'too fucking sober to sing.' Well speak for yourself Polly, because the champagne has certainly lubricated my throat perfectly well. It's a tight squeeze with the six of us in here. I notice with a strange detachment that I keep finding myself next to Alex; he keeps thrusting the microphone between us, leaning against me. Whenever I sit down, he does too. He dances with an easy charm, and takes my hand to get me to join him. It feels pleasant to be flirted with in this unmistakable way, but nothing more.

During a song far too modern for me to be able to join in or even sway convincingly, I scuttle out to find some signal.

To Ed
Children? What children? I am in karaoke bar. I have a tambourine and I am not afraid to use it. If you were here, what duet could we sing? Jx

Immediately - READ, 'Ed is typing....'

Oh that sounds like a leading question.... Erm, I've Had the Time of My Life? (NB is jk about Jennifer Grey. Hmmm better press send. PS. Hope you're drunk enough to find this amusing.)
Hahahaha <drops tambourine in hilarity>
What about a little Disney – I Wanna Be Like You?
OK but only if I get to be Baloo.
Sure, I'll be the monkey. Though you have the facial hair for it.
True true. Any more ideas?
Alright then, Fairy-tale of New York? Anyway I don't mean to nag but shouldn't you be running for your train.

I check the time. SHIT, yes he's right. I had better get a move on. I shove the phone back in my bra, but feel it buzz again almost immediately.

Oh I nearly forgot, my favourite duet of all time: Elton John and Kiki Dee - Don't Go Breaking My Heart.

Those words are still burning and flashing on the inside of my retina when I climb into a cab ten minutes later. Alex is with me, because it's 'on his way' - to Chelsea? Really? He is chatting away and I am nodding and smiling, but I am already half way home in my head. I keep my eyes on the red numbers of the clock ticking away. Please, please hurry. I need to get this train. Please don't let me miss this train.

The cab pulls up outside Paddington and I scramble out in the most dignified way I can in this rather tight dress and wedges. Alex is on the pavement next to me, and as I turn to say goodbye he wraps his arms around me and almost scoops me up. He feels huge and solid, like a wall of flesh; the feeling of being enclosed by someone so broad and tall is unfamiliar and disconcerting.

'Thanks so much for coming Jen. Honestly, it was great to have you here. Even if you didn't know that it was my launch.' He laughs to show he bears no grudge. He pops me down on the pavement again; I feel a little bit Fay Wray.

'Can I call you?'

'Yes, of course. Well goodbye.' In my head I am screaming I NEED TO GET MY TRAIN! but he is a little too drunk and blissful to notice that I am itching to go. I feel like a heel; this is his big night, he is a lovely gorgeous man and I am an ungrateful bitch.

He leans forwards, and downwards, to kiss me; I keep my mouth closed and firm and we kiss on the lips. I pull away, smile broadly, turn and start to run.

I don't stop running until I am on the train; the guard is already blowing the whistle for departure. I slide open my phone to message Ed again, to tell him I am on my way. He messages back immediately.

Good, I will see you about 1.30. I can't wait to hear all about it.

And I can't wait to be home to tell you.

Now you're just saying that to make me feel better about being stuck at home like Cinders while you go to the Ball.

And in this analogy I am, what, an Ugly Sister?

Well if the shoe fits.....

Thanks for that. I hope my fairy godmother appears and turns you into a pumpkin.

God, people are always saying that to me.

I bet.

(My finger hesitates, just a little, but I am a little drunk and a lot over-emotional.)

Actually if it makes you feel better I would have had much more fun stuck at home with you doing the washing up.

Send.

Wait.

Panic.

Buzz.

Well thank you. Actually if it makes *you* feel any better, you were far from the Ugly Sister tonight. You looked beautiful.

I stare at that message for so long that the little black characters start to swarm around like ants. I think I should turn the phone off. I should definitely turn the phone off. This conversation is in dangerous waters and I'm too drunk to negotiate them safely.

Buzz.

This one makes me jump so much that I almost drop the phone. I try to focus on the screen.

Message Chris

Oh, what?? What do you bloody want??

Sorry, I am trying to wait and be patient but I am not doing very well. It would be great to speak to you, or maybe I could come round, perhaps take you out somewhere, if you can get a babysitter.

From the seat behind me, I can smell the greasy stench of fried chicken and chips. I suddenly feel very very sick. God please don't let me be sick on a train. I turn off the phone and then I rest my head on the table in front of me and close my eyes until the spinning feeling passes.

I wake up suddenly, with the motion of the train pulling out of a station. But when I look out of the window, nothing looks familiar. In fact everything looks appallingly unfamiliar. The countryside looks pitch black; we are a long way from the city.

I look around the carriage; the once-full train is now pretty much empty. My stomach lurches in dread. This is not good, not good at all. The ticket collector passes.

'Excuse me, what station did we just stop at.'

'Chippenham.'

CHIPPENHAM? Oh crap.

'So the next station is...?'

'Bath Spa.'

Oh dear. Oh dear oh dear oh dear.

Well at least I'm sober now. Pretty much.

Reluctantly I fish out my phone, press the button and stir it into life.

Oh dear.

Ed missed calls 14
Voicemail 3

Oh dear. I can't face listening to any of those. Better face the music instead. Return call.

'Jen? Jesus, thank God.'

'Ed I'm so sorry. I can't tell you how sorry I am.'

'I have been so bloody worried.'

'I know, I'm so so sorry. I fell asleep.'

'I was thinking about calling the police. It was horrible. I wanted to come and look for you but I'm stuck in the house with the children. I was just about to call Carrie to sit with them while I drove out to look for you.'

Oh dear lord. Close shave there then. That would have caused some comment for sure.

'So where are you now?'

'I'm still on the train. Next stop is Bath.'

'Bloody hell, you really did fall asleep.' He is trying to make light of it, but his voice is still sounding a little shaky and he can't quite manage to hide it. 'I was rehearsing what I would tell the children in the morning. I had got as far as 'Your mother was a reckless drunk...' when you phoned.'

A hit, a palpable hit.

'Will you try and get a hotel? I guess it's too late to get a train back.'

'Too late for a hotel too I think. I'll try and find a taxi to take me home. Although it will bankrupt me.'

'Shall I come and get you? Get Carrie to come round, or put the children in the car?'

'No, that's kind but it's OK. I'll be home quicker this way. Ed.'

'Yeah.'

'I am so sorry.'

'I was bloody worried sick. Jesus. Don't do that again.'

Sheepish, 'I won't, I promise.'

I think about pointing out the ironic role-reversal of this conversation, given our relative ages, but I guess it hasn't escaped his notice. Age, as he never tires of pointing out, is a very very ambiguous concept.

It takes me about ten minutes to persuade a taxi driver to take me back home. He has to go and ask for a price from the controller in the office: £100. Such is the price of my drunken shame, I guess. The driver is very confused about where he is to go; he finds it difficult to get his head around the concept of a place that is 'PAST Swindon? Beyond Swindon?' By the time I finally reach home, the first azure tones of dawn are on the horizon and the birds serenade the return of the prodigal mother.

Ed is still up; he makes me a cup of tea and offers to make breakfast, but I decline. I am shuddering into a well-deserved hangover. I feel I need to make some more profuse apologies.

'I really am very very sorry.'

'Honestly Jen, don't apologise. It was very enlightening to be an anxious parent. Now I know how Mum and Dad felt when I was out all night clubbing.' I manage a snort at this.

Ed hands me my tea and says, 'Chris phoned.'

I look up, 'Really? God he's persistent.' Shut up Jen, you're still a little drunk.

'Yes, he wanted all the details about where you were.'

'What did you tell him?'

'I told him you were at a drug-fuelled orgy. Well I told him you were out with Polly, I think he filled the rest in for himself.'

He stirs his tea. 'He left a message.' He pushes the pad towards me.

Chris called. Can he come round tomorrow? Please call.

I am too tired, too drunk still, too over-emotional to hide what I am feeling. I close my eyes, breathe in and out through my nose.

'Jen.'

I open my eyes and look at Ed. 'Mm?'

'Don't let him get to you. You've come really far.' He reaches across and, very gently, pushes my hair behind my ear. The tenderness of the gesture, the lightness of his touch, makes me shiver.

I nod. 'I know. Look, I really need to get to bed. I must try and get some sleep before the kids wake up.'

'Of course. Take your tea, and I'll get you some water.'

'Will you go home? It's so late.'

'I think I'll try and sleep for a bit on the sofa, I don't want to wake everyone up. And I can look after Rosie for a bit so you can get some more sleep. I will go home in a few hours.'

I try not to think about what might be said, behind closed doors, about this in the Becker household. Best not to dwell on it.

'Just... Try to get some sleep.'

I try, but despite my physical and mental exhaustion, sleep eludes me. In the cold azure light of the early dawn, I replay the events of the evening in my head, and count my stupid mistakes. Almost too many to count.

BEFORE YOU START PAINTING, CHECK THE CORNERS FIRST

Chris and I are sitting, around the kitchen table. The children are with Carrie for the afternoon, because we want to talk. Well, Chris wants to talk. He really wants to talk. I am pretty ambivalent about the idea, but nevertheless, here we are.

The urge to run away is very strong right now. I fantasise about walking out of the door, getting in the car, and driving driving driving, far far away. But I can't. I have to sit here and listen while Chris justifies himself and his weakness, his selfishness.

Why are we talking about this now? I mean, he was living with us for weeks afterwards, and we never talked about it, not really. Months and months have gone by. A divorce petition has been served. Why now?

Well he wants to, he's asked to, is the first reason. So why have I agreed? I don't know, I guess I am ready to. I am feeling OK, strong enough. I guess that means, it's probably too late. I don't say this, but I am thinking it. It probably means, I don't care enough, I'm just not as bothered as I used to be. I don't say this either.

'I just don't know, I just let it run out of control. I mean, we seemed to have a lot in common and she made me laugh.'

MADE HIM LAUGH? Seriously, Romily? Look, really, this is too much. I'm the bloody funny one, OK?

I say, 'Yes.' This is the maximum, the absolute limit, of what I can bring myself to say. I am trying to really listen, really empathise.

'I mean, we had grown apart, don't you think? You are so wrapped up with the children. I just seemed like a spare part.'

Really? Can he hear himself? Hear what an unmitigated pile of crap this sounds? Such a string of clichés. I try and think of something substantial to say.

I say, 'Yes.'

'I had started to forget who I was. And I didn't ever intend for it to happen the way it did. We just talked and I found myself telling her about my life, things I didn't tell you. Things I hadn't told you for years.'

I say, 'Yes.'

I am not sure how much longer I can manage this. Calm. Calm.

'And then there was one PC meeting and I had been having a really difficult time. You know, at work. I didn't feel I could even talk to you about it by then. I was travelling so much and by the time I got home I was so tired. I couldn't find the energy to explain it. But Romily, she seemed to understand, without me needing to explain. And she suggested a drink afterwards.'

'The Red Lion?' He looks startled by my question.

'No, we went to The Dog.'

'Right, so, you got in your cars and you drove past the pub

100 yards away and drove through the countryside for - I don't know - 5 miles and this didn't seem in any way strange? I mean, this didn't ring any alarm bells?' My voice is rising; I don't much like the way I sound, but I can't seem to stop myself.

'Jen, I don't know. I wasn't thinking straight.'

'Oh come off it Chris. You were thinking bloody straight. You knew what you were doing.'

'Jen, I....'

'There's always a moment. Always a moment when you can stop. You just ignored it. You wanted her, and she wanted you and you just ignored your conscience and did it anyway.'

Now he's crying. Jesus. I still don't stop. 'And don't give me that bull about my wife doesn't understand me. You made a choice, to open up to her, and not to me. I was always there.'

(Is this bit true? It feels good to say it. But I don't know, perhaps I was distant, perhaps I was too wrapped up in myself. Polly seems to think so, but she's not the most reliable in these matters. I can't think about that now. I am on a roll, galloping along on my high horse with the wind in my hair. Well, he deserves it. I'm not sorry.)

'Jen, I am just so sorry. I don't know, it seemed so natural.'

'Natural?' God I sound vicious. 'Natural. Like rutting? Like lying? Like cheating? It was just weak, you know, weak and selfish. That's all.'

'Jen it was a mistake.'

A silence enters the room, stealthily, insinuates itself between us. A mistake?

'What kind of mistake? A mistake to do it, or a mistake to get caught?'

The silence slithers, slides. Expectantly, it stretches, taut and tense.

'A mistake to risk everything. To risk losing you and the family, for nothing.'

Nothing, a mistake. God, this is strong stuff. This is new.

'Chris, I'm not sure what you want me to say.'

'I'm sorry Jen, I'm really sorry and I want you to forgive me.'

Ah yes, there we are. Chris's problem, is now my problem. A problem I need to find a solution for. Forgiveness?'

'I know it's a lot to ask.'

I don't say anything. There's nothing I can say. I have nothing to say to this, nothing at all.

'Jen, could you forgive me?'

'I don't know. I don't even know what that means. You've hurt me really really badly.'

'Yes, I know. I know.'

'You really really don't.'

I hate this. I hate feeling so angry, I hate knowing how long it's going to take to shift this feeling when he's gone. I hate the feeling that I am back to square one, back to the miserable hole he left me in. I've come so far, so far and it's taken so long. If I go back now I might not be able to find my way out.

I am trying to conserve my strength now, trying to keep something back for when he's gone, for the 3am waking, for the 5.30 panic attack.

Then he says,

'Would you have me back? Would you at least think about it?'

Well, would I?

Maybe I should make a list, of the pros and cons; a sensible idea, of the sort that the Just Seventeen problem page might suggest.

Or, I don't know, toss a coin?

The idea of putting everything back to normal, sweeping all the accumulated pain and hurt of the last few months onto the floor, under the carpet. Have a normal family life. Well, that would be nice, wouldn't it?

But really, seriously, how would that work? How would I start? How could I face it, every day, knowing that he lied, over and over, and wondering if he was doing it again?

How could I bear it if, every time his phone went, I was wondering who was calling, who was messaging (sexting! Oh God). Could I really pretend it was OK, that I was managing? How could I be sure that I would ever shift that feeling in the pit of my stomach?

That moment when you wake up, and there is a minute, maybe two when everything feels normal. Then somewhere in your brain, a thought starts to form. No, everything isn't normal. Why? And your synapses struggle to grasp the thought, to mould it into a stinking, lousy globule of truth.

Well, recently the normal feeling has been there for longer. I have three, five, maybe even ten minutes' respite in the morning. And when the reality-blow hits, as it always does, it isn't quite so painful, not quite so deep, the feeling inside is not quite so hollow.

It's taken months to get here. Can I really bear to start again?

WHAT ARE FRIENDS FOR?

Poll says. 'Oh God Mare I don't know. Why are you asking me?'

'I don't know really. I guess I wanted to hear your opinion, or something. It seemed a good idea at the time.'

'I've nothing for you Mare. I don't know. Never been married, never had children.'

'No, but. Well.'

Your Mum and Dad split up, is that why you are a total fuck-up Polly? I really want to know.

I say, 'You have experience, I mean.'

'You mean of divorce? Yeah I guess. The thing is, it's hard to compare isn't it? It's not like I have a lovely fluffy childhood to look back on, like a control sample or something.'

'No, but...'

'No I mean it Mare. Listen to me. My childhood was fine, really. I mean the bits I remember, the crappy bits, weren't anything to do with the divorce. My brother shoving my head through a window, shaving my hair off for a laugh - that's the kind of stuff I remember. And I can't blame Mum and Dad for that.'

I am not sure whether I should laugh or say something sympathetic. I keep schtum.

Poll goes on, 'And I guess the question is, can you be happy together? I mean, can you get back together and be a decent Mum? Can you hold it together? If it all goes tits up I mean, or, if it doesn't - well, either way. Can you still promise yourself that you will be able to get up in the morning? Without cracking up? Because I tell you what I do remember, when Dad finally left, we weren't upset, not really. We were relieved. I mean being together, it isn't everything.'

I think this is the longest speech I have ever heard from Polly without some sort of expletive punctuating it. I think I might cry.

She says, 'If you want my honest opinion, then be by yourself for a while. If he still wants you in a year, then you can try again then. Because you can't trust your judgment now. It's too soon. You just want to feel better. This would definitely be a 3am decision. Wait till the morning. That's a metaphor by the way.'

'Yeah thanks, I got that. What with my English degree and all.'

'And, you're forgetting the most obvious reason.'

'Which is? Enlighten me.'

'You just don't want him any more.'

Is that true? I don't know.

Polly's right and it's 3am and I just want a cuddle. (That's another metaphor by the way.) I want everything to be alright.

So I talk to Ruth. I wouldn't say that Ruth and I are close. She's not like Polly, Polly who has known me since university and has held my forehead to stop it banging on the loo seat when I was throwing up. I haven't bailed her out of a police station, or even mopped up her blood with my pyjama bottoms and driven her to A&E.

She's not even like Mel, sweet dippy Mel who tells me everything about her life, but blinks a little rapidly if I start to disclose anything personal like she has forgotten I am an actual person. I don't take offence at this; Mel doesn't mean anything by it. She is just wrapped up in her own world, and she's so used to having everyone take care of her that she doesn't really comprehend that other people might need taking care of occasionally. She's never really grown up.

Ruth leads a deliberately straightforward, simple life. She doesn't get involved, keeps it all in check. Of course she's a doctor, so she has plenty to deal with at work, maybe she needs to keep everything else simple.

We share our lives on the surface, look after each other's children and drink a lot of tea in each other's kitchens. But I don't know what's going on inside her head, because she doesn't want to share it. But I want to talk to her about this. I trust her judgment, and I trust her to be straight with me. Carrie can't get her head around the ambiguities; she wants a black and white answer. Ruth knows a bit more about how the world works, really. She sees real life, one casualty at a time, through her GP surgery door.

When I have finished telling her how I feel, Ruth says something I find startling.

'Do you remember your wedding vows?'

The truth is, no. I don't remember them. We wrote them together, Chris and I, in the tiny living room of our first house, barely wide enough for our hand-me-down sofa. We sat on that vile orange sofa, the sofa where we first got off with each other, then, six months later, where Chris got down on one knee, emboldened by too much wine and asked me to marry him. We talked through each vow, taking care to consider each and every word.

And now I can't remember a single word of them.

'No, I don't. I really don't.'

'I'm not saying that's significant or anything. I'm just saying, what did you think you were promising? I mean, thick and thin? Forever, whatever? Or was there a get-out clause? Are there limits, and has he gone over them?'

She stops talking, lets me process the words and the meaning. Then she adds, 'And what did you expect from him? Maybe that might help. Just to get your head around it.'

'I guess... do you mind if I just talk this through?

'No, of course. Please, go on.'

'I promised to stay with him, if our circumstances changed. We talked about, if he was paralysed in an accident or something.' I pull an embarrassed face at this memory, reflecting on the overdramatic tendencies of the newly in-love, and the characteristic blindness to the mundane. 'But I can't say I thought about what would happen if he was unfaithful. We definitely didn't talk about it. Does anyone? I don't know. It would have been weird to talk about it. It still feels weird.'

I think some more, harder this time. This is what's good about Ruth: she just lets me think, and I need to think.

'I guess I would have said, if you had asked me, that being unfaithful was not necessarily the end. That it didn't necessarily mean anything significant. That it wasn't necessarily a sign that it was over. Maybe? But, and God I can't believe I am saying this out loud, I guess I was thinking about me, and not him.'

Ruth smiles, 'Yes, that might have been easier to take.'

'So I think I would have said that, yes, it's possible to forgive. That you shouldn't, that I wouldn't throw something away for the sake of, I don't know, wounded pride?' I stop for a minute, to contemplate this admission, this remembrance of ridiculous naïveté. 'I mean I wasn't wrong, but listen to me! Listen to me, who knew so little. Pride, like it's just a little something to get over, something self-indulgent.'

'Jen, you know this happened to me, don't you?' Her tone

is so quiet, so unassuming, so calm that I don't really catch her meaning for a few seconds.

'Last year, Tom had an affair. I mean, he was seeing someone. It lasted a few months and then it ended.'

'God Ruth I had no idea. Jesus, I am so sorry. I mean sorry it happened and sorry I didn't even notice. And sorry for making you listen to my endless droning on about my troubles. How insensitive.'

'No, don't take it like that. That's not what I mean. You've nothing to be sorry for, really. I didn't tell you because I didn't want anyone to know. I thought you might have guessed, and that's why you wanted to talk to me.' I shake my head, no. 'It was a bad time, but we got through it. And yes, you're right, it needn't be the end. It was a mistake. And if you love someone enough, you can love them enough to overlook their mistakes. Even massive ones, that hurt you.'

I am trying to gauge if I should stroke her hand, maybe try a hug, but Ruth's body language suggests not.

'Sorry, Jen. I know this isn't about me. But I did it, you know, I'm still doing it. Forgiving, forgetting. It's taking it out of me. I feel - shattered.' Ruth, strong and solid, passes a hand across her hair, a gesture touching in its minimalism, resonant with meaning and emotion. 'I see it all the time, women come to see me. They make the choice to stay, to try again. I can see it's a mistake. But they do it, we do it. I like to think it's for love. Love, and duty maybe. But... I don't know.' The hand again, across the hair, as if trying to soothe her troubles, calm her thoughts. 'Maybe it's because we're scared.'

I feel I should say something, but my head is too empty and my heart is too full.

'And you know, I have absorbed it all. Moved on. But, what's it cost me? Really? I mean, you're my closest friend.' I open my mouth, and shut it again. 'My closest friend, and you don't know what's going on. I think I might have numbed myself, permanently. You can stop yourself feeling the pain, but then can you feel anything? Ever again?'

She looks at the floor for a while, and I think of something to say. Nothing.

Eventually, she looks up. 'Think about it Jen. Think about what it will cost you, and if you're prepared to pay that price.'

And that's it - the end of the list of people I can talk to about this. I can't risk speaking to Mel; she'll only freak out. And Carrie – well, let's not even begin the list of reasons why I can't talk to Carrie about it.

But of course it's not the end of the list. Not really. There is one person who I can't talk to; there is one person I can't talk about, either. The one person who really knows me, knows what the last year has been like for me, because he's been there throughout it all. Taking care of me the best he can. I can't ask him about whether I should go back to Chris, although in fairness I don't need to ask, because I already know what he would say, what he thinks.

So all these conversations about what I should do next, about what's in my heart, it's all doomed to failure. Because to no-one, to no-one at all, not even myself, I am telling anything close to the truth. I am keeping the truth all wrapped up tight, deep inside my heart.

MOVING ON, MOVING UP

So I tell Chris - yes, I can forgive but no, I can't give it another go.

What reasons do I give him? What version of the truth do I offer? In the end, I go for this version: that I haven't got the strength to face trying again, in case we break up again and I have to go back to the start. This is pretty convincing, and it's not untrue.

It's not the whole truth, though.

I don't say, 'If we were to start again, I would have to leave the village, because I couldn't face seeing everyone, including your lover, every day. And that's what I really don't have the strength for: looking for a new house, moving the children to a new school, finding new friends. No, that's too much to ask.' I don't say this, although this is the absolute (although not the whole) truth, because I think it says a great deal about the state of my love for my husband. If I loved him, still, with all my heart, then I could face all this. I would do it, if it was worth it. But it's not worth it. I don't want to say this, because even though he has hurt me, deeply, painfully, I don't want to return that particular favour.

I also don't say, 'I don't want to try again, because I can't trust you not to do it again.' Because, actually, that's not true. Because I've given that one some thought and I think I could trust him not to do it again. I think Chris has learned his lesson; he got himself stuck in a situation that he didn't really want, that he didn't think through. I honestly don't think he would be stupid enough to do it again. He's not a natural risk taker, not a player; he's naturally faithful. I think if he found himself at the top of one of those steep paths again, he would walk right past. This would be a lovely, neat, tidy excuse, but I can't bring myself to use it.

Then there's that bigger truth that I don't say; I come at it obliquely sometimes, but I can't approach it head-on, so I can't be sure what it really looks like. It's too big, and too dangerous. This is the massive boulder in the path of any reconciliation: I've moved. I am not sure whether I've moved on, and I definitely haven't moved up, but, for sure, I'm not in the same place that I was a year ago. Really Chris, you can't just leave me here and expect me to be where you left me. I am not a parking space, reserved with your name on it. If you leave my heart broken, expect it to be mended. I dragged it around for months, like a dead polar bear on a sledge, but I haven't seen him for weeks and I don't ever want to see him again, not ever.

Chris, you're too late, my darling, you're way way too late. I don't say any of this, but he knows it. I don't want him to suffer, even as I have suffered. I still love him, but the time has passed and all the wishing in the world won't get it back.

LETTIE IS NOT A FOUR LETTER WORD

Ed says, 'I have a favour to ask.'

'Sure, of course. What is it?'

But I'm distracted by sorting out the washing, and I haven't clocked the significance of Ed's request.

'Can you come and sit down? Please?'

'Hold on, give me a minute.' I still haven't really picked up that what he means is 'COME AND SIT DOWN NOW!'; in my defence, there really is a terrific amount of washing to distract me. Where does it all come from? There are only three people in the house, can I justify employing a laundry maid, or even sending the washing out like they do in books?

'Jen, will you please come and sit down.' Suddenly, I'm concentrating; my eyes snap up from the socks-and-pants chaos. Ed is sitting at the table; he is biting the side of his thumb and looking at me in a way that can only be described as pleading. He looks, from here, young and vulnerable and startlingly beautiful. I know his face so well, and the sight of him sitting in that seat is usually so comforting, but in this minute I am not comforted. I think about putting my hand against his forehead to smooth away the frown creasing there; I start to think about taking his hand away from his mouth and holding it. And then, just for a moment, I imagine lifting his hand to my own mouth, and putting his thumb between my lips and tasting what is left of him on there.

Jesus, no. I must under no circumstances let that thought in, or out, ever again. I must get a grip.

'Sorry,' I say. 'Just give me one second.' I shove the washing hurriedly back into the washing basket; sod it, that can wait till later. I can get the children to sort it out. Ha ha ha.

'Shall I make a cup of tea?' I ask, wondering if hearing about this favour might require me to drink some tea, to calm my nerves. Because my nerves are jangling. His tone, his expression, they are making me anxious. His tone, in fact, is making me think of one of those scenes in films where the boyfriend says, 'We need to talk.' And then he dumps her.

(Does that happen in real life? I don't know. It's never happened to me, but then again I have, until this year, led a fairly uncomplicated romantic life. Obviously I am making up for it now, big time.)

I wonder about making a joke about this - 'Am I dumped?' - but Ed's expression suggests that this is not the appropriate time for my particular brand of crass humour to avoid dealing with difficult emotions.

(Is it ever the appropriate time? Answers on a postcard please.)

'I'll put the kettle on,' he says. 'Will you please just sit down?'

I sit down. I watch him as he fills the kettle and begins the tea-making ritual. Like my own surfer-geisha. Stop, Jen, stop. Control yourself.

Rosie comes into the kitchen; she is just about to ask for a snack, but Ed pre-empts her with an outstretched hand before she has even opened her mouth. 'Don't even ask Rosie, it's nearly tea-time. You can have something afterwards.' And she leaves again, without a murmur.

On another occasion I might find this vignette amusing. But right now it seems unbearably poignant. Just one push and I might cry. (I have been feeling close to tears pretty much all the time, for about the last week. On Tuesday I had to pull the car over because something I heard on the news made me weep so hard that I couldn't see. I know it's just a matter of time before Ed is out of here. We are on the countdown, like a bloody missile launch, but I have no idea what number we've reached.)

Watching Ed from here, like an outside observer, I am freshly struck by the ambiguities of his appearance, and his presence. He looks, and is dressed, like a teenager. Blue and yellow checked shorts, a garish yellow t shirt, bare feet; the hair is long, tousled, gelled in that artfully casual way that typifies the young man feeling a little too self-conscious about his appearance and spending a little too much time in front of the mirror fretting about it. If anything, he looks younger than 18 from here. He reminds me of Becker; a skinny, dark Becker. But he isn't Becker, far from it.

And contrasting with this outward appearance of youthful vulnerability is the sense of poise, control and calm powerfulness. He belongs in this kitchen, not as a guest, not as a child I am looking after, but a man who is helping to look after this family, the centre of our family's gravity, keeping us all balanced. Well, looking after the tea in any event, and controlling the snacks – but we all know that tea and snacks are what fuels and soothes this family.

Considering this contrast gives me a rushing sensation, a feeling of danger. Danger for whom? Ed is so much part of my family that the thought of him leaving it is almost too much to bear. If he goes, what will happen to us? Will we fall over, all of us scattered across the pavement like a market stall in a car chase? What will happen to Ed? What will happen to his sense of purpose? Will he able to go back to being what he looks like from here? A child. A serious child with a lively taste in surfing clothes.

If he goes? When he goes. 3,2,1...

He brings the tea and places a mug in front of me.

'Will you come for Sunday lunch,' he says with immense gravity. I laugh, the comic appeal of this juxtaposition of words and tone too much to resist.

'God no, that's far too much to ask. You must be joking.' But he's not smiling.

'This Sunday, at Auntie Ruby's. Bring the children,' he adds, sensing that I am trying to remember if this is an on or off week. 'All of us. All of you.'

'OK, sure. That would be great.'

He smiles, but the smile gets nowhere near his eyes.

'Well I doubt that. Dad will be there. And Lettie.'

Lettie? Really? Almost a taboo word, very rarely spoken.

I say, 'That would be lovely. I can't wait to meet them.'

His elbow resting on the table, he pushes one hand in his hair, the other against his face. The thumb is in the mouth again, his teeth biting down hard on it. I can see it's going white from here.

His tone is agitated. 'Oh, you can be sure it won't be lovely. The best we can hope for is that we survive it without anyone needing an ambulance.' He laughs, with that bitter tone that makes me wince when I hear it. No-one this young should be that bitter.

'I didn't know Lettie was over. How long is she over for?'

'She's here for a wedding. Arrives tomorrow, then she's going down to see Becker. The wedding's on Saturday, then Ruby's persuaded her to stay for Sunday. She goes back on Monday.'

Right, OK. Shall I ask the obvious question? Yes, I think I will.

'Is she going to see your mother?'

'No, I don't think she is.' His voice is tight with emotion, so tight in fact that I can't distinguish what emotions are there in his tone. 'She says she won't have time.'

We let that sentence sit on the table between us for a good long while. It's there for so long I think about offering it a seat, making it a cup of tea. It's hard to know what to say next. I wait, to see if he wants to vent anything, but he says, 'Do you mind, about Sunday? I know I am not selling it to you.'

'Of course. Did Ruby suggest it?'

He nods, 'She said would I like to invite you. She thought it would be a good opportunity for Dad and Lettie to meet you, to say thank you for everything you have done this past year.' He laughs, 'She's a nice woman, Auntie Ruby. Clueless, but a nice woman. She doesn't really appreciate what a totally fucked up family she's married into, even after all these years. I guess that's one of the reasons why Uncle Jim married her. Anyone else would have run away screaming, long ago. But she is very good at pretending that we are a normal family. She even convinces me sometimes.' The thumb is back in the mouth again, chewing on the nail. 'It's not just Ruby though. I'd like you there. And Rosie and Michael. I'm dreading it.'

'Is Becker coming?'

'God I wish he was. No, he can't leave the school. This is a busy time, and he has a hen party or a 40th or something this weekend. Would it make a difference if Becker was coming?' A little edge to his voice.

'No, no I was just curious. You know I'll be there, of course. What time? Shall I bring something?'

And we talk about the practicalities. And I wish I could ask him the real questions - What do you think is going to happen? What can I expect? Why is your sister travelling thousands of miles for a wedding and won't even take a short detour to see her own mother, who she hasn't seen for over a year? And what about your Dad, Ed? How's he going to be? What exactly are you dreading? I can speculate about all of these questions, and have a pretty good stab at them, but I hold back. Ed doesn't want to talk about it. Asking him would only upset him, more than he is upset already, and I won't do that. Ed is always so careful of my moods, so responsive to what I need, that I have to try to match his sensitivity. It's not always easy.

He's getting up now, stacking the dishwasher, getting the tea things ready. The conversation is closed. What he wants is for me just to be there, take it as it comes. And that's what I have to try to do.

What do I want? What I want is to hold him, protect him, to snarl in a tigerish fashion at anyone who comes near him, anyone who threatens to hurt him. What I want is for Sunday to come right now, and for Sunday to never come.

SUNDAY BLOODY SUNDAY

My waking thought on Sunday is: oh please let someone be ill. One of the children, perhaps, or me. Or, ideally, Lettie. Ha. No, I can hear the children arguing downstairs; they sound in the peak of health. Slightly too well, if anything.

I message Ed:
There's no chance that you all have food poisoning or anything? <hopeful>
Ha, no. I am looking forward to it too EBxx

No, there's no escape. And, first job of the day, wardrobe decision, and never more agonising has it seemed. I flick through the hangers in a desultory fashion. OK, so what's my role today? Christ, ambiguous doesn't even begin to cover it. I choose some jeans and a white top - I am going for Extra Normal - and some white plimsolls. I choose a swimsuit too, although the choice is pretty limited there, in case I can't avoid getting in the pool.

Rosie is jumping around with excitement about the prospect of this 'pool party', and even Michael has already put his swimming bag by the front door. They have been frequent visitors to the Becker's house all year; Ruby is a very kind person and has always made them hugely welcome, exclaiming that 'it's good to have the pool in use, otherwise it just sits there!' I bet it doesn't; I bet Ruby is out there doing twenty lengths before breakfast, all year round, but it's a nice thing to say and makes me feel less guilty that my children spend so much time at her house.

As we enter the front garden, I can hear Ruby's voice, and Ed's low rumble underneath, from behind the fence. I decide not to knock on the front door but shout a cheery, forced 'Hullo!' to warn of my approach, and open the side gate. The children pile past me; they are at home here, and they make straight for Ed, Rosie grabbing his hands excitedly and pouring out her news, describing her new swimsuit and what she did at school and does he know her friend Millie? Well she has a new hamster called Roxy. And Ruby's delighted to see them too, laughing indulgently and bringing them drinks, but apart from that - in the words of Jarvis Cocker - I can't see anyone else smiling in here.

Ruby comes over to take my food contribution, offering me a drink, saying how well I look. 'Let me introduce you, everyone's dying to meet you.' God bless you Ruby, I can see from here they aren't. If only the world was full of people like Ruby. If only I was more like Ruby.

Jim is dispatched inside to fetch me a cup of tea - I've declined the offered booze for now, I need to keep my wits about me - and Ruby walks me over to meet Dave Becker and Lettie. They are on adjoining sun loungers, with the Sunday papers spread between them. Although Ruby is heralding our approach with plenty of loud preamble, Lettie doesn't choose to look up until we are standing right by her, intending to signal her indifference to me loud and clear. Not very convincing, love, I think. Such a deliberate choice gives you away. Dave's indifference, though, isn't faked at all, that's easy to tell. He looks up, briefly, before returning to the sports pages; I don't even register with him. I am of no significance at all.

Lettie's studied nonchalance tells me that she feels the opposite. I am, it seems, particularly significant. With a surreptitious glance to make sure that Ed's looking, she gives me her beautifully-judged cold shoulder.

'Hey,' she says.

Honestly, love, who do you think you're dealing with? Do you think that's going to intimidate me? Try harder. Bring. It. On.

'Oh no don't get up, you look very comfortable there. How lovely to meet you both, Ed has told me such a lot about you. I feel I know you already. I am sure Ruby will make sure I am next to you at lunch, so we can have a proper chat.' I turn to Ruby, whose smile doesn't falter. 'Can I help you with lunch?'

From the kitchen window I have a good view of the pair of them, skulking by the pool. Jim looks just like Becker, even more so from this distance, but balding and running a little to fat. (Watch out Becker, this is what happens when your metabolism catches up with your taste for chips and beer.) He is deeply tanned and the blonde hair faded to ash. Still very good looking though, but with a heavy sense of edgy tension about him, like an often-kicked dog just about to bite back.

In contrast, Lettie is like one of those sleek black cats, entirely certain of their own beauty. Her features are almost too perfect, her neat face framed by short black hair, cut at a length and in the gamine-style that only the stunningly-beautiful can get away with. She's tiny, too, the kind of frame that makes me feel enormous and lumpen in comparison. Dressed in a skimpy black bikini, stark against her alabaster skin, she has artfully arranged herself on the sun lounger; something in her pose reminds me of Olympia in its self-consciousness, though for whose benefit I'm not sure, as she's a blood relation of every male here except Michael. I expect she is so used to the male gaze that she can't imagine that it isn't focused on her. But all this ravishing beauty, and still she isn't attractive; there is something about her face, and in particular her eyes, of the spoilt, mean child.

It's possible that opinion may not be entirely unbiased, but even Michael is indifferent to her, and he's normally a connoisseur of the adult female: terrifically keen on Polly, and even a little tongue-tied around Mel and Ruth.

Ed, Ruby and I potter around the Becker's enormous kitchen; Ed and I are setting the huge farmhouse table ready for lunch, while Ruby finishes the final preparations. Ruby is a fine and generous cook, and I am slightly embarrassed at my slightly feeble offering of a potato salad next to the groaning bounty of the buffet table. ('Couldn't quite face a Sunday roast, darling, sorry,' she grimaces in apology, though why she thinks I might have been expecting meat and two veg, or might be disappointed, I'm not sure. I am, as always, ludicrously grateful when anyone cooks for me, or even makes me a sandwich.)

Ed is not exactly in chatty mood; his face is grimly set, and he is concentrating hard on the very serious business of getting cutlery in the right place at the right time. Ruby, boundlessly cheerful, is singing along, but not quite in tune, to the radio. As she attempts to match the pure voice of Karen Carpenter - with mixed results - I use the moment to see if I can open up a little chink in Ed's armour.

'How has it been, I mean with Lettie and, everything,' I say, sotto voce.

He looks at me quickly, then down again. 'Don't ask. Worse than I imagined, and that's saying something. Luckily she was out all day yesterday at this wedding and came home, late and drunk. Woke the whole house up when she got back. Then she slept in late, and since she got up she's been moping around feeling sorry for herself and moaning about her hangover. Pretty much vintage Lettie. Not changed at all.' He pauses to concentrate on a particularly complex napkin fold. 'I can't bear how rude she is to Ruby. She's such a child,' this last part almost a snarl.

'I'm sure Ruby doesn't mind.' I am trying to be reassuring; what I mean is, I am sure Ruby doesn't notice.

'I mind.'

'And what about your Dad?'

'Well, you saw what he's like. Half asleep, basically. I am not sure, well, how long he's going to last.' This remark is a little too cryptic for me, but I understand the basic idea.

'And you, how are you?'

'Oh I'm chipper, just chipper thanks for asking.' He hesitates, 'I know everyone has a lot on their mind and everything, but you'd think at least one of them would have remembered I'm right in the middle of my bloody exams. I mean it's a bit of a big deal, you'd think. Apparently not.' He laughs, 'Listen to me, now I sound like a child.'

'I quite like it when you act like a stroppy teenager. I feel like sending you to your room.'

'Oh yeah,' Ed challenges, laughing. 'I'd like to see you try. And anyway, what would you do with me when you got me there? There!' He balances the final napkin swan on the plate, 'I'll just go and check the kids haven't drowned or anything. You can guarantee Lettie and Dad wouldn't notice.' And he goes out of the kitchen door, leaving me to wonder exactly what he meant by that particularly ambiguous remark, and whether he noticed how much I am blushing.

I am rather regretting my bravado by the time I sit down for lunch, as I am seated between Lettie and Dave Becker. Ed is up the other end of the table; Ruby has him by her side, lucky cow. Rosie and Michael are between us, acting like a buffer zone. Ruby and I are sharing the role of making cheerful conversation; we are managing it quite happily between us, with Rosie's support as apprentice. (She's a natural.) The Becker males are talking about sport, even Ed, although his role in that conversation is as side-kick rather than apprentice. I am suddenly very hungry - tension always makes me ravenous - and I am piling my plate with lamb couscous and roasted vegetables enthusiastically. With any luck, I think, the children won't need anything but a snack. That would be marvellous, the perfect end to a Sunday: cheese on toast for dinner.

Lettie eats little, says little, drinks steadily. The first course is cleared by me and Ed and Ruby and a number of lavish puddings appear. I work my way through a helping of the meringuey one I remember from the Boxing Day Bash.

'So, Jenny, I hear your husband left you for another woman.'

Really not necessary to speak at that volume Lettie, I'm sitting right next to you.

Even Ruby baulks at this as a potential conversation opener; I can see her hand, poised over the cream jug, pause and shake a little. I catch her eye and smile, reassuringly. I think, you're right Ed, of course. You should mind about Ruby, and so should I. She doesn't deserve this. She's taken in Ed for the year, and I am willing to bet that no-one has offered her a penny in recompense or a word of thanks apart from Ed. And now she has to put up with this unpleasantness around the table she has worked so hard to fill with delicious food. My mother would say this girl needs a slap. I hate to say it, but I think I agree with my mother.

'Yes, that's right. We are separated.'

'How did that happen? I mean, why?'

Ed starts to say something, but I give him a look, and shake my head. No, I'll deal with this. Don't worry.

'Well, these things just happen sometimes. Unfortunately, it's just part of life, isn't it? People fall in and out of love, and times move on. We all just have to deal with life as it is. You can get used to it.' I keep my concentration on my dish. (I am actually vain enough to want to add: actually my husband wants me back, so stick that sunshine.)

'But surely you can pin something down. These things always happen for a reason. I mean, did you put on weight when you had kids? It happens a lot, I hear. Or was he just looking for someone younger?'

'Lettie,' Ed warns.

'No, it's fine. It's an interesting question. I have given it some thought of course. It's definitely not the last one, as my husband left me for someone ten years older. And no I'm not any fatter than I was when I met him. So no, neither of those theories work.' I turn and look at her, proud of my control. I give her a tight smile.

She looks away first, back to her plate, although it's empty. 'Some people do like to form relationships with people who are much younger. People with low opinions of themselves, poor self-esteem. People who need to feel better about themselves and can't face a relationship with someone their own age. Or so I understand.'

OK that's too far. I need to get the children out of

hearing.

'Kids, how do you fancy going back outside? Ed, do you think you would mind taking the children?'

'Christ, do you never look after those children yourself? I don't know why some women have children.'

I say, 'Ruby, that was really delicious. Thank you.' I turn to Lettie, 'Are you finished eating? Would you come outside with me?' I look at her levelly. 'I think we need to talk but I don't really think this is the place.'

'Well I am happy for everyone to hear, but OK if you insist.' She discards her napkin onto her virtually clean plate, picks up her wine glass and follows me outside. I am trying not to catch anyone's eye, but I can sense Ed's rigid tension as we pass him.

We move round the side of the house, to the same patio table where I sat with Ed at the Boxing Day Bash. I pull out a seat for her with the familiar scrape and nod for her to sit down with what I hope is a dominating and mildly intimidating gesture. I am remarkably calm; actually I am not bad at confrontation. I avoid it, if at all possible, but when the time comes it doesn't scare me. Years of practice of dealing with my mother have given me a reasonably good immunity to high drama and attention-seeking behaviour.

'You obviously have something on your mind Lettie, why don't you get it off your chest. I am happy to hear it.' I set my face to 'neutral' and my voice to 'reasonable, with extra calm'. I have a little twinge of sympathy for Ed; God knows I'd rather be here taking part in this conversation than around the corner imagining it.

But she needs to get this out, and I need to have to deal with it. No point getting all het up about this now, Ed. This is what you brought me here for, to get her to butt out. You had just better let me get on with it, get it over with, although I have a feeling it's going to take it out of me.

'No, I've nothing to say. No, I'm fine.' Flustered. Excellent. I feel the superiority of my self-control and I am glad. I hold the silence. If she gets up, if she bottles it and leaves, well that wouldn't be perfect but it would be OK.

She cracks first, 'But I can't say I am happy that you are taking advantage of my brother. I just don't think it's right.' Her tone is aggressive but she is shifting in her seat, uncomfortable.

'Taking advantage?' My tone is calm and I keep the volume knob turned right down. 'Is that what Ed said? That he thinks I am taking advantage?'

'Yes.'

Oh you really are a liar, Ms Becker. I am going to give you a minute to see if you are really going to go with that one.

'Well no, not in so many words. That's obvious though. He doesn't want to spend time with you.'

'Is that what he said?'

'He doesn't need to say it! He's bored with you, but he's too polite to say so.'

OK, so far, so easy to absorb. I am pretty certain that's all lies.

'It's obvious. And I know why you keep him to yourself. You're just lonely, that's really obvious.'

Hmm, less easy to take. Tiny bit of truth here.

'The whole village is laughing at you. You're just pathetic.'

Yes, that's quite possibly true. Absorb, absorb, deal with this later.

'I just wish you'd leave him alone.' She pauses.

I say, 'Is that it? Are you done?'

'For now, yes. I'm sorry but I am just protective about him. He's my baby brother. I hate to see him taken advantage of. You just treat him like an unpaid babysitter. And he feels sorry for you and can't say no. He's not a replacement husband for you, you know.'

God that's is going to take a lot of absorbing. I feel, momentarily, a bit fearful of how hard it's going to be to process this. Suck it up, for Ed's sake. Christ, Ed. I feel a momentary wave of anger that he has left me to face this. I know he thinks I'm strong but this is tough, and getting tougher by the minute.

'That's what everyone thinks but no-one dares to say it, in case it upsets you.'

'OK. Well first of all, I know he's your brother but believe me I have only his best interests at heart.'

Lettie says, 'What do you know about his best interests! You barely know him.'

Oh well this is safer territory.

'I know him very well, actually. We spend a lot of time together. And he comes of his own free will.'

'That's what you want to believe. You can convince yourself of anything if you want to. We are his family and you can't ever replace that.'

'If that's what you're worried about, then you can stop worrying. I don't want to. I really wouldn't want to.'

'God, I'm not worried. Why do you think I'm worried? I'm not.'

Lettie is really agitated now. I am not sure if it's the drink but she is sweating and shaking. I start to wonder also if there might be something else in her system, something that is affecting her judgment. Ed has never indicated that he thinks she takes drugs, but he might not know or, more likely, might not want to talk about it. Another taboo subject, especially given his mother's history.

I think of Ed, and their mother, and I try to reach out a little to this girl. She may be brittle and aggressive, but what has she seen? What kind of damage is she hiding under this spiky exterior? Ed, Becker, Lettie, Dan, Liberty. Christ, what a mess.

'Well you are obviously worried. I don't blame you. It must have been hard to be so far away for the last year. To be so many miles away, not knowing what's going on with Ed or anyone. Not being able to give him your help and support. I can see that's been on your mind. Of course it has. Maybe you've even felt a bit guilty. But I give you my absolute reassurance that I have not, and will not, taken advantage of Ed. I promise you that spending time with my family has helped him. I know this because I have been here, with him, all these months. And you, with the best will in the world, haven't.'

Lettie has run out of steam. I am not sure if she is listening, but she has lost the will to fight. There is a long pause, during which I can hear her trying to control her breath, even over the noise of laughter from the pool. Eventually, she says.

'I know I haven't been here, but I do love him. I do. You know?'

'Yes, I know.'

Do I? No, I've no idea if she loves him. It helps her to say it, to justify her guilty outburst, to give it a more legitimate intention. What the hell does it even mean, to love someone? The idea becomes harder and harder to pin down. Chris said he loved me, says he still does. Look where that got us. And between me and Ed, what's that called? That thing where you like each other, take care of each other, look out for each other, put the other person first, day in day out, even when it's hard. Especially when it's hard. Remind me what that's called again?

She is struggling to control her emotions now; it's not hard to see why she's been keeping out of the way for the past months. Good job you stayed in South Africa, because you couldn't have hacked it here anyway. He may be your baby brother, but the idea you could have supported him these last months - well, that's just sentimentality. You don't have it in you to support anyone; I can see from here, you're shattered. It takes one to know one, and you're a major fuck-up.

Now, she's crying. Quietly but insistently. I am not deluded enough to think that she's sorry, that any apology will be forthcoming, but I offer to hold her, to comfort her. She accepts, wordlessly, and I hold her while her body is racked with sobs. She has a smell of neglect about her, of unwashed hair and stale cigarette smoke; her body feels tiny and fragile, like a child's. I hold her for a long time, thinking about everything she said, trying hard to sort her accusations into those that have an element of truth, and those I can dismiss. All my anger is gone, and I am just holding a tired, damaged child. Eventually, she stops; I hand her a tissue and we go back into the garden.

Later, when the children are exhausted and the kitchen is tidy again, I say my goodbyes and thank yous. Lettie is back on the sun-lounger, puffy eyes behind her sunglasses. When Ed offers to walk me home, she snipes, 'God it really isn't that far. I'm sure she can manage,' without looking up from her magazine. Dave doesn't say goodbye either; he's upstairs, I think. He has not said one word to me all afternoon. The warmth of my hug with Ruby is entirely genuine; I admire the woman more and more, and hope that we will still be friends when Ed goes.

When Ed goes.

3,2,1...

I need to keep that thought out of my mind, because otherwise it's going to make me crazy. I think I'm starting to lose the plot already.

As the door closes behind us, we let the children run on ahead, with shouted warnings to watch the road. Once they are out of earshot, he covers his face with his hands.

'I can't tell you how sorry I am, really. If I had any idea it would be that bad, I wouldn't have put you through it. Or the kids. She was so completely out of order.'

I manage a laugh, 'Yes, it was pretty bad. I didn't know if that was par for the course.'

'Well I thought she might be a bitch. She's frequently a bitch. Being a bitch is her thing. Her USP.'

'She's a natural. See, now I'm a bitch too.'

He laughs, 'Oh come on, you're an amateur compared to her. You can't even aspire to her levels of bitchiness.'

'True, she is the undisputed queen of the bitches. I am in

awe at her bitchhood.'

'She's always been like that. Mum let her, encouraged her, even. Made out like she was some sort of free spirit.'

'You know, it would have been nice to have a little bit of a heads up, about the Queen Bitch thing? Just for the record? Forewarned and all that.'

He smiles, apologetically. 'Yes. I was thinking that too. Sorry.'

We turn the corner into the drive, and walk into the back garden. I send the children up to get ready for bed. When I return, Ed is settled at the patio table.

'I'm going to hide here for a bit. Do you mind?'

I hesitate, thinking about what Lettie might say, what she might think, if he lingers here. Then I think, fuck it. What do I care? The boy wants to stay, let him stay. The fact that this coincides with what I want, well, that's irrelevant. More or less. The boy will be gone soon enough. Let him stay.

'So, can I ask you what she said?'

'Oh I bet you can guess, if you think about it.'

'Just tell me. Please.'

Don't make me Ed, don't make me.

'I'd rather not repeat it. It was hard enough to hear it once. And you will only get angry with her, which won't be helpful. And you'll end up trying to reassure me, which I don't want.'

He isn't happy with this response, I can tell. I can hear Michael and Rosie chasing each other, shrieking with laughter. Still, Ed's silence persists, insists.

'Alright, I'll give you the gist. She thinks you are bored in my company, that I keep you here although you don't want to be and that you are too polite to say no. That I take advantage of you as a free babysitter and because I need someone to replace Chris, and because I am lonely.'

Not any easier to hear second time around, from out of my own mouth.

'You're right,' he says, 'I want to reassure you. Can I?'

'No you can't. Definitely not. I don't want to put that on

you.'

'It isn't a burden to reassure you. Don't think that.'

The church bells start to ring for the evening service. A reassuring sound, that the rituals and routines of village life continue around us, ignorant of the crises and high emotions and low, low points.

'Some of that is true, though isn't it?' I am not sure I want to start this, and I definitely don't want to finish it. I can't even blame alcohol; I have been steering clear all afternoon. I think the adrenaline rush from the confrontation with Lettie has left me feeling a little weak, vulnerable. And Ed wants to talk, and that rarely happens. For whatever reason, or reasons, I carry on.

'I am lonely. Or I would be, if you weren't here.'

'And I would be too, you know that. But that's true for everyone. We're all just one friend away from loneliness.'

I say, 'Lots of people would look at us and say the same thing as Lettie did. We might even say the same things, looking from the outside. I am not saying that means we should pay attention to what other people think. I am saying the opposite.'

Ed says, 'I know. It's easy to say - I don't care what people think. But sometimes they might have a better perspective than you.'

'Yes, although I am not sure that applies to your sister. I don't trust her judgment. She is biased by her own guilt, that she hasn't been here. I told her that.'

Ed looks startled, impressed, 'Did you? How did she take that?'

'I don't know. I was kind of subtle about it. Ish.' I laugh, 'I am not sure if she got it, to be honest.'

'Self-awareness isn't her strong point.'

'No we've established her strong point is being a bitch. She's a one trick pony. She can't do self-awareness AND bitchiness.'

'Exactly,' says Ed, 'she should stick to what she's good at.'

Ed puts his feet on a chair, stretches out his legs. He is almost glowing in this half-light, his white t-shirt reflecting the last of the sun. He says, 'So. I've lost track - are you taking advantage of me or not?'

I say, 'The short answer to that is, yes. And no. And, also, you should be so lucky.'

And the tension of the impossibly difficult day is released, and we laugh and then the children come to find us, and we are pulled into the comfort of the bedtime routine and then I test him on his French poetry paper and normality, for now, is restored.

IT'S COMPLICATED

One of the things I like - liked - about being married was the quality, the frequency, and above all the certainty of the sex. Does that make me sound shallow? Well, it's true. Once I was married, it was one less thing to worry about; I could rest easy. Six weeks, is about my maximum, before I start getting edgy. Before I start flirting with barmen and traffic wardens and lusting after bus drivers.

Well it's been nearly a year and frankly I'm way past that stage. I am craving physical contact; I find my mind wandering at inappropriate moments.

My mother's illness, the brush with mortality, doesn't help either. I feel the urge to grab life, to rage against the dying of the light. At the end of a long and difficult year, my reserves of energy are very low. My first thought on waking is, how long Till Ed Goes. The fear and the dread, that the day is drawing closer when I will be on my own again, is wearing me down. I want comfort, to feel alive, to feel safe. I want love, and connection with another human being.

This is not an excuse for my behaviour, but it does explain why, one afternoon in the hazy midsummer, I end up in bed with my husband.

He has taken the morning off work to come to sports' day. Because we are civilised now, I refrain from pointing out that this is the first time he's managed a sports' day. He is trying, really trying, to recover some ground. To prove he can be a good father and, I guess, a good husband.

(There's a whole lot of ground to recover there. I think he understands that I have made up my mind that I won't take him back, but at the same time he holds out hope.)

He brings a picnic - hamper and everything - and even runs in the Dads' race, not realizing (as a sports' day virgin) that his suit and shoes combination is not really going to cut it in this crowd; the Dads in this village will start training for next year's race tomorrow. Maybe even later today.

But you know, it's nice. I don't ask about Romily; I don't really want to know, and he definitely doesn't want to talk about it. Rosie powers her way through the qualifying heats, and we both cheer her on, unashamedly screaming with delight at her second place in the final race.

(Rosie is pretty delighted too: 'I came twice mummy!' - and even sardonic Michael, a very half-hearted relay runner, manages to look pleased about his sister's performance.)

So it seems entirely natural to invite him back to finish off the picnic lunch in the garden - amazingly for sports' day, it is neither pelting with rain nor roastingly hot, and we enjoy a very companionable couple of hours talking about nothing much. Once we open a bottle of wine, the writing is pretty much on the wall. And after the first tentative moments, the pains and tensions of the recent past are forgotten, just for a while, overlaid with the habits and patterns, the passions and desires, of the years we shared, before. It's much easier to be with Chris, these days, when we don't have to talk.

Afterwards we lie on top of the duvet, drowsy and still a little pissed, when I hear the scrunch of gravel, followed by the click of the door.

I sit up. 'Shit.' It's Friday, and Ed is here. He's due to collect the children and bring them home because I am supposed to be at the library, researching an article. 'Shit.'

I hear the children's chatter, and behind it, Ed's voice, a

little tense.

Strained, unsure, he shouts 'Hello?' He would have been expecting a locked door. I feel like a teenager, caught shagging in her Mum's bed.

'Hi! I'm up here! Hold on.'

Chris, I think, has dozed off. I had forgotten his ability to sleep through every crisis. Of course, to him this is no crisis. He has just slept with his wife in his bed. To me, this has the lurching potential for disaster. Flushed and flustered, I pull on my jeans and shirt, trying to assess the potential damage to the hair and face. 'Shit, shit.'

Ed shouts, 'Are you OK?' A little anxious.

'Sure, hold on, I'll be down in a sec.' Don't come up, don't come up.

They are in the kitchen, opening drinks and snacks negotiations. I say, as levelly as I can, 'How was the revision class?'

'Good yeah, good, fine. Only one more to go. Thank God.'

'Yes and we will have to celebrate, in style!'

What's wrong with me? Why am I talking like this? He looks a little startled at the false jollity.

'Is Daddy here?' Rosie, sharp as ever. I feel Ed's eyes on me. Calmly as I can manage, I reply, 'Yes, he stayed after the sports' day. He was so proud of you!' I turn to Ed, 'Rosie came second in the final. I don't know where she gets it from!' Jesus, shut up Jen, bloody shut up. He is looking at me, steadily, but with something behind the eyes that I don't want to see, don't want to name.

'Where is Daddy then?' Oh shut up Rosie, shut up.

'I'm going to play on the X-box.' Does Michael need an excuse to leave, or am I reading too much into this timely exit?

'He's upstairs darling, having a sleep. He's very tired.'

'I'm going to wake him, tell him that I came twice!'

'Sweetie, he was there remember?' But she's gone, and now it's just me and Ed in the kitchen.

I can't bear to look at him. I can hardly breathe. With my back to him, to give myself something to do, to pass this endless minute, I take the kettle to the sink, fill it, put it on, fiddle around with mugs and tea bags.

'So, what's your last exam?' I know, of course. There's a list on the fridge; I have committed it to memory. It's just something to say, to fill the echoing silence. But silence is the only reply. I know before I even turn around: the kitchen is empty, and he's gone.

When I finally hear from him, it's hours later. Chris has gone back to his flat, the children are in bed and I am sitting outside, alone again in the dusk. The heat of the day is gone, and I am shaking with the start of a miserable late evening hangover. I am trying to read, but my concentration is shot. The Fear is hovering, ready to pounce. I have my phone resting on my lap, and although I am trying to ignore it, every cell in my body is focused on it, waiting for the buzz.

When it comes, it still makes me jump.

I already know it's going to be bad news.

> *Message Ed*
> *I'm sorry, that was incredibly rude. I should have said goodbye. Speak soon x*

Christ, that's it? OK, well let's have a go at replying to that immense iceberg of a message. About 5% above the surface.

> *No don't worry. Let me know when we can celebrate.*

CHAPTER FOURTEEN
AFTER

THE FOREST

I step closer, one step further. Except it isn't a step, it's a stumble. The rhythm and the beauty of the moment is jarred but at last I am close enough to touch you. I close my eyes again, to try to regulate my emotions. I reach out my hand, outstretched and trembling. I feel the white-hot heat of your fingertips against mine.

There is a moment, just a moment of connection. A synaptic connection that judders through me, changing the chemicals in my blood forever and then.

The silence is gone.

The soft velvet warmth rushes away, driven out by screeching clinical white noise. The noise of pain, the cold of loss.

My eyes snap open but I already know what I will see. Nothing. You're gone. Not even a glimpse through the trees. For a moment, for the briefest moment, I can catch the very last scrap of your scent before the wind carries that away too.

My strength is gone and I feel the onslaught of the pain. My legs buckle and I lie on the ground. The threads of our thoughts have woven themselves into a mat, a shining tapestry of astonishing richness. I pull it over me, to blot out the glare and the noise. Underneath it, the pain recedes a little.

Carefully, I look inside my heart and start to read the words you left there, picking each one up and turning it over. It makes the pain worse, but easier to bear, and it passes the time.

There is a lot of time to pass.

IT WILL NOT SAY GOODBYE, JUST LIKE IT DIDN'T SAY HELLO

But we don't speak soon. And we don't celebrate. And I never even get to say goodbye.

A week later, I hear on the grapevine that Ed has moved out of the village and is living with his Dad in the new flat. We exchange messages that bear less and less relationship to the truth with every day that goes by. Full of cheery promises to 'get together soon!' and assurances that he would 'love to' see us again. After a few weeks of this miserable bullshit, I give up. I would like to explain, I would like to find some way to get back the friendship we had, but how to even begin that conversation?

A hundred times - more than that - I sit staring at the phone, trying to phrase a message that will open up communications again. I fight the strong urge to phone him, several times a day at first, to make sure he's OK. His sudden absence, his overnight disappearance from our lives, suggests that it's caused him some sort of upset. Did I hurt him? The idea, the guilt, was unbearable.

But then, is that just my ego running away with me? Maybe, all along it was, for him, nothing really significant. It didn't take much imagination to paint the scene another way - me as a temporary mother-substitute, providing a little company in a difficult year. Just a filler to pass the months in a dull village until real life started. He certainly seemed to leave our friendship behind without too much trouble, after all.

Then, in the middle of the night, the darker thoughts. How I used our friendship as a comfort blanket, to protect against the emotional onslaught of the past year. I needed some help lugging that bloody polar bear around, and there he was, young and strong and kind. The horror of this thought was enough to give me a vertiginous lurch whenever it entered my head.

Or maybe the whole thing existed only in my imagination. This idea was a stomach-tightening combination of comforting and humiliating. Comforting, because if I made it up, then there could be no harm done. Humiliating because, in truth, now he was no longer here, the idea of a friendship between us seemed ludicrous. Utterly unbelievable. What could we possibly have in common? Did I just imagine it all? Was Lettie right all along, that he was bored and just too polite to say no?

The search for truth in all this conjecture seemed exhausting and impossible. Like some epic quest into the world of the video games Ed played with Michael, a world of infinite darkness, with no guide and myriad dangers. Snake pits, infinitely deep wells, thorny pathways.

And although I wanted to speak to him, to see if he could shine a torch into this wilderness, to see if he could shed some light, I knew that this was pointless anyway. Even if he knew the truth about his role (and mine) in this mess, then the barriers to telling me were too deep, too wide, too opaque.

And the further away I get from that brutal day, as time goes on, the harder it is to distinguish any form of truth from the confusion.

The way we make sense of the horrible mess of our lives, the structure we use to prop up and hem in the sprawling chaos of our lives, is influenced in countless ways by the books we read, the films and TV programmes we see: the stories we are told, and the stories we tell. This is what they told me at university, and this is what I tell the students of Lasso the Muse. And this is what I believe, too. The stories we live by, they shift and change as time passes, as we learn more about the world and more about ourselves. But our story, mine and Ed's, makes no bloody sense at all, and less and less sense as time goes on.

The best I can hope for, and I hope for this fervently, is that Ed will look back on the last few months and feel, maybe, nostalgic? Happy? Or at least, glad that I was able to help him with some difficult days, and that he was able to help me too. Because, my God, did he help me. I don't like to think about how I would have got through the year without him. If it was just me and the polar bear, how would I have dragged it along by myself all year? I have this vision of me, crushed and motionless under the weight of that dead polar bear, right in the middle of the village green, and everyone walking by, completely oblivious.

Because they were, completely oblivious. That's exactly what they were. I don't blame them. Most of us, almost all of us maybe, bumble through life totally unaware of the pain and misery everyone else is suffering, so caught up are we in our own suffering. All of us, dragging our own bleeding carcasses around, ignorant and heedless that we are surrounded by millions of others, hefting their own burdens. Exhausted and miserable, and thinking they are the only ones. No wonder we all feel so lonely.

That's what struck me most, after he was gone: how few people even registered it as significant. No-one had the first clue that for me, Ed's absence was unspeakably painful, impossible to bear. To nearly everyone else, even after all this time, he was nothing more than my babysitter. No-one cared, no-one noticed, no-one really registered. Or, they chose not to, because it didn't fit in with their view of the world. That story made no sense, after all. Why would I miss Ed Becker? If I thought I was alienated before, well I was mistaken. Nothing is more difficult to face than the loss that can't be shared, that must be kept secret.

So if the truth is so slippery, then what can we trust? Must I just resign myself to living in the centre of this ambiguity, in the kaleidoscope of shifting reality? Just look at the pretty patterns, Jen, and stop trying to make sense of them. Well, I don't know. I may not know his truth, but, on the other hand, I was there. I was a first-hand witness. I saw it with my own eyes, close up, personal. Sometimes, in the lightless wilderness, I can find a glittering, sparkling memory. Something infinitely pure, pulsatingly true. A word, a phrase, a shared moment. We shared a lot of love, as well as a lot of other things - tea, biscuits, jokes, poems, thoughts, hopes, pain, loss, games of Top Trumps - this past year.

Love is word that's hard to describe. But if you look into someone's eyes, hard and carefully, then you can see it. If you listen closely to the words they say, you can hear it - not necessarily in the words themselves, but the voice, the tone. And if you stand near enough to someone, if you keep your heart open, then you can feel love. The heart can speak to another heart, if you are brave enough, if you can forget your fears for long enough to hold your heart open. And what the brain forgets, what the memory edits and overlays, the heart remembers. The heart remembers.

And as the days and weeks passed, if I forced myself to look at the situation objectively, clear-headedly, then - whatever the truth, whatever the story - this was surely the right time to end it. It was, of course, time for him to go. But strip away everything else, the fear and the pain and the barriers, and actually, we just liked each other. And God, I missed him, when he was gone.

I found out scraps from Carrie, caught what I could. Which was precious little. With the emphasis on the precious. I heard he was back together with Charlotte, that they were travelling across Europe. I found out his exam results - three bloody A*s after all - and that he had his place to read English at Oxford. I received all this news, as I was forced to, with the equanimity of the casual acquaintance.

I found myself grateful, stupidly grateful, for the experiences of the last year, which had taught me the gift of tight emotional control. That had built up my emotional muscles, my stamina, so that I had the strength to get out that bloody sledge again, to drag that dead polar bear around, this time even more silently, stealthily, secretly. And at least this time, I knew that the day would come when I could ditch that carcass and walk again, unencumbered and free. I couldn't mark the date on a calendar, but it would come. Until then, I just had to keep walking, keep walking towards the horizon. One minute, one hour, one day at a time.

And, though I lay in bed, night after night, fretting over his poor, precious heart, it was mine on the line all along, too. My bruised heart that got wrung out again, then thrown downstream, fast and hectic, bouncing on every sharp rock.

I don't expect your sympathy. It was what I signed up for. And yes, I'd do it again tomorrow. Or even, God help me, today.

Because today I saw him again. In the Covered Market, shopping for my pre-Christmas party.

(Chris is coming to this party, as a matter of fact. Who would have predicted that we could move so quickly into the amicable zone? It helps, of course, that things are off with Romily, for good. In fact, Romily is back in the Big House with lovely, kind, wonderful Edwin, whose capacity for forgiveness, it seems, is considerably greater than mine. Chris is in a nice little flat in town, with room for the children to stay. I stay there sometimes, too, bunking up with Rosie if we are out late. And tonight he'll stop at mine, in the spare room. It's a fragile peace, I guess, but it's holding.)

I am queueing up for lamb shanks, when I see him. In a moment of clunky unintended symbolism, I am standing right by a torso of venison carcass, soft and vulnerable and eviscerated. He flashes by, in one of his usual lively shirts, garish and loud against the pastels and beiges of the middle-class, middle-aged shoppers. Our eyes catch. I smile. He looks startled, frightened even, and looks away. The pain of this reaction, this rejection, after months of numbness, is like a punch in the stomach. I almost double over, leaning on the butcher's counter to give myself a little stability.

Just one more thing. Just one more blow to take on the chin. I'm the adult, the grown up. Like I said, I signed up for this, a long time ago. I agreed that I could take it, and I now need to just take it. But now I just want to go home, to lie down, to lie under my duvet until I can absorb this new wave of pain. I half-jog, half-stride to the car park.

I feel my phone buzz in my jeans pocket.

Ed – message

Not yet, not yet. I can't face it yet. I slide the phone back into my pocket, and hurry to the car, throw the shopping bags into the carnage of my boot. I stare at the screen for a long long time, slowing my breath, deepening it to calm my jangling nerves.

Slide, press.

Can we pretend I didn't just behave like an absolute child and that I said hello like a normal person? EBxx
Sure. We can pretend whatever you like.

Bit harsh. Whatever. I press send anyway. I am angry and hurt and frankly Ed yes, you may be 19 but that's no bloody excuse: you're still a coward, a selfish self-centred coward and I didn't deserve that.

I turn on the engine, but can't quite bring myself to leave. Not yet.

Can we just pretend that I asked you out for tea, to catch up?
Sure we can pretend that too. Really, there's literally no end to what we can pretend.
And can we pretend you said yes?
Yes we can pretend that. Why don't you let me know what we chatted about?
Why don't you let me buy you tea, and you can find out.

OK now what I really want to reply to that is WHY DON'T YOU FUCK OFF?

Except I don't. I don't want to reply that. And I don't want him to fuck off. I want to see him, to talk to him. I want everything to be right, everything to be fixed, between us. Because he is my friend, and I miss him still, more than you can imagine, every single bloody day.

And to be honest I wouldn't mind a cup of tea either.

By the time I get to Starbucks he's already there, sprawled on a leather sofa, soft-edged and languid. I stand at the door for a moment, press the pause button.

He looks up, straight at me, straight into me. And smiles.

I press play.

A Dead Polar Bear on a Sledge

Read the beginning of my next novel Cover Version... released Spring 2021
RORY

Of course I shouldn't have told them. I knew that even as I started to spill out the story; my gut started churning, telling me loud and clear to stop. The trouble is I've never been very good at knowing when to shut up and yet so very **very** good at ignoring what my gut is telling me. That's what's got me into trouble, and to be fair some pretty good times too, over the years.

So I say (stupidly, ill-advisedly), 'Forgive me ladies and gentlemen, I am a bit distracted this evening. I have had the weirdest day.'

I should have just shut up, tuned the guitar, checked the set-list and sang the songs like a sensible person would. They're here to listen to the songs after all, not to hear my pathetic drugs-bust story. Not even a cool drugs bust either: no Marianne Faithful wrapped in a rug, no Mars Bar, not even a fun-size one. Just me, a tatty messenger bag, 20 fags and a copy of the Telegraph. (For the cryptic crossword - how rock and roll is that? What can I tell you? It's the best one. Ask anyone.)

I'm not usually nervous when I'm stage - to be honest, being on stage is the very least of my worries. It's everything else I'm afraid of. Like, getting up in the morning. Going to bed at night. Writing songs. Checking my email. Checking my bank account. Opening my credit card bill. Talking to Lexie. Being left alone to entertain my daughter Mirabelle for more than ten minutes – if only there was a set-list for that.

But singing the songs - that I can do. Well, at least I can usually. Just as long as I have about ten minutes between each song to tune up the guitar and crack a few bad jokes.

That's the great thing about being on stage: they always laugh at your jokes, no matter how bad they are. The same cannot be said for my home life, I'll tell you that.

I think it was looking out at those familiar faces in the audience that made me tell them. Faces I've seen for years, on and off.

Since the old days.

It was different in the old days though. They were much further away, separated by barriers and burly blokes holding walkie-talkies. A blurry sea of upturned faces. I even wrote a song about that once: 'singing the lines for the benefit of / the blur of the back row'.

Now, in these poky venues, they can be very close. Very close indeed.

Why am I thinking about the old days? The old days have been old for a long time.

We used to call them fans, but I'm not sure that means much any more; it definitely doesn't mean what it used to mean. These days it means - some people I might recognise, some people who have probably read an interview with me in a magazine somewhere. Often they will repeat some fact back to me from one of those interviews, something flippant and probably untrue I said to an interviewer off the cuff ten years ago, and it gets repeated back to me as gospel. I try not to look too confused; normally I just laugh. I think I get away with it most of the time.

Fans these days are the people who might buy another t-shirt even though they've got a drawer full of them at home, and probably won't wear any of them anyway except to sleep in.

They are the kind of people who might buy a CD just for me to sign it with that Sharpie I always have with me for this very purpose, just to have an excuse to chat. Will hand over £15, even though they haven't got a CD player and everything's on Spotify anyway. Well, apart from those last two albums caught up in that expensive and lengthy legal dispute.

But that's another story.

Thank God for fans. God bless them. They are the only people keeping the increasingly-ravenous pack of wolves from my door.

They are the only people who might actually care that I've had a shitty day.

And really, it's been a shitty day.

They aren't a blur any more though. At these solo gigs they are so close that they will be able to see I'm sweating, really sweating; it's pouring off me now. My throat's dry, not helped by the crappy dry ice left over from the previous act. I've got nothing to drink but the cheap white wine in a greasy plastic cup left by the mic stand. Who bought that? Not me, that's for sure. Was it that nice looking blonde girl with the hopeful smile and the tight t-shirt? Probably. She came over as soon as I arrived, introduced herself. Melanie. Very pretty. Very nice too, if she's bought me a drink, because I really do need a drink.

I take a sip and give her a grateful smile, tip it to her in a gesture of thanks. She smiles back. Cold, too sweet, but cold.

If only I'd had time to shower, to change even, but the shittiness of the day has left no time for anything but a mad dash to King's Cross for the last possible train to wherever the hell I am playing tonight - somewhere North of London anyway - and a quick fag in the car park. I couldn't see much of my face in the grimy mirror in the dressing room (for which read - broom cupboard with a stool, some coat pegs and a rickety old bar-table). Then again, I'm pretty sure seeing it wouldn't have helped. I can feel my face is stubbly, possibly a little shiny, almost certainly flaky. And very very sweaty.

The sight of these faces, especially those very familiar faces at the front, at the end of the shittiest day in a lengthy parade of endlessly shitty days, is an actual comfort. The only real comfort I've had in days. A hell of a lot more comforting, and certainly a lot closer to *feeling* like home than all the other places I might be tempted to refer to as home at this moment.

The house in Clapham, quite near the common, for example - the one I put down a deposit on when the first album got to number 3, but which I really **really** can't afford to pay the mortgage on anymore, especially since I had to remortgage to pay some very pressing tax bills. The house which I used to share with Lexie and Mirabelle. That house has been out of bounds to me for the last few months, ever since Lexie decided she needed 'some space'. But it's still hoovering a massive amount of money out of my bank account every month.

Money, let's be clear, which I don't have.

A lot closer to home, for that matter, than the box room at my brother Declan's house, the one he shares with his wife Cheryl and their two kids, and now (reluctantly) with me. The place where I've been sleeping since Lexie chucked me out, on a mattress jammed into a space on the floor against the stacked suitcases and boxes of old baby toys.

Certainly more like home than wherever I'm going to sleep tonight. Wherever that might be. I had hoped Steve might have booked me a hotel room against tonight's fee, because I sure as hell can't put one on my credit card.

Come on Rory, you can't carry on pretending to tune this bloody guitar for ever. But I can't quite face starting a song yet. I poke the set list with my toe.

Yea, not quite yet.

I say, 'It's just some bad luck, nothing but bad luck. I'd like to tell you, but I know what you lot are like, with your Twitter and suchlike. You can't keep a secret.'

A ripple of laughter from the crowd. I hesitate. Start the song, Rory. Just start the song.

The blonde girl, Melanie, catches my eye, and signals to offer to buy me another drink. Should I have another drink? Definitely, no. But also - yes. Yes please, friendly Melanie. I need all the friends I can get.

Statement of PC Jones

On Friday 22nd May I had been attending an incident on the Thornbury Estate. At around 10.45am I entered the Spar convenience store on Station Road. I had been asked to speak to the owner about some damage he had experienced to his shop.

When I entered the premises, I waited behind a man I now know to be Rory McLean. Mr McLean purchased a newspaper. When he removed his wallet from his bag to purchase the newspaper he dropped a plastic package containing what I reasonably believed to be a quantity of cannabis.

On the basis of this reasonable suspicion I spoke to Mr McLean and asked him what was in the package. He replied, 'It's not what it looks like. It's for my brother. He's letting me stay at his house so I thought I had better bring a present for the host.'

On the basis of this conversation, I informed Mr McLean that I was arresting him on suspicion of possession and supply of a controlled substance and returned with him to the Thornbury Police Station ...'

'And that's how I managed to get busted at 11 o'clock in the morning ladies and gentlemen. Don't worry though I'm a professional and still managed to get here. So now if you can all pretend I never told you that story because that's the kind of thing that could get me into a bit of trouble with that child custody case that's surely coming my way so, keep it under your hat ok? Cheers!'

I raise my plastic glass to them, more cheap sweet white wine courtesy of Melanie. A toast to those familiar upturned faces, and indeed to Melanie herself. I touch the set list one more time with my toe for luck and finally, finally, I start the first song.